MY LIFE, A NOVEL

By

Gene Cowen

© 2003 by Eugene S. Cowen. All rights reserved.

No part of this book may be reproduced, stored in a retrieval system, or transmitted by any means, electronic, mechanical, photocopying, recording, or otherwise, without written permission from the author.

ISBN: 1-4107-3827-2 (e-book)
ISBN: 1-4107-3826-4 (Paperback)

Library of Congress Control Number: 2003092192

This book is printed on acid free paper.

Printed in the United States of America
Bloomington, IN

Cover: *Interior of the Pantheon, Rome, 1977*. Photograph by the author.

1stBooks – rev. 04/29/03

For Phyllis
Ne plus ultra

Acknowledgements

I am much indebted to the following people, publications, and organizations for their assistance:

First, my wife, Phyllis, who pored over countless drafts and then had to listen while I read to her "good parts" that I had just written.

Karen Pershing of Mybookedit.com, who did a first-class job of editing the manuscript.

Joseph Fanelli, dear friend, who helped me with the Italian language.

The People's Chronology, by James Trager, a year-by-year record of human events, which told me what was happening in the world as I went through life in fact and fiction.

And Google.com, the ultimate Internet search engine, which took me by the hand and led me through the thicket of everything from .50 caliber machine guns to the Watergate burglars.

Author's Note

This is a book written literally in two types. One is My Life, which appears here in Times New Roman type. **The other is A Novel, fiction which appears in Arial.** Everything in My Life is fact to the best of my memory. Everything in A Novel, however, is fantasy.

As Jeanette Winterson wrote in *The PowerBook*, "It used to be that the real and the invented were parallel lines that never met. Then we discovered that space is curved, and in curved space parallel lines always meet."

My Life, A Novel

PART ONE: 1941

Gene Cowen

My Life: Chapter One

When the Japanese bombed Pearl Harbor, some friends and I were at the Polo Grounds in the Bronx, watching a professional football game. The public address system announced, "Colonel William Donovan, come to the box office at once. There is an important phone message."

We heard the call, but it didn't register with us until later that day that it was for "Wild Bill" Donovan, the nation's spy chief. We were more concerned that our New York Giants were being trounced by the Brooklyn Dodgers, 21 to 7.

We had used student tickets for those games, waited on line for a long time, and got pretty good seats in the lower stands at about the twenty-yard line. As we left the stadium, kids were hawking copies of the *New York Inquirer*, as sensationalist a weekly newspaper then as it is today. We didn't have any money to buy the paper, but we read the headline saying, "Japs Bomb Pearl Harbor," and laughed. "Yeah, and somebody married a six-hundred-year-old man and had a two-headed baby!"

When we got home and heard the same news on the radio, we realized we were at war.

I was sixteen at the time, and it was clear that once the United States declared war, not only against Japan but also against Germany, this was going to be a long conflict. Two years later, I signed up for the Army Air Corps Reserve, thereby assuring that I'd get into the Air Corps and not something worse, which could have happened if I'd waited until I was drafted. It was a hell of a lot smarter a decision than I realized at the time. When I was finally called to active duty, it was September, 1943, and because of all the training necessary to become a navigator, I did not get shot at until March, 1945. In any other service, I could very well have been dodging shells at the invasion of Normandy and slogging through the mud of European battlefields.

When my parents learned that I had been called up, there was much wringing of hands about what would become of me. I was as worried as they were and I should have understood the concern that parents have for children. But I was worried more about *how* I'd perform under fire than I was about getting hurt and I was afraid that all this family angst would weaken my resolve. I said to Phyllis Wallach, whom I had been dating for two years, "Why doesn't anybody just say, 'Give 'em hell'?"

Phyllis was just as worried, but the last thing she said to me before I left was a half-hearted, "Give 'em hell!"

The army was a shock. I had spent all eighteen years of my life in the Bronx, living in apartment buildings, rarely traveling any farther than other parts of the city in rattling subway cars, and knowing very few people who were not Jewish.

When I got to boot camp, the drill sergeant often railed against us with the scream, "You New Yorkers think your shit don't stink!" In our barracks were young men from all over the country. They talked differently. They ate differently than I did. Some would not sit down to a meal if it didn't include red meat, and they thought it was funny that I liked vegetables and fruit. Many knew how to drive. Many were farm boys and were comfortable with guns because they had hunted. I had never seen a gun any closer than on a movie screen, and I did not drive a car.

I made a few friends who were also from big cities and who liked to read and write. But not many. About four days after the excitement of being in the service wore off, I announced to a barracks-mate, "I'm not a soldier. I'll never be one. I'm just a civilian in uniform."

The preliminary tests the Air Corps gave me made it pretty clear that I was never going to qualify as a pilot. I had played almost no sports and my coordination was lousy. I did take a training plane up with an instructor alongside me and managed to bounce it into a landing without tearing off the landing gear. But I was clearly not cut out for this, and when I was asked, I said I'd like to be a navigator. I was fairly good at math, had taken some pre-engineering courses at the City College of New York and eventually qualified as a navigator. But I wasn't enthusiastic about it, and I was still a civilian in uniform.

So I was officially designated a flight officer, not a second lieutenant. Our uniform, rights, privileges, responsibilities and pay were the same as the lieutenants, but we got blue-and-white bars that looked like flattened-out Celebrex medicine capsules to wear on our uniforms instead of a commissioned officer's gold bars. When I was assigned to a crew, my pilot and co-pilot were also flight officers. It comforted me a little that they had apparently not achieved the ultimate, as I had not.

Those two were interesting characters. Roy, the pilot, was from Wisconsin, a bedrock Republican with a cutting, acerbic tongue. But he was a careful pilot, prepared meticulously before every flight and took a paternal interest in his crew. He managed to get us into the air and back on the ground without incident, and, as we'd say often about combat flying, "If you can walk away from the plane, it was a good flight." Roy was married, puritanical about pre-marital celibacy, and would lecture us about that from time to time.

Bill was from the Dakotas, grew up on a ranch, loved to hunt, wore his officer's hat at a rakish angle and fancied himself a lady-killer. He was a good co-pilot, stayed sober most of the time, and had a certain taciturn pleasantness about him.

Flying

We flew a B-17 heavy bomber. Civilians called it a Flying Fortress, but that was uncool for us military types. Besides, various models of the plane came with additional letters (B-17F, B-17G, etc.), and also, we gave our own ships really distinctive names. Ours, when I was flying out of Foggia (at the spur of the Italian boot) early in 1945, was called "Gin & Juice." That name came from a drink at the officers' club bar that was made with sour canned juice and raw-tasting gin. I drank it only once.

I was a navigator, which put me in the Plexiglas nose of the plane. It had two .50 caliber machine guns protruding from the nostrils, even though the Air Corps called them the cheeks, of the plane. They were probably the most inaccurate weapons of the war, because they could be moved only a few degrees in any direction. This was to prevent excited navigators from shooting off their own planes' propellers. Because of the lack of fighter opposition, I never fired one in anger, but often in disgust when I missed practice targets in training.

(About four years later, when I was a reporter on the Syracuse NY *Herald-Journal*, I typed on a balky typewriter made by the same

Gene Cowen

Remington Company that manufactured those machine guns. I asked the repairman during one of his frequent visits why a company that could make weapons that rapid-fired .50 caliber shells couldn't also make a little old typewriter that didn't break down so often. He said patiently that a machine gun, although it performed an important and lethal function, was really a much simpler device.)

Late in 1944, we arrived at MacDill Field outside of Tampa for transition training, where we got to know our plane and each other. Part of the navigator's job was to calibrate instruments. For instance, an airspeed meter told you how fast the plane was traveling through the air. But it was invariably off by a few miles an hour. As long as you knew how much off it was, it was easy to correct each time. So we flew the plane to an area in Florida where we were to fly across two parallel roads that were a known distance apart.

The plane had to fly low over the roads to get an accurate measure. I looked into what was called a "drift meter," but was simply a steel pipe pointing straight down. In its center were cross-hairs, and on the end of the pipe where you pressed your eye socket, it had some rubber cushioning so you wouldn't hurt yourself during a bumpy ride.

It was hot and the thermals coming up off the ground were creating a lot of turbulence. I paid little attention to that. At 120 miles an hour, as the cross-hairs showed us crossing the first road, I clicked on my stop watch. When it passed the second road, I stopped the watch. Then, back again over the same course at the same speed to nullify the effect of any wind that might have been pushing the plane. I'd make a fast calculation, and if it would turn out that, say, when the airspeed meter registered 120 miles an hour, we were actually traveling at 124 miles an hour, I'd paste a tiny "+4" note at that point on the face of the airspeed meter to remind me to add four miles an hour each time I used the airspeed meter during regular flight.

Then back again at 125 miles and hour, and so forth, all the way up the scale. I was busy clicking and calculating, and all I noticed was that my eye socket was getting sore from hitting the rubber cushioning when the plane bucked. Roy was busy flying the plane, keeping it straight, level, and at the speeds I required.

After about half an hour of that bumpy drudge work, I heard, "Pilot to navigator," in my earphones. "How much longer are you going to be nutsing around?" he asked.

"Not much longer. Why?" I said.

"You'd better stop pretty soon," he said, "because you and I are the only two members of this crew who aren't throwing up!"

Another incident was much less funny. We were to take a training flight out of MacDill Field, fly over water for an hour or two, perform some maneuvers, and return to the base. We did and I navigated the plane back—to Orlando, instead of Tampa. I was mortified.

The commanding officer later arranged for an instructor to take me up for a test flight, and it turned out that when I saw the "+4" on the airspeed meter, instead of adding four, I'd subtracted four. Fortunately, the test navigator decided that was not a hanging crime and that I understood the error, so he didn't wash me out.

After several months of that training, it was time for us to fly the plane overseas. First stop would be Goose Bay, Labrador. Just before leaving, I called home and spoke to Phyllis. I told her we were leaving, I couldn't say to where, but we'd probably fly over New York City en route, and I gave her an approximate time. She said she'd watch for the plane. I said I'd ask Roy to waggle the wings. She said she'd be waving a big white towel. It was all very romantic, and I was looking forward to the air-to-ground encounter.

We flew north, rerouted ourselves over New York City, waggled the wings over Manhattan, couldn't see any pretty dark-haired girl waving a towel, but left, hoping she'd seen us. Phyllis told me later that she stood on the roof of her apartment house on 74th Street for hours, waving a towel until, seeing nothing, she began crying.

I have no idea what happened, but with my prowess as a navigator, it's entirely possible I routed the plane over the wrong city.

Flying to the Azores

Frigid Goose Bay, Labrador, was a big change from the warmth of Florida. We had to wear fleece-lined clothing, and the snow squeaked under our boots as we walked from the tarmac to our barracks. But the weather was not on our minds; the war was. We were on our way.

We took off late one evening to fly to the Azores in the North Atlantic, about nine hundred miles off the coast of Spain, on our way to North Africa and eventually to Italy. We flew at night because we would be over water all the way, and the stars were our only navigational points of reference until we could pick up a radio range-signal when we got fairly close to the Azores.

I used a bulky, clunky sextant to get the angles of certain specific stars; those readings, matched against the precise time of day, gave me the data I needed to draw lines on my map. Where three lines intersected was our location. But since a plane moves quickly through the air, I had to adjust each line for our movement forward, I had to assume my sextant was drawing a bead on the right star, and my watch had to be precisely accurate. I also had to be a better navigator than I was.

In view of all those variables, neither the crew nor I were very sanguine about the accuracy of this groping through the dark over the icy Atlantic. Roy, the pilot, watched anxiously for his radio range-finder to pick up a signal from the Azores. When he did, he heaved a sigh of relief. Now, all he had to do was to point the plane so that the needle on the range-finder scope was glued to zero, and it should take us all the way to the transmitting station. When the plane was above the transmitter, the needle was supposed to flop down, indicating a "null," telling him that we had arrived.

Several hours out, but long before my celestial navigation told me that we had reached the Azores, I heard on my intercom, "Pilot to navigator, I've got a null. We're there!"

I looked down at my map and said, "Something's wrong. We should be at least an hour or so away."

Roy had a lot more confidence in his radio range-finder than he had in his shaky navigator, so he said, "I'm taking us down to have a look."

He lowered the plane through the clouds, but all we could see was night-black water. He began circling, certain that he'd find the little island. After about half an hour of searching and finding nothing, he said, "Navigator, there's obviously something wrong. Give me a new heading."

I looked in dismay at my map and said, "Roy, you've been nutsing around and circling. I think I knew where we were when you started losing altitude, but I have no idea where we are now. I'm going to take a good guess and give you a heading and let's keep our fingers crossed."

I did some fast calculations and told Roy which direction to fly. We climbed above the clouds, and I began nervously taking more sextant readings and rechecking our position.

After about thirty anxious minutes, my headset brought the joyful news, "Navigator, I've just picked up the signal again. We're on our way!"

What had happened? We guessed that it had been a German submarine screwing up the signal. Enemy subs knew the transatlantic routes of the thousands of planes being ferried to Europe. They would surface and jam radio range-transmissions. If that sub had thrown us sufficiently off course, we would have ended up out of fuel and in the water. Roy, my doubting pilot, forever after had new confidence in my navigating abilities.

Our final destination was an air base outside of Foggia. Our air base was a tent city, where we slept on cots—about eight of us to a tent. We heated with airplane fuel. Crews who had occupied those tents before we got there had scrounged abandoned airplane wing tanks, mounted them outside the tents, run piping into empty metal drums inside the tents and affixed little valves to the ends of the pipes. The gasoline dripped from the valves and we lighted it. That was a pretty herky-jerky arrangement, and there were stories of those tanks occasionally exploding, but we went right on using them.

They had to be refilled periodically and, when it was my turn, I went down to the flight line with a friend and we began to roll a drum of gasoline back toward our tent.

An indignant sergeant came running toward us. "Where are you going with that?"

We told him.

"Don't take that. It's jeep gas, and we never have enough of that. Take some of that high-test crap for the planes. We have more of it than we need."

Gene Cowen

On dry days, heavy dust blew into our tents, and on rainy days, the ground turned into lumpy mud. But anyone who complained was reminded that we were living in luxury compared to the "doggies who are slogging their way in the infantry."

When we weren't flying, we sat on our beds talking to one another, whittling sticks, writing letters, or waiting for letters to come from home. I wrote to Phyllis every day, trying to think of what to say that—in conformity with censorship regulations—would not reveal where we were or what we were actually doing. So I wrote about how much I missed her and tried to recreate the good times we'd had in our puppy-love days.

She answered less frequently than I wrote, but with warm and welcome letters. In later years, I told her that I'd kept wishing that she'd write more often. She explained that she was busy at school and with an active social life. Not a satisfactory answer, I thought, to someone who had been pining away.

#

Our outfit was the 15th Air Force's 463rd Heavy Bombardment Group, 773rd Bombardment Squadron, which local tradesmen memorialized with leather patches that showed screaming eagles flinging bombs. I bought one and sewed it onto my flight jacket and was very proud of the symbol until I visited Switzerland on leave one day. There, the locals didn't think much of those belligerent patches, since it reminded them of how often they had been accidentally bombed by the wild American air crews who wore those patches.

In combat, however, my job was not to fling the bombs, but rather to get the plane to the target, so a bombardier could do the flinging. In the B-17, I was seated just behind the bombardier, who crouched over his bombsight inside the tip of the plane's nose.

My desk was a table that was bolted to the cabin wall. On it were papers and a cardboard-like circular slide rule that did quick multiplication and division and had a center section where we drew lines to compute angles and other simple geometry. It was called an E6B Calculator.

I sat on something that resembled a secretary's posture chair: The four little feet that touched the floor came together at a post, which supported the seat, which, in turn, supported my rump. Rump and the rest of me were encased in coveralls, then a zippered, insulated flight jacket and, for the coldest weather, a lumpy, fleece-lined leather jacket and pants.

But there was more. We then strapped on a parachute harness which, about breast-high, held two steel rings designed to hold the chute itself. On one strap was a tiny first-aid kit which included morphine. But the chute was generally attached only to one ring, to keep it out of the way of more layers to come. If we had to bail out, we were supposed to remove the additional layers, snap the chute to the other ring and head for the doors. Fortunately, I never needed to use a chute.

Are you still with me? Coveralls, flight jacket, fleece-and-leather jacket and pants, parachute harness. And then the Mae West. (Good old Mae, noted in her time for prominent breasts, now memorialized mostly for the yellow life vest, which still bears her name.)

On my head went the traditional aviator's cap, with flaps that snapped beneath the chin. Over my face went an oxygen mask, which was attached by hose to a pipe in the wall of the plane. When I inhaled, life-giving oxygen came from that pipe, but when I exhaled, where did it go? Out from an exhaust vent under my chin, too close to the Mae West and the neck of my jacket. Therefore, at high altitudes, my warm, moist breath often froze onto those articles of clothing. And when the plane descended and the temperature rose, the crystallized vapor then melted down my chest in a slow chilling drip.

Finally, when we were under anti-aircraft attack, I would buckle on top of all that gear a flak suit of steel mesh covered in fabric. It looked somewhat like a baseball catcher's chest protector, giving the chest, groin and back some protection against anti-aircraft shrapnel. And on my head went a flak helmet. It was desperately heavy. Also, much in demand at the time were thick sheets of scrap steel that we put on the seat itself, to give the family jewels more protection, even though it made that part of us colder.

We bombed in daylight, which meant that the preliminaries started on the ground before dawn. Wake-up call; mess hall,; briefing on what our target was to be; what the alternate targets were if we couldn't get to our main one; climb aboard the big silvery bombers; taxi down the runway.

Gene Cowen

On my very first bombing mission, as the big plane bumped along the taxi strip, I looked out through the Plexiglas nose and saw two men in uniform standing on the grass, looking forlorn in the cold. One was making some kind of motion with his hands as each plane rumbled past. I asked the bombardier, who had flown combat before, what that was all about.

"They're chaplains," he said. "They're praying for us. The Catholic one crosses himself as each plane goes by."

I thought that was nice of them, but neither my own praying nor someone else's could do very much to calm my nerves.

"Wave at them," he said. "It makes them feel better."

I did.

Linz

My first four missions turned out to be uneventful. It was late in the war. The German air force—shot-up in flight, pounded on the ground, and without the fuel that our bombers had destroyed—couldn't put any fighter planes into the air, thank God. The anti-aircraft fire over targets in northern Italy was thin and inaccurate. But my fifth mission to Linz, Austria, was going to be different.

We flew in squadrons of seven planes that formed themselves into Vs; four squadrons clung together as a "group" of twenty-eight. The group was supposed to stay tightly bunched, so that, when the bombardier in the lead plane drew a bead on his target and his bombsight released his bombs, all other bombardiers in the group would throw a switch which released theirs, and the bombs would make a tight pattern of hits on the ground. (We were essentially shoveling the bombs out of the plane. What a far cry it was from today's electronically guided, precision bombing, which can put a missile down a targeted chimney.)

Linz is a city in northern Austria, straddling both banks of the Danube. It was an important rail hub for the Germans (and also Hitler's hometown), and on this cloudless, sunny morning on April 15, 1945, we were going to do something about that.

It was a long flight from Foggia near the spur of the Italian boot. After we took off, each plane joined its squadron; then squadrons

My Life, A Novel

formed themselves into groups and groups into larger flights of bombing units.

The men who flew B-17s liked them. The planes were four-engine bombers which could deliver three tons of bombs and were armed with thirteen .50 caliber machine guns and had a crew of nine or ten. The planes were sturdy, with a reputation for being able to withstand lots of non-lethal hits. If they did come down into the water—which was all around the Italian boot—they would float for a few vital seconds while the crew scrambled into life rafts. But Flying Fortresses were pitifully slow, even for the 1940s. Their cruising speed was 187 miles per hour. The most elementary enemy radar could target us while we were creeping through the sky at that speed.

We flew north over the Adriatic Sea, where there were no enemy gunners to fire at us while we were at low altitudes. I fiddled nervously with my E6B Calculator to keep track of our position. We climbed slowly, and as we passed eight thousand feet, we snapped on our oxygen masks. The planes flew in one direction for a few miles, zigged slightly in another direction for more miles, then zagged in yet another direction, all in an effort to confuse enemy radar as to our ultimate target.

It confused nobody. By the time we made a landfall at about where Italy borders Yugoslavia, the Austrians had little doubt about where we were heading that morning. Hundreds of U.S. bombardiers were waiting to put Linz into their bombsights. Each group of twenty-eight U.S. planes was scheduled to arrive at a precise time, separated from one another by minutes and a few hundred feet of altitude, so they could crowd into the same limited air space above the city. As we approached Linz thirty-two thousand feet below and the bomb bay doors opened, we could see that the Austrian gunners knew precisely where our planes would stop the zig-zagging and fly straight and level from the "initial point" (where we began the actual bomb run) to the point of the bomb drop.

We all buckled on our heavy flak suits. The enemy gunners were tracking each flight of planes coming in for the bomb run, but it seemed as if they were also filling the sky ahead with bursting flashes of fire, forcing us to fly through their Nazi-manufactured hell.

I could see ahead of us a great dirty cube of smoke and fire, with trails of what looked like phosphorous bursting high in the cube and worming down through it. The phosphorous looked very much like the burning snakes you see during fireworks, which is why, to this day, I get an uncomfortable feeling in the pit of my stomach whenever I see an Independence Day fireworks display. We headed right into the black churning cube.

(Stephen Ambrose wrote in *The Wild Blue* that over Linz that day, "the flak over the target was extremely intense. The Germans were using their box system—firing 88s' shells into an area 2,000 feet on each of the four sides and 2,000 feet deep, just in front of the formation so that the planes would fly into it." Then Ambrose quoted B-24 pilot George McGovern, later to be a Presidential candidate, as saying, "The sky just became solid black. Then in that solid black you'd see these huge, angry flashes of red, which was another shell exploding...It was terrible...Hell can't be any worse.")

Except for our pilots and the lead bombardier, the rest of us were miserably without anything to do, except to toss chopped-up aluminum foil out of little portholes, which was supposed to confuse the enemy radar. Our seven-plane squadron dutifully bunched together more tightly to give the bomb strikes a tighter pattern on the ground, but this also gave the enemy gunners a more compact target.

I looked out the Plexiglas window on the left side of the plane and watched the flak burst with sickening regularity off our left wing. As we flew, the fiery puffs accompanied us, as if they were walking alongside. Whoever was doing the aiming was a fraction too far off to the left to make a direct hit, but he certainly had our speed down pat. Since the gunner must have known he was missing, he would probably adjust his settings—which he must have done just then. Something hit the plane and it rolled to the right. I was suddenly no longer looking at the flak. The Plexiglas window on my left showed me a lot of sky that was supposed to be above us. Then the plane rolled the other way, and I was looking out the window at the ground that was supposed to be below.

A Novel: Chapter One

There was a hole in the cabin, and wind blew over the body of Jerry, the radio operator. The left inboard engine was smoking and the plane rolled crazily.

"We've been hit," shouted Roy on the intercom. "I'm having trouble controlling it, but I think we're still okay. Crew, stand by to bail out, but don't do anything until I tell you. Let's do a quick check on how everyone is."

Everyone in the crew answered present and unhurt except the radio operator. "Bill," Roy said to the copilot, "go back and see if you can help Tommy. Navigator, give me a heading."

"Swing around and go south," said Navigator. "Take a heading of a hundred-and-eighty degrees. That'll get us started. But give me a minute to look at my map." His hand was shaking as he tried to smooth the rumpled map.

"For Christ's sake, Navigator, what the hell do you have to look at? Just get us back to the base!"

"Roy, back-to-base takes us over the Adriatic. You're losing altitude now. If you have to go down, you don't want to go into the water. Roy, correct the heading to two-hundred-and-twenty-five degrees. That'll put us southwest, over land, north Italy."

"You mean into the Alps?" said Roy. "We're losing altitude and you want me to put this into a mountain?"

Roy didn't wait for an answer, but turned the plane southwest. "Attention, crew, we have to start unloading weight to help me maintain some altitude. Bombardier, release all the bombs. Everyone else..." He stopped while the plane rolled crazily and then settled down. "Everyone else, toss out anything that ain't nailed down—machine guns, flak suits, everything. But keep your sidearms. You might need 'em."

Bill, the copilot, came into the nose of the plane and Navigator handed him the cold, heavy machine guns to toss out the bomb bay. He pointed toward the radio operator and Bill just shook his head.

Navigator felt his stomach churn as he watched the bombs head down to God-knows-where. *Too bad we couldn't put them on the target*, he thought, then went back to his maps. The plane seemed to be heading past the mountain country. Just as he was thinking, *We might just make it*, the smoking engine flared and smoke filled the cabin.

"Prepare to bail out," Roy shouted on the intercom. "We're on fire."

Navigator snapped off his flak suit, pulled the intercom wire out of its socket, disconnected his oxygen-mask hose from the wall pipe and reached for the small, yellow, emergency bottle of oxygen. That would last while he jumped out of the plane and fell to breathing altitude.

Connect the oxygen-mask tube to the bottle, he said to himself. *Connect, damn you, why don't you connect!* It jammed. He tried to stay calm. You don't last long at thirty thousand feet with no oxygen.

In training, the crew had sat around wearing oxygen masks in a cabin pressurized to oxygen-scarce altitude. Each in turn had removed his mask and recited "Mary had a little lamb..." Before you got to "whose fleece was white as snow," you were unconscious and someone put the mask back on your face, and you were not even aware that you had passed out.

Don't breathe. Stay calm. You must be doing something wrong, he thought. Yes, he'd forgotten to twist it into place. Finally, he fixed the connection, inhaled deeply, and stumbled toward the bomb bay. As he passed the radio operator, the plane rolled and Navigator slid across the blood that was leaking across the floor.

The bomb bay looked welcome. Bailing out was a last resort. You stay with a plane when it has any chance of making an emergency landing but not when it's burning. He reached for his chute. *No chute!*

That's impossible, he told himself. *Be calm. You always wear the chute attached to the ring on the right side of the harness, so it hangs down and gets out of the way of the heavy flak suit.* Thank God, there it was, hanging by one ring!

As he swung the chute pack over to the left and connected it to its ring, the plane lurched and he slammed into Fred, the tail gunner, who was pushing his way toward the bomb bay. The gunner shoved him aside and jumped out the bomb bay. *Some nice guy. Rat leaving the ship.*

Bill, the copilot, was shouting into his ear, "For Christ's sake, what are you waiting for? Roy is trying to keep the ship under control while we get out. Get your ass out."

And Navigator dropped through the bomb bay.

Wait with the chute, he told himself. *Don't open it too soon, or it'll snare on part of the plane. Free-fall as far as you can. You mustn't hang there so the enemy has plenty of time to fire at you while you swing slowly from side to side. But watch the ground; open it in plenty of time for it to open before you hit.*

"No one ever complained of a chute that I packed not opening," flitted through his mind. That was the sick joke the chute-packers used to tell.

Whap! The chute opened. He didn't know how high he was, but he couldn't wait any longer; he had just pulled the rip-cord ring and there he was, floating down to God-knows-what.

Not bad, he thought. He had probably waited until he got to five thousand feet. He hadn't thought he had the guts to free-fall that far.

Below him, he could see the tail gunner's chute. Above him, another, probably Bill. On the ground, he could see a house and a barn, trees and an open field. *Jesus*, he thought, *I don't want to hit those buildings. If there's a wind, I'll be slammed against the walls. Or I could be hung up in the tree, a sitting duck for shooters on the ground.*

But how could he avoid them? Something about twisting the chute cords one way or another, but he couldn't remember which way. *Now, let's remember what you do when you hit. You come down hard; you have to hit, roll forward and try not to break something.*

They'd never had any chute practice. Too dangerous. Would lose too many airmen, just taking practice jumps. So they'd rehearsed by climbing to the top of a ladder and falling into sawdust on the ground. *Some rehearsal!*

Then he would have to get out of the harness. It was strapped between his legs and over his shoulders and came together at about his belly into a device that held it all together. The device had a disk in its center. It was twisted clockwise to prevent accidental opening. When ready to release it, you must twist the disk counter-clockwise. It still stayed fastened, but when you were ready to release, you hit the disk, and all four straps would fall away.

But was it clockwise to open or counter-clockwise? He couldn't remember. God, he was frightened. He decided it had to be in the locked position, which it always was, and he'd just twist it the other way and pray that it would open.

He missed the house, which was off to his right, and hit, rolled hard on his left side, slammed the disk on the chute harness with both fists, and heard his left ankle crack as the harness fell away. *Damn, that hurt!* But now, he had to get the hell out of there. *First thing, get rid of the chute, roll it up and bury it, so they won't find where you landed.*

Not a chance. He couldn't maneuver with a broken ankle, let alone give a decent burial to his chute. But he did pull the little medical pouch off the harness and stuffed it into his jacket pocket. He reached down and touched his left ankle gingerly. Broken, all right, but not a compound fracture. At least, no blood was showing.

He heard gunshots and began crawling with his elbows toward the house. He reached for his holster and pulled out his .45 caliber automatic, pulled back the hammer. The gun was cold in his sweating hand. Powerful weapon. If you hit any part of a guy's body, it would knock him off his feet.

If you hit. It was a defensive weapon. Good for maybe ten or twenty feet. It was a powerful weapon with such a strong recoil that you were aiming high after you fired your first round.

More shots. *If whoever is firing at me is a local, he'll shoot me*, he thought. *These guys have a score to settle for us dropping bombs on them and their families. The .45 maybe would hold him off until soldiers came and then I could*

My Life, A Novel

surrender to them—stand more of a chance of being captured alive as a prisoner of war. Or maybe the solders would shoot me down, as they had so many other prisoners.

But he couldn't die. Remember that? He had that special power. When he was born, the world began, he repeated to himself. History had already been written, the stars were in the skies, the pyramids had been built. Instant off-the-shelf-universe. And when he dies, the world ends. Everything stops. Everyone dies. The good guys and the bad guys. That would be the end of his mother and father and brother, and the pretty brunette who had waved a towel at him from the top of her apartment house and cried because his plane hadn't shown up. He started to cry.

He crawled on his belly, dragging his broken ankle as he headed for the barn. He was in a field that had been abandoned to climax growth. He worked his way to the cover of a tree. Nice thick trunk with graceful branches, lush green leaves and strange fruit.

An airman was swinging slowly from parachute cords that had caught in the branches. Slumped over, bleeding, and dead. It was Fred. So much for leaving the ship in a hurry.

The tree was surrounded by high green weeds with nice lacy flowers that he remembered from the vacant lot in back of his Bronx apartment house. When you snapped the stems, they leaked a milky fluid that smelled very "green."

The weeds provided him with some cover as he worked toward the barn. Still on his belly, he reached for the door and groaned as the pain in his left ankle went screaming all the way up his back. So he put his gun back into its holster and pushed the door open.

A bullet hit the door about six inches above his head. He crawled painfully into the dark interior, smelling hay and manure. A chicken cackled. His eyes were beginning to adjust a little to the dim light.

Something creaked and he heard, "Sst!"

He pulled out his gun, rolled left to face the noise, and a shooting pain drove him back onto his stomach. When he recovered, he moved more slowly and was able make out a disembodied little head coming up from the floor. He kept blinking his eyes to try to make out what this was all about.

The head said, "Sst," again, and alongside the head, he could see an arm with a hand that was waving at him.

But it wasn't waving, he thought. That was the way Italians say "Come here," palm down with fingers moving toward the wrist—the opposite of the way Americans motion.

By now, he could make out the child clearly. She was inviting him to come down a trap door.

Why not? he thought. *I might be Alice going down the rabbit hole, but the only alternative is for me to stay up here and get shot at by whoever is firing at the barn.*

He crawled under the open trap door and closed it behind him. Then, awkwardly, with the gun in his right hand, he lowered himself face-first down a rough wooden ladder, trying not to put any more pressure on his throbbing left ankle.

There, in a dim, smelly, room, lighted by a smoking lantern, were three people with their hands in the air.

The man wore a shirt that used to be white. His trousers were trussed up with a rope under his big belly. He needed a shave. He smiled nervously. The older woman wore an apron over a black dress and stared straight ahead. And the child hid behind a younger woman, whose face was obscured by a kerchief that was knotted under her chin. No one said anything for a while.

Navigator looked around the room and couldn't see anyone else. His ankle was pounding. He put his gun back into its holster and motioned to them to lower their hands. "I'm hurt. My ankle. You understand, capish?" He knew no Italian at all.

The man hiked his pants up and said, We give up." It came out "upa." "*Siamo vostri prigionieri.* We you prisoners," he said, motioning to all of them, "*Vogliamo arrenderi dai Americani.* We want to be captured by Americans."

That sounded reasonable. The forward Allied infantry lines must be pretty close.

Navigator sat down gingerly on an empty packing case. "Okay, you're my prisoners. Can you help this ankle? Look, it's broken and it hurts like hell."

My Life, A Novel

The older woman, who had pushed her hands into her apron, raised one hand tentatively and said, *"E possible aiutarsi."* She motioned toward a shelf and asked in sign language whether she could open a toolbox that sat at one end.

Navigator's eyes had adjusted now. The shelves in this makeshift bolt hole held jars of food and water, several white candles, stacks of rough clothing, some books and a bag of what appeared to be old rags. There were no weapons in view.

He nodded, but rested his hand on the butt of his pistol. The woman removed a pair of scissors, held them up and approached slowly. Then she removed his shoes, cut away his left pants leg, looked at the man and said, *"Da me la chiave."* He slowly removed a long flat wrench from the toolbox and asked in sign language whether he could approach.

Keeping his hand on his gun, Navigator nodded again.

The woman went back to the wall, dug some rags out of a bag and cut them into long strips.

Damn, he thought, *she's going to splint my ankle. Thank God! This one is probably a nurse or a midwife or something.*

In minutes, Navigator's left ankle was splinted to the wrench. He groped in his jacket for the medical pouch he had salvaged from the parachute harness, removed a small syringe and jabbed the needle into his exposed left thigh. The long soothing fingers of morphine began working their magic on his body.

He lay back and strained to see the face of the younger woman, but the kerchief hid her face. All he could see was her back as she moved to shelter the child. But the rhythm of her hips rolled past the morphine and the pain in his ankle.

The older woman straightened up and said *"La!"* Throughout the whole procedure, she had never made eye-contact with him, never smiled. It was as if to say, "I did my job. Now it's your turn."

Navigator groped around in his pockets and pulled out the package of papers given to all airmen for use if they got shot down. One page was a red-white-and-blue reproduction of an American flag. The other said in English: "This airman will write out an obligation to reward you for the help you have given him.

Upon presentation it will be honored by Allied authorities and with it is expressed the extreme gratitude of the Allies for any assistance which you have given our airmen."

He looked through the other languages, pointed to the Italian version, which started, "*Questo aviatore...*" and showed it to the woman. She read it slowly and nodded. Still no smile.

Navigator found a pencil in the outside of his jacket's left sleeve and looked up at the ceiling and thought for a moment. The morphine was making him groggy. He'd have to hurry.

"This good lady," he wrote, "splinted my ankle after I bailed out here over northern Italy, and her husband and daughter gave me shelter from hostile fire. Please reimburse them in accordance with the importance of what they did."

He dated the note and decided he really ought to put the woman's name in it. "What's your name?" he said. No response. "Your nomay. What are you called? Signora what?"

"*Signora Tedesco*," she said.

He reached over and kissed her hand. "I doubt if I'll ever see you again, but I owe you, madam, I owe you."

Then he fell asleep.

My Life: Chapter Two

Our plane finally righted itself, and I could see through the Plexiglas window that we were one of only three planes flying in a ragged V-formation. Four other planes had been knocked out of our seven-plane squadron. We didn't learn until we got back to the base that three had managed to limp their way home. All I could see was that one plane from our squadron was slowly circling below us, losing altitude. We had been instructed to watch for chutes from any damaged plane, so we could later say where the crew members might have come down.

I saw no chutes and the plane kept circling lower and lower. I could see no smoke either, a small hopeful sign. Why, I wondered, didn't those damned fools bail out? Then it exploded. Just a big puff of fire and smoke thousands of feet below us. The plane either had been hit again or something internal had blown up. We watched for a while longer, but still saw no chutes.

Our decimated squadron managed to get over the target and we released our bombs. The K-20 bomb-strike camera in our plane's belly got the required pictures of the strike pattern (no pictures, no mission credit).

Then we surveyed our own damage. Only one hit. A lone shrapnel fragment had slammed through the side of the cabin and hit the radio operator in the chest. He said he felt the warm blood running down his leg. But it was just his imagination, not a penetrating hit. The flak had bounced off his flak suit. Other than scaring the young man half to death, it had done no damage. Those steel-mesh garments actually worked sometimes.

On the way back to our base, I was miserable. The returns from bombing runs were always a letdown. This time, we still also thought that we had lost four planes from our squadron.

The frozen vapor from my oxygen mask began thawing, and the cold water leaked down my chest. When we were low enough, I snapped off my oxygen mask and lit a cigarette. I thought about the bomb run. I remembered that navigators were supposed to record cloud and weather conditions at various points of the trip. I couldn't remember much of it, so I made it up.

After we landed at our airstrip in Foggia, we were driven to some prefabs, where we reported our unhappy tidings. I also turned in my fictitious weather reports. Most navigators did the same thing. I'd once asked a debriefing officer what the hell they did with those cloud and wind reports.

"We use them to forecast the weather," he said.

That would explain why the forecasts were so often wrong. Ironically, fifty years later, weather-forecasting is still pretty inaccurate, and meteorologists don't have the excuse that they work with fictitious reports.

At the end of each mission, we were offered a "medicinal" shot of whiskey. I usually declined because I didn't drink much. That day, I took the whiskey. It did nothing for me.

After the debriefing, several of us climbed into a truck and sat on hard benches while a manic driver bounced over the hard, rutted ground and then caromed crazily down the narrow Italian road that led to our tent barracks. I said to someone sitting next to me that it would be a fitting end to that day to have survived enemy fire only to die in a truck that missed a curve.

He didn't answer me, probably because he was thinking what all the rest of us were thinking: What would the next mission bring?

There was no next mission. I asked out of the one that succeeded Linz because I had been shaken by that experience. You were allowed a "bye," if you didn't do it too often, but I was warned by a sarcastic companion that if the navigator on that mission died, it would haunt me for the rest of my life. He didn't, but the fact that I had asked for a bye did bother me, just on the principle of the thing.

I suited up to fly the next mission, and we rolled out onto the flight line. It was May, 1945. Suddenly I saw one of the most welcome sights of my life: red flares bursting over the control tower. The flight was aborted. The war was over.

Much celebration at the air base; lots of drinking; guns were fired in the air; some guys got hurt, perhaps more than they would have if they'd flown another mission. But, what the hell, it was over, and there were only the Japs to contend with and we wouldn't be there for a while.

I was in combat only a couple of months, flew five missions, got an Air Medal for doing nothing more than staying alive, and never got closer to the flak than to see an occasional piece ricocheting around the inside of the cabin. But the combat experience is still uncomfortably in residence deep in the back of my memory. The bursting flak doesn't keep me awake at night, but every once in a while, when I'm flying in a comfortable passenger plane and looking out the window, I imagine fiery black puffs walking alongside the left wing, and I wonder how long it will take that gunner to correct his aim just a little bit to the right.

Rome

One of the watering holes for Air Corps officers on leave in Rome was the Excelsior Hotel. The first time I was there, I went to my room, changed into a clean shirt and went down to the bar. It was crowded with young men drinking steadily with pretty young girls. It could have been a college fraternity party, except that all the men were in uniform and all the girls were Italian.

I asked a buddy where all the girls came from and how these guys managed to line up dates so fast. He said, "Take your pick. They're all for rent."

The price was usually quoted in cigarettes. We paid fifty cents for a carton of a major U.S. brand, but were rationed to one carton per week. The same carton sold for twenty-five dollars on the black market. One night with one of these young girls usually cost a carton of cigarettes. During the evening, couples would pair off and leave. Toward the end of the evening, there was often a raucous, drunken auction, and if you were not too choosy about taking leftovers, you could often get a night's companion for less than a carton.

Roy, my ascetic pilot, avoided this kind of ribaldry, but Bill, our feisty co-pilot, got involved with several girls. One day, I was scheduled for some leave time in Rome. I was looking forward to the rest, to doing a little sight-seeing, maybe a little drinking, but especially to calling Phyllis in New York. Rome was the only place where we could place international telephone calls.

Before I left, Bill took me aside and asked for a favor. "Gene," he said, "can you help me out with a whore in Rome?"

"Help you out how?"

"Well, I've seen her a couple of times and I think she's in love with me."

"Congratulations!"

"Cut that out. She's expecting to see me at the Excelsior Hotel tonight, and I just don't want to get involved. Would you tell her that I'm not going to be there…that I've been reassigned…that I've died? Tell her anything, but just get her off my hands."

Her name was Maria, and I remembered her from the last time Bill had introduced me to her. She was an attractive young girl with a shy smile and arms and legs that were painfully thin, but she could keep up with my exuberant co-pilot's dancing. So I agreed, not really knowing exactly what I was going to do. But you don't turn down your co-pilot in his time of need.

When I checked into the hotel I searched the bar, but no Maria. So I went to the dining room, ate a dinner that cost all of fifty cents for men in uniform, and went to the bar and nursed a drink for about an hour before we spotted each other.

"Where's Bill?" she said. She pronounced it "Beel." Maria had dark curly hair, bright dark eyes and a face that looked as if it had seen a lot of lousy things in this loser of a country. She couldn't have been any older than nineteen.

I was embarrassed by this whole thing. I told her Bill wasn't here yet. Her face fell, and she asked me if I knew when he was going to come. I said I didn't and asked her if she'd like a drink. She said she would and, as she drank, she occasionally looked around the room.

After about another hour, I screwed up my courage and finally told her that Bill wasn't going to be there at all. She looked at me with a resignation that spoke of having been brushed off before.

As she slowly got up from the table, I said on impulse, "Have you eaten?"

"No," she said, and started to leave.

"Hey, come join me."

After a pause, she did and we went back to the same dining room. When she ordered her meal, I told the waiter I had already eaten, and Maria turned to look at me. When the food arrived, she began to eat hungrily.

"You are very *gentile*," she said when she had finished, "to give me a meal because your friend is a bastard."

"Well, it was just because I figured you were planning to eat with him, and I didn't want you to go away hungry," I said. This whole thing was beginning to sound pretty maudlin, but I didn't know what else to say.

"You come sleep with me tonight?"

"No," I said, "I really can't."

"You so *gentile*, I won't charge anything."

I got up to go, taking her by an arm. God, it was thin. I wondered how much she ate in a day. I wondered if she was supporting anyone else. Many of the young prostitutes had children and occasionally one would bring a child around to meet her "friends." What a hell of a way to make a living, I thought. Then we walked out of the Excelsior.

Gene Cowen

A Novel: Chapter Two

They walked to the bottom of the big hill where, that morning, he had given a kid three Old Gold cigarettes to carry his duffel bag up to the Excelsior Hotel, then into a back street. From there, she led him through an alley, smoky with the smell of foods being cooked over little fires by raggedly dressed Italians.

His left ankle, now healed but tender, made him stumble a little on cobblestones that were just like the ones that lined the Boston Post Road where he'd grown up in the Bronx. It was dark, but that didn't worry him. Italy was a defeated, occupied country, but the Italians generally liked Americans. The U.S. fed many of them; it seemed as if half of them had relatives in Brooklyn. There were hardly any crimes of violence against the occupying Americans—lots of pilferage, but nothing worse.

He knew they were getting close when some people on the street nodded to Maria and she nodded back. They climbed a staircase and she knocked on a door.

A smiling fat woman in a housecoat let her in without a word, and Maria led the way down a dim hall to a door, which she closed behind them. The room had a bed, made up with a clean worn sheet, a blanket and a pillow, one chair, and nothing else on the floor. A painting that he couldn't identify hung on a flaking wall. His one visit to the Louvre in France hadn't included Italian religious art.

She undressed quickly and climbed under the covers. So did he and put an arm around her.

"How often do you do this?" he asked.

"You mean not charge?"

"Well, that, too. But I mean how often do you go off with soldiers?

"You going to reform me?"

"No, I didn't mean that."

"I like you, so I tell you a few things," she said. "I gotta live. There's no work here. No jobs, no money. So it's this or starve. If I get one good meal a day, I'm lucky. That's why I like you for giving me dinner. Besides, I got a kid." She pronounced it "kidda."

"You wouldn't be pulling my leg?"

"I can do that, too."

"No, I mean this sounds like a story you tell people who want to know about your life."

"No, I don't make up stories. My story is simple: I told you, I gotta eat. Listen, I thought we come here to make love. No charge. You want to talk, maybe I charge you," she said, and then she laughed. And then they made love.

When he got out of bed, he asked if there was some warm water. She got the lady in the housecoat, who brought a battered tin bowl. He performed the ablutions that the medics at the base said you should do after every sex act, and he squirted a tube of antibiotic into the right places.

She watched with a bemused expression. "That for VD?" she asked. "You don't trust me to be clean?"

He laughed. "I trust you, honey, but cut the deck," he said, but only to himself, because Maria wouldn't understand cowboy-movie jokes.

She slipped cotton panties over her hips, the only thing fleshy on her thin frame. "Mediterranean hips," his family used to call them. Not what chic women wanted, but appealing in bed. Her lips were sensual and animated.

She stuck her tongue out of one corner of her mouth as she wriggled into a simple, pleated black skirt and buttoned on a plain white blouse. She tied her full curly hair back with a headband.

As they left the room, Maria handed the fat woman a bill.

"Here, let me get that," Navigator said to Maria and reached into his pocket.

"Not part of our deal," she said. "No charge tonight." Then, as they walked down the steps she said, "You, I only charge for conversation." Another smile flickered across her face. A curl had escaped from the headband and she brushed it back.

As they walked back to the Excelsior, a breeze rustled the pink oleander flowers. There was a faint, sweet scent in the air. A lemon slice of moon hung in the umbrella pine tree to his right. He was feeling happier than he had for a long time. He was finally no longer a virgin. He had handled it like a pro. No hesitation, smooth moves. There was no way she could tell.

When they got to the foot of the hill within sight of the Excelsior, Maria said, "Can I ask you something?"

"There's a charge," he said.

"When you fly in this war, are you afraid you die?"

She didn't realize how complicated that question was. As they continued to walk, he reached into his pocket and pulled out his pipe and a tobacco pouch. Filling a pipe was a great way to buy time while you thought of an answer. He pressed the tobacco into the bowl slowly, flicked open a Zippo lighter and drew in some smoke.

The bowl had a rough finish because of what had happened when he'd bought it a few weeks ago. He had spent a day on Gibraltar, climbing hills and looking into shop windows. In a tobacco shop, the shopkeeper had seen the name on his wristband and asked if he were Jewish. Yes, he said.

Well, so was the tobacconist! Therefore, he was going to give him an especially good deal on this fine pipe made in Gibraltar.

When he got back to the base and lit up the pipe, the finish ran down the side in blotchy streaks. So much for *landsmen*!

"No," he said to Maria. "Not dying. I'm afraid as hell when I'm being shot at. I'm afraid I'll be wounded, that I'll lose an arm or a leg or an eye. But not dying."

"Why not dying?" The oleander gave her black curls a halo glow.

He sighed. He had never discussed this with anyone else, and here he was, about to unburden himself to a whore. But why not? Here was someone he'd never see again. So he explained that he thought he had this special power. The world had started when he was born and would end when he died, and he was pretty sure that it was not yet time for the world to end.

My Life, A Novel

He watched her closely through the pipe smoke. She smiled, leaned against him and said quietly into his ear, "Navigator, you got this thing wrong. The world is going to end when *I* die, not you."

The air was still. A cloud hid the moon. He stopped walking and slowly blew a perfect smoke ring. "Damn, that was a good answer!" he said.

By then, they were at the Excelsior Hotel.

"I hope the first time for you was good," she said.

He flushed.

She reached into her purse, wrote on a piece of paper and handed it to him. "My whole name is Maria Tedesco. This is my phone number. If you come back to Rome, call me at that number. Maybe we talk some more. No charge. *Arrivederci*."

He stared at the name. "Tedesco," he said. "Are you related...?"

Maria laughed a conspiratorial laugh. Her face softened from that of a young hooker to a girlfriend who had a secret. "You some dummy, Navigator. I'm the one, and you never recognized me. That was my mother who fixed your leg and my uncle who helped. I was off in the corner, protecting my daughter from the crazy American who was waving a pistol at us. You were in such bad shape, you probably couldn't even hit the wall with that gun, but I wasn't going to take a chance. The child never should have invited you into our cellar."

He was having trouble absorbing all this, and he felt like a fool. This was the girl in the kerchief at the back of the cellar, the one with her back to him and the sexy hips.

"How did I ever get out of that cellar?" he asked. "When I woke up, I was in a field hospital and the medics said some locals had handed me over to the troops who took the town. They took me to the medics and continued on their way. The medics didn't know any of the details. They put my leg in a proper cast and said to stop worrying about who put the wrench on the leg. 'You're alive,' the head guy said. 'So be thankful and stop asking questions.'"

"The morning after you came," said Maria, "your soldiers arrived, and we came out and said we had a soldier with a bad leg in the cellar. They got you out, and that was all."

"Well, I wrote that message about your mother. I hope they gave you something."

"No, they said her name was not on it, so we couldn't collect. What do you expect?"

He was angry now and confused and embarrassed. Those people had saved his life. "Look, babe. That's awful! Tell me what to do. I can send you money."

"No. *Questo e la mode da mia vita*. This is the way life has been for me," she said with a shrug. "Don't try to change it." Then, pointing to her note that he still held in his hand, she said, "Call me some day when you're back here."

My Life: Chapter Three

As Maria and I walked out of the Excelsior Hotel, I looked at the undernourished girl with the shy smile and dark curls and said, "You know, you're really very kind. I know you mean well, but I can't sleep with you tonight. I planned to call my girlfriend in the States; I just can't."

She shook my hand solemnly and said she understood. I wished her good luck. I never saw her again.

Gene Cowen

My Life: Chapter Four

The *Foggia Occupator*

When the war in Europe ended in May, 1945, we were transferred to Naples with our planes, which were stripped of their weaponry and converted into jerry-built transport craft. We flew the American Fifth Army from Naples across the Mediterranean to Port Lyautey near Casablanca in Africa. The Fifth Army was on its way to the planned Japanese invasion, but President Truman, may his memory be blessed, authorized the dropping of atom bombs, and the war finally ended—with the horrors of Hiroshima and Nagasaki, but without the carnage to both sides of an invasion.

So we continued flying the ground troops out of Italy, now on their way home. We were told that after we'd flown out the last of those troops, we were to fly ourselves out and go home.

One happy night, the orders were posted for my crew to leave. There was a great air of celebration. Lots of the guys took their extra uniforms, which they had paid for themselves, and even some of their side arms, which they had not, and sold them to black-market operatives in town. I hesitated, not out of a sense of patriotism, but rather because I felt uncomfortable shipping out with nothing more than the uniform on my back.

Later that night, our orders came down off the bulletin board and up went others that directed us to be posted back to Foggia. It seemed that the air crews who had had longer combat duty than we had complained like hell that the low-pointers were going home before they were, and they'd gotten shipping orders in our place. It was only fair, but some of our guys, especially the ones with wives waiting for them at home, were bitter. For me, however, it turned out to be the introduction to a wonderful experience.

We were a heavy bomber outfit. Did the United States need Flying Fortresses in Italy? What for? To stop petty pilfering? To drop bombs onto food protesters? Hardly. It was only later, when we saw the Cold War divide the former allies into rival camps, that I deduced that our bombers had been kept at Italian airfields, just a few flying minutes away from the Soviet-bloc countries, as a stern signal to the Russians.

Whatever the reason, we were there, and there wasn't a damned thing for us to do. Air crews got fifty percent additional pay for flight duty, and four hours a month in the air qualified as flight duty. So the enterprising folks at headquarters organized "time flights," in which planes loaded with crewmen like rush-hour buses took off once each month, flew around in big circles for four hours, and then landed. That meant that for the other 716 hours in each month, we had a choice of sleeping alone, looking around for local girls to sleep with (few of whom were available in and around prim Roman Catholic Foggia), drinking the inexpensive and plentiful U.S. whiskey, or going stir crazy—which some poor fellows did.

Or find something creative. As a student, I had been interested in writing, so I followed up a rumor that someone was starting a weekly newspaper and found Milton Hoffman, a quirky sergeant in charge of the Information and Education Department. He was an older man (I was twenty, so Milt must have been pushing thirty), short, balding and wonderfully irreverent. He thought the base needed a journal of some sort, and he gave it the inelegant name, *Foggia Occupator*. It was our hometown weekly, covering the doings of a bunch of airmen who were marking time until they could get shipped home. We reported on the troops' basketball and softball games, boxing matches, and the weddings of GIs to local Italian girls.

After Milton was shipped home, I became the editor and I loved the job. I wrote some short stories, stirred up a little trouble about the maltreatment of some black troops, and I covered one hell of an Italian food riot.

Our stories were typed in Foggia; then we drove the copy and photographs to Bari, about sixty miles south. There the words were set in type by a method which had not advanced much from Gutenberg's time, which amounted to picking metal letters out of cases. The upper case held the capital (upper-case) letters and the lower case held—guess what?—the lower-case letters. Letters formed words and words became a line of type one column wide. They were picked out of the cases one letter at a time and held in a little metal device that became a "stick." To "justify" a line, so that both right and left edges touched the borders of the column, the typesetter dropped the requisite number of wafer-thin pieces of metal between the words. Nice and neat.

Several lines would be bound together tightly with twine and placed carefully onto a flat chase until the typesetters—working with layouts we provided—had a page, with headlines, borders and metal halftone engravings that had been made elsewhere.

Italian printers set the metal type, based upon the written words we gave them, few of which they understood. So they read the copy phonetically ("the" was sounded out "te-hey" and so forth). You can imagine our hilarity as we read proof—and Editor Milton's apoplexy when we missed occasional errors.

Now, about the riot.

One afternoon, I was walking down the main street of Foggia when I found myself surrounded by angry marching demonstrators. Marches were not unusual. Italians marched in religious parades, political parades and apparently parades just for the hell of parading. But this time the marchers were combative and carried signs saying, "*Pane e Lavoro*" (bread and work). Some marchers were swinging clubs, and others were stopping trucks and beating up the drivers.

The belligerent crowd was friendly enough toward Americans in uniform, so I asked a demonstrator what was going on. He explained that, even though people were starving here in southern Italy, those bastards in the north were shipping grain out of the country to get higher prices, and the demonstrators were going to put a stop to that.

That was a story I wanted to cover, but it needed pictures. I ran back to our office to look for our contract photographer but couldn't find him or his camera. Damn! I wasn't going to miss this one.

I searched around and found a K-20 aerial camera on a shelf. It was a heavy blunderbuss that looked liked a small steel pig. On the left of its snout was a handle and on the right, a lever, like a slot machine. You aimed the snout, cranked the slot-machine lever to move the film and pulled a trigger to click the shutter.

It had been used to take bomb-strike photographs from bomber aircraft, but once I had asked a Signal Corps photographer if it could be used to take pictures on the ground. He said, "I suppose you could.

Its focus is set at infinity, but I guess if you got back about fifteen or so feet, you'd get a picture."

So I picked up the monster, got back out on the street and began following the crowd that had by now gathered into a seething mob at the train station. They were going to commandeer a train, get grain off that was being shipped out of the country, and then deal with those black-marketers on board.

I stepped back and waited until the train arrived. It was not really a station, just a place where the train stopped. A boarding party climbed aboard, and then I heard shots, but couldn't see who had fired at whom or whether any one had been hit.

Suddenly a man came running off the train. The crowd closed in, clubs flew, and then the crowd parted in front of me. The rioters wanted to punish these people, but apparently not kill them.

A badly beaten figure limped miserably toward me. When he saw my camera, he took his hands away from a bleeding face and said in Italian, "Look what they did to me!"

Crank, click, and I got a picture.

Behind me, jeeps with U.S. military police pulled into place to contain the riot. One drove up and hauled off the victim, then moved back to monitor the action.

Another man came running off the train, the crowd closed in, delivered its punishment and I cranked and clicked. From somewhere, a horse-drawn cart showed up and men began loading sacks of grain off the train. Atop the cart flew, of all things, an American flag. *Crank, click.*

Then the people on the train apparently decided to fight back. They leaped off, picked up rocks from the other side and began pelting us. I watched rocks fly, decided I could dodge them, and pointed my camera at more action.

Crank, wham! A rock had hit the blunderbuss camera. I looked at the welt in the steel snout and wondered what would have happened if that had been my head.

Just at that time, the MPs came up with the answer, and a jeep roared up beside me. "Lieutenant," said a G.I. with a sub-machine gun, "you'd better get your ass out of here before you get hurt."

I agreed and left, happy that I had apparently gotten some good pictures and pleased that not once during the melee had any Italian protester threatened this screwy American soldier who was taking pictures in the midst of shooting, flying rocks and flailing clubs.

Shooting in Cerignola

Covering the Foggia riot story was one thing. Getting the story printed was another. I gathered up the news copy and photographs, got a jeep from the motor pool and drove south to Bari to have our little newspaper printed. It meant that I had to run a gauntlet of sections of southern Italy that were boiling with angry people facing starvation.

Getting there was no problem, but as I returned from Bari with my jeep full of newly-printed *Foggia Occupators*, I picked up a Polish soldier who was hitching a ride. Transportation was hard to come by in those days, and I always gave a lift to anyone in an Allied uniform.

My passenger was a friendly fellow, but he spoke only Polish and I spoke only English, so we conversed in a fractured pidgin-Italian.

It was nighttime and, as we drove through Cerignola en route to Foggia, we noticed that the streets—normally bustling with strolling people—were empty. Suddenly, we heard automatic gunfire in the near distance.

I reached into the jeep's glove compartment and pulled out a .45-caliber automatic and put it into my lap. The Polish soldier offered to protect me if I'd give him the gun. But I told him that I would carry it and protect him.

I continued driving cautiously and had hopes of getting through whatever was going on when the jeep coughed and died. My Polish friend and I looked at each other and agreed by hand signals that we needed to seek help.

I put the pistol under my jacket, careful not to let it show because the sight of a gun might itself draw fire. We were walking along the deserted streets, staying close to building walls, when I saw the welcome sign of a police station. I called out loudly that we were "amici" (friends), knocked on the front door and opened it.

We were greeted by several Italian policemen, who explained that they were not involved in the turbulence outside because the national police and soldiers were handling the situation. They let me call our air base, and I got in touch with someone in the motor pool. I told him where the jeep had given up the ghost and said, "Please get someone to get us out of this shooting gallery."

He said he would try, but that it might take a while at that time of the night.

The Italian police graciously offered us some wine while we waited. I had to laugh when I saw an early example of glass recycling: the wine had been bottled in old Coca Cola bottles.

We waited and waited. Finally, I decided to take my chances on the deserted streets and find out whether some local might have stripped the wheels off our abandoned jeep. When I got there, there was no vehicle at all, but far down the street, I could see someone towing what looked like my jeep.

I pulled out the .45 and began running after the convoy shouting, "Stop" in English, Italian and any other language that came to mind.

The convoy stopped and several of my crew mates jumped off with their guns drawn, ready to do battle. Fortunately, we recognized one another before anyone fired. I was angry with them for being so late, and they were angry at me for having abandoned the jeep. When they found it, they'd assumed I had been kidnapped.

Everyone calmed down quickly, and my Polish friend and I got a ride back the base, much happier than we had been for several hours.

#

We distributed the *Foggia Occupator* to our readers and we also posted copies of the pictures—which, I must say, were very good—on bulletin boards for the locals to see. Editor Milt Hoffman said a number of residents of the area were delighted to see how well they photographed.

We had a long-standing arrangement with the *Stars and Stripes* in Rome. That was a "real" newspaper, and we often phoned in stories from southern Italy, in exchange for which they gave us supplies, such as flashbulbs, which we never seemed to have enough of.

The day after the riot, I had called the story in to them, and I later sent them, by courier plane, negatives and prints of the riot pictures that I had taken.

Gene Cowen

About a week after the event, I got a call from the editor. He apologized for not using the pictures, but said they had run the story several days earlier and that, by now, it was stale news for the *Stars and Stripes*. However, Mortimer Belshaw, the Associated Press correspondent in Rome, wanted to talk to me. He said he liked the pictures, his photographers were all off covering the Greek elections, and would I mind if he offered the pictures to New York? I said I would be honored and promptly forgot the incident.

About two weeks later, I got a letter from home. In it, Mother asked if I had seen those terrible food riots in Foggia. In the envelope were tear sheets from the New York *Daily News*, the *Mirror* and the *Journal-American*. There were my pictures. I was famous! Or was I? The credit lines said simply "AP Photos."

Well, if not famous, then maybe I was rich. I had heard of news organizations paying large sums of money for good pictures. I quickly took the next Air Force plane to Rome to look up the AP correspondent.

My Life, A Novel

A Novel: Chapter Three

The phone rang. It was someone from *Life* magazine. The caller wanted to talk to "that guy who took the riot pictures."

A frisson of excitement tingled down Navigator's neck. "I'm the guy."

"Those were good pictures, and we have what AP moved, but we need one more, something that no one else has."

"They only used seven. I can send you a few more to pick from."

"We're in a hurry and I'd like to see them. You in your office? Stay there. I can get a plane down to you in about two hours."

Wow! This was what he had dreamed about. He pulled out the riot-pictures file and spread them out on his desk. For a panicky moment, he couldn't locate the negatives. Fortunately, they were in another drawer, tucked carefully into glassine envelopes.

The *Life* guy arrived about three hours later, complete with magnifying glass and release forms. "I like this one," *Life* said. "Jeez, look at that one with the American flag. Sonny, I think we've got a cover."

It took Navigator about ten seconds to focus. "Did you say cover? On *Life*?"

"Well, don't get your bowels in an uproar," said *Life*. "You never know with magazine covers. Maybe somebody will take a shot at the President and that would bump you. But we've got a shot at it. Fiorella LaGuardia is in Europe on a mission to discover the extent of food shortages and starvation. This should tie in nicely. I can offer you only two thousand dollars for exclusive use of this negative. No dickering. Take it or leave it."

He took it with no dickering, but his hand shook as he held the two-thousand-dollar check. It was all over in about thirty minutes. He never even got *Life*'s name.

Gene Cowen

This was more money than he had ever seen in his life. What should he do with it? The first thing was to get it out of this country and into a bank somewhere. Who knew how long the check would be good? Maybe *Life* would go out of business. Maybe somebody would stop the check.

He endorsed it over to his mother and quickly posted a letter.

Three days later, another call. Could he come to Rome? The picture was on the cover and *Life* wanted a little story about this courageous young soldier who had taken the picture.

He changed into a clean uniform—the one with the word "PRESS," which he had stitched onto the epaulets. He told the office where he could be reached in Rome and got on the next courier plane, thinking, *Courageous, my ass. All I did was stand there and wind that camera. Everybody was friendly. The MPs saved my neck.* But he wouldn't say any of that.

The *Life* offices were in a cramped office in a Mussolini-modern building. People worried over papers on a desk; others pushed photographs around a layout sheet; phones rang. No one paid any attention as Navigator entered.

A guy in a fedora came over and introduced himself as the one who had talked to him on the phone. "Let me introduce you to some of the people here," said the *Life* guy. "Shake hands with Bob Capa and Henri Cartier-Bresson. Capa took that great picture during the Spanish Civil War, the one of a soldier falling a moment after he'd been shot. Cartier-Bresson's work has been exhibited in the Louvre, but he spent most of the war in a German prison camp. They've just formed the Magnum photo agency, and we're doing a lot of business with them."

Capa was a wild-eyed guy, who said hello in some sort of accent that Navigator couldn't place.

Cartier-Bresson said in a soft French accent, "Those were nice pictures you took—good geometry, nice tension in the frame. You could teach something to American photographers."

"Me? Teach photographers?" he asked.

"Yes," said Cartier-Bresson. "You can teach them that you can take a good picture without flashbulbs. Almost everything the Americans do is with a Speed Graphic and a monster flash.

They don't know that using a flash is like shooting a gun in church."

Navigator wanted to ask these world-class photographers more. He wanted to learn, to find out if they really thought he had that special talent that converted a photographer into a photojournalist. But he never did because the phone rang and the *Life* guy told him there was a call for him. It had to be the office. No one else knew he was there.

"Pal," said Captain Piccozzi in a voice that crackled more than the static on the line, "just what in the hell are you up to?"

It was the first time during the year that Navigator had known the officer in charge of Information and Education at the air base that he had ever heard Mike Piccozzi sound agitated. He'd always been a congenial, supportive guy, who left the little newspaper staff alone to do its thing, except that occasionally, he would ask that they not do anything to get Piccozzi into trouble. He hadn't seen his wife and children for three years and couldn't wait to get home.

"Well, for one thing, Mike, I'm in *Life* magazine," Navigator said proudly. "You know those pictures of riots? AP moved them, and they appeared in a lot of stateside newspapers. Then *Life* decided they wanted a cover shot."

"Buddy, you have no idea what a can of worms you've opened," said Piccozzi. "When those pictures first appeared in the States, the credit line said only 'AP Photo.' But then comes *Life*'s cover and they credit you. Army Air Corps command in Washington just called me and wanted to know how you come off self-dealing with a magazine. They're especially ticked off about that picture on *Life*'s cover of those Italians waving an American flag while they're beating up train passengers and hijacking sacks of grain. They want to know if it's true that that picture was a set-up and you gave the Italians the flag."

"Shit, Mike. I didn't set up anything. I don't know where they got the flag. There are American flags all over Foggia. They probably swiped one from some Army building."

"Listen," said Piccozzi, in what sounded like a conspiratorial voice over the line static. "AP and *Life* usually pay freelancers for those kinds of pictures. You didn't happen to get any money, did you?"

"Well, as a matter of fact, I did," he said. He felt a dream beginning to evaporate.

"Buddy," said Piccozzi, "listen to me. Give back that money. You and I are going to deny that any money ever changed hands. I've got too much at stake to let something like this ruin my chances of going home. Those were pictures taken by an officer in a U.S. Army Air Corps uniform while he was on duty, and they were taken with equipment that is the property of the United State Government. They're not your pictures; they're the Air Corps' pictures. Go back to reporting on the basketball games that the guys on the base play. Take pictures of the reformed whores they marry. But get the hell out of this big-time photography crap. If you don't unscrew from this, buddy, you are going to be court-marshaled."

Navigator hung up the phone and left the office without saying goodbye to anybody. He had to make two calls.

My Life: Chapter Five

Belshaw

I got the next plane for Rome and looked up Mortimer Belshaw, the AP correspondent. He greeted me warmly and said that when he offered the pictures to New York, it was coincidental with former New York mayor Fiorella La Guardia's taking over as roving ambassador to deal with food shortages in Europe. So the pictures were timely and lots of papers used them.

"What are they worth?" I asked Belshaw.

"We have a standard free-lance rate of three dollars a picture," he said. "New York took seven of them, so I can give you twenty-one dollars."

I don't cry readily, but I had a hard time fighting back tears right then. I thought about it for a while and realized there wasn't a damned thing I could do. AP had the pictures, which I had taken while on duty with a military camera, so they weren't even my personal property.

"I don't want the twenty-one dollars," I said. "But could you give me twenty-one dollars worth of flashbulbs for the paper? We never can get enough of them."

He agreed readily and I got up to leave. The transaction behind us, Belshaw invited me to have a cup of coffee with him. No, I was soured on my whole relationship with that news organization, so all I did was tuck the flashbulb packages under my arm and head for the next plane back to Foggia.

Gene Cowen

A Novel: Chapter Four

"Mom, it's me," he said on the transatlantic call.

"Are you all right? What time is it where you are?" she asked.

He told her he was fine and that he hoped he hadn't awakened her. He had, she said, but she was delighted to hear from him.

"I saw your snapshot on the cover of *Life* magazine," she said. "I hope they gave you a pretty penny for it."

"Snapshot? Mom, that photograph was..." But he didn't pursue it. "Listen, I just mailed you a check I got for the pictures..."

"Good for you. How much?"

When he told her, there was a pause.

"But you have to tear up the check," he said and he told her why.

A longer pause.

"Listen," she said. "You know how good Uncle Manny is about those things. I'm sure if I talked to him, he'd figure out some way to cover up..."

"No, Mom, tear it up. If you don't, I'll be the richest man in an Army prison."

"I could also write to Senator Lehman again."

"Again? What have you been writing to Senator Lehman about?"

"I said that now that the war was over, the government should be shipping you home."

"Did he answer you?"

"Sort of. His letter said, 'Thanks for your letter and I'm pleased you agree with my strong stand on government shipping.'"

"Tear up the check, Mom."

"Okay. Take care of yourself. Come home as soon as you can."

My Life: Chapter Six

<u>White Christmas</u>

A.J. Leibling once wrote that the power of the printing press belongs solely to those who own the presses. That could also apply to the editor of an army publication in southern Italy in 1945. As editor of the *Foggia Occupator*, I began publishing my own short stories.

One was called "White Christmas" and was about a GI who meets this attractive young prostitute at the Hotel Excelsior bar. They negotiate a cigarette price, go to bed, and later talk about love and truth and the meaning of life. When he returns to his base, he decides he is in love and wants to marry her. On Christmas Eve, he meets her again in the bar, and while the band is playing Irving Berlin's classic song "White Christmas," asks to marry her. She says no. So, with a heavy heart and the music in the background, he asks to go to bed with her one last time. She says she doesn't do those things on Christmas Eve, but maybe she would after she goes to church for Christmas Mass. The end.

That was my "White Christmas" short story. Not a bad story, if I remember it correctly, and the guys in the outfit who read it liked it. The Catholic chaplain, however, told me forcefully that he didn't like it, but I could understand that.

Shortly after "White Christmas" was published, I read in *Camp News Service* that a publication in the States was running a short-story contest and I entered my story. After several weeks, I got a letter saying that I had come in third and that my prize was a three-week subscription to the publication, the *People's Weekly World*, which I had never heard of. I was delighted.

One of my compatriots on the *Foggia Occupator* said that if third prize in the contest was a three-week subscription, first prize was probably one week. But I was still proud of the award. I told the paper to send the award to my home, since I was shortly to ship out. When I did get home, I learned to my dismay that the newspaper was a direct descendant of the Communist *Daily Worker* and copies were coming to me by mail.

Mother was very upset. "I'm ashamed for the mailman," she said. I told her that not many more copies would arrive and not to worry.

But I must say that even I was nervous about it. In later years, whenever I needed FBI security clearances for government positions, I shuddered at the thought that someone might accuse me of having written for a Commie publication.

A Novel: Chapter Five

Navigator looked at his watch, reset it to local time, and realized he had a couple of hours to kill before the meeting. It was a navigator's "hack" watch, which could be stopped on the second to conform to the time counted down by the briefing officer before each flight. For bombing, it was always "hacked" on Greenwich Mean Time, so that all crews' watches agreed.

Navigator folklore was that you were supposed to leave it set on GMT and then sit at a bar next to a pretty girl with your sleeve pulled back. She would then say, "Oh my, I had no idea that was the time," which was supposed to be a good entry line to making a date. But this navigator never met girls at bars. The only bars he frequented were officers' clubs, and the girls there were already spoken for. The few girls he met outside of his fantasies were young Italians. and they couldn't have cared less what time it was.

So his watch was dutifully set on Rome local time, and he passed that time by taking a Red Cross tour of a cameo store with its own workshop. He was fascinated by the lovely shells, which he had often admired when raggedy kids hawked them on street corners with the assurance that they were "real cameos."

When the group got to the workshop, they were introduced to the owner, a Mr. Appa.

Navigator asked him, "How can you tell if it's a real cameo?"

"They're all 'real." said Mr. Appa. "Cameos are shells, very delicate and beautiful. What separates the good ones from the poor ones is the quality of the artisan's work. You judge a cameo the way you do any piece of fine jewelry."

Navigator followed the owner to a display case.

"Look at these three trays," said Mr. Appa. "Here is the work of apprentices." It was obvious that the workmanship was rough. "Now, here is the work of my journeymen. See the better quality? And here are the master craftsmen's."

They were beautiful and dramatic, with multi-colors that had been brought up by the level at which the artisan had dug into the different colors of the multi-layered shell. These were not just the pale-faced ladies' heads he remembered his grandmother wearing. They were beautifully-etched Roman warriors, scenes of the Three Graces, even a contemporary head copied from a photograph supplied by the person who had commissioned it.

Navigator negotiated a price with Mr. Appa and took several that were matched to make a bracelet and ear rings for his girl friend in the States, as well as a pendant for his mother. Finally, he bought one more, a dramatic head of a Roman warrior in a battle helmet with a shimmering feathered plume. He had that one put into a separate small brown jewelry envelope, which he dropped into his pocket. Then he stopped off at a PX and picked up a box of candy bars.

Maria had said on the phone that he could visit her in her "real" home. It was obvious what she meant. The address she had given him was in a lower-middle-class neighborhood, but the building was a lot more respectable-looking than the hovel where they had bedded down weeks before.

The door to Maria Tedesco's apartment was opened by a middle-aged woman whom he recognized. She looked hard at him, frowned and motioned him inside. It was a cramped apartment. The living room was simply decorated with inexpensive and well-worn furniture.

"*Buon giorno, Signora Tedesco,*" he said. "I want to thank you for protecting me and for splinting my ankle. I also want to apologize for the American troops' not giving you any money. Please take this as a small measure of thanks. I wish It could be more, but that's all I could raise." He drew from his pocket two hundred dollars in lire, which he had scrounged up before he left the base, and handed it to Mrs. Tedesco.

The woman simply nodded, pocketed the money and stood aside so he could see Maria standing alongside a couch. Behind Maria's skirt, he could see the feet of a little girl.

My Life, A Novel

"Hi, Navigator!" Maria said. All he could see of her daughter was dark curly hair and one eye peeking from behind her mother's skirt.

"I know you, *bambina*," he said. "We met in the barn. You really saved my life, and I should have given you some of this money, but I know your grandma will be sure that you get your share. What's your name, dear?"

The head disappeared.

"Her name is Anna," Maria said, reaching back to ruffle the curls. "I'm glad you've come. I see you've brought me something."

"I don't know if it's for you. I think it really is for Anna." He reached into the bag and pulled out a chocolate bar.

An outstretched hand came from behind the skirt, and he could see the three-year-old whose head had materialized from the cellar trap door. She whispered, "*Grazie,*" and disappeared again behind the skirt.

"Oh, yes, I guess I do have something for you," he said to Maria, and handed her the brown jewelry envelope.

When she undid the flap and the unmounted cameo dropped into her hand, she glowed momentarily.

"I'm sorry I couldn't get more, but at that point I ran out of money," he said.

"I don't believe that," said Maria. "The picture you took is on the cover of *Life* magazine, which I just saw, and you must have made a lot of money making us Italians look like train robbers."

Little Anna came forward with a shy smile to ask for more candy, which he gave her. He looked at this little replica of her mother, with the same hair and eyes, but not the bitter lines around her mouth.

She stood next to him while she munched, and he ruffled her hair. Then she said something to her mother. Maria shook her head and answered abruptly. All this in Italian, which he could not understand.

"Well," he said, "I want to tell you about those pictures, but not here. First, tell me what Anna said."

"She wanted to know if you were the man who would marry me and take us to America. And since you probably want to know what I said, I said you were too smart for that."

"Tell her I can't take her to America, but I can take her to dinner if her mother says its okay."

"It's okay if you also take her mother."

They walked down a street that was crowded with early evening strollers. Most couples either held hands or walked arm-in-arm in the Italian tradition. Anna took her mother's hand, and then Maria quietly put her arm through his.

At the restaurant, he and Maria ordered broiled fish and the three-year-old asked for fish and chips. Before starting to eat, the child offered him a chip, which he took with thanks.

"Are you originally from Rome?" he asked.

"No, Palermo."

"How did…?"

"Navigator, you ask too many questions. So let me answer all at once while you chew your fish. Anna's father—yes, we were married in church—was in the Italian army. He died at Salerno. Then my father was killed during your bombings."

That hit home, but he said nothing.

"So my mother decided we should get away from the invading American army and come live with her brother who you met when you dropped in on us near Verona. Then we recently moved to this apartment in Rome. You can understand why she wasn't happy to see you when you came into our cellar and now to our apartment. Momma scrubbed floors and took in laundry until Anna was born. Now, she also takes care of her. I look for work. There is no work in this country. Once I got work in a restaurant, once in a bookshop. That's why sometimes I work nights, as you know."

The waiter cleared the dishes and asked what they wanted for dessert. Anna said *gelato*. He said he would like ice cream, too, but could he have it in a half-melon?

The waiter shrugged and brought his melon in one bowl and the ice cream in another. He reached over, dumped the ice cream into the melon half, and began to eat.

Anna giggled and whispered something to her mother.

My Life, A Novel

"She said you're a crazy eater," Maria translated.

"Tell her that if she talks like that, she's never going to get to America."

"No, I won't. She's too young for wise-guy American jokes."

Later, the three of them walked back to the apartment. After Maria had tucked Anna into bed, they left for a stroll.

Again, she took his arm "My daughter said to tell you you're the right guy for me."

He didn't want to pursue that line of conversation, so he told her what had happened with *Life* magazine.

"So you fucked up," she said.

"Maria, can I ask you a favor?"

"Not tonight," she said.

"No, that's not what I mean. I just wonder if you would mind not using gutter language."

Her face flushed and she began shouting. A couple near them looked at the lovers' quarrel.

"Listen, Navigator, who the hell do you think you are? You fly to Italy and bomb us—yes, you personally. You come to Rome and hop into bed with me. You take pictures of Italians beating each other with clubs like savages. And then you say, 'Don't use gutter language!' What's with you? Are you Jewish or something?"

"As a matter of fact, I am," he said. "Not a very good Jew, but one just the same."

Maria looked away. Long pause.

"Hey, Navigator, I didn't really mean it that way." Another pause. "I don't know how to say this in English. My English is bad. But let me think a minute and try to translate what's in my head."

They walked quietly. A motorcycle roared past. The couple that had been looking crossed the street. A mangy dog sniffed the curb.

"I used to be a person," she said. "I married a dear man and we had a baby. Then the war came. My husband and father were killed and we had to leave. Now I'm in Rome. I'm a whore. I'm dirt. I hate what I do. I hate the men who pay me with cartons of cigarettes and talk to me in gutter language. I have to take my daughter and get away from here. I'm not asking you to help. You're a nice guy, but the wrong person. I just want you to understand. That's why I invited you to see us. I want to become a person again." She turned her head away and blew her nose into a handkerchief.

He didn't have a clue what to say. This girl was obviously determined to find an American who would marry her and get her out of here. It certainly wasn't going to be this American. Besides, he wasn't even sure he could believe this Excelsior Hotel whore. But it would be worth thinking about.

They walked back to the apartment and at the door he said goodbye with a discreet kiss.

"Maria, let me think. If I can help you at all, I will. I've enjoyed today. You are a good mother and I think you are a nice person."

A Novel: Chapter Six

Navigator thought on the plane all the way back to Foggia and then called *Life* magazine.

"I'm the guy who took that picture of the riots that were on your cover last week. Someone from your office came down to Foggia and gave me a check. What was his name?" he said.

"Lou Brovyard, our bureau chief," said a male voice.

"Can I talk to Mr. Brovyard?"

"Hold on."

"Hi, this is Lou," said a gravelly male voice. "Say, that was a good picture. We got some nice comments on it from New York. It's not often we get a cover out of the Rome bureau."

"Lou, can I ask for a favor?"

"You can ask."

"Can I trade in that two thousand dollars for something else?

"Depends on what kind of else."

"I'd like you to use that money to hire someone."

"Who, and to do what?"

"It's a girl. Could she be a copy girl or a runner or anything?"

Brovyard laughed. "A girl. I guess I can talk to your honey. I suppose we could use somebody as a gofer if it won't cost me anything—and if she behaves. I'll see if she works out."

"How much work would two thousand dollars pay for?"

"As a gofer? Probably a couple of years."

He gave Brovyard Maria's name and phone number.

"Does she know I'm going to call her?" said Brovyard.

"No."

"Should I tell her you're the sweetie?"

"No. Just tell her you heard from a friend she was looking for work."

"I'll call you if this works out," said Brovyard.

"Don't bother. Just stop the check and I'll tear up mine," he said and hung up.

#

Lou Brovyard looked at the attractive nineteen-year-old who was crossing and uncrossing her legs nervously as he fiddled with a pencil. *This navigator out of Foggia not only knows how to take pictures, he knows how to pick the babes*, he thought. *Nice piece of ass. I wonder why he didn't marry her and take her home with him. He's probably already married, or maybe she is. Well, he probably wants to keep a bone buried here for when he comes back to visit. But this is not getting me anywhere. I've got her for about two years on that navigator's money and I have to give her something to do that won't make New York wonder if I've got someone on the side.*

"Do you take dictation?" he asked.

"What is that?" said Maria.

"Do you type?"

"No."

"What the hell do you do?" he said.

"I read, I write..."

"In Italian."

"In Italian," she said. "I worked in a library and a bookstore. I can deliver messages and packages. I can answer your telephones."

"I can answer my telephones," he said.

"Your Italian accent is terrible," she said.

Brovyard laughed.

"The people who call you in Rome like to hear a good Italian spoken; that should be worth something."

"I guess you're right about that," he said.

"I also need the work," she said nervously. This interview was not going well at all. She hoped she wouldn't have to prostrate herself to this smart-ass. "I'll be on time. I'm honest. What more can I say?"

"Fair enough," he said. "I don't know anything about you, but you sound honest, and if you want this job bad enough, I

My Life, A Novel

assume you'll work hard. We'll see. I'll give you a try. But please remember, we're a bureau for a big U.S. magazine. Our home offices are in New York, and when they pull my chain, I have to break my ass to be sure that they get what they want. If you can make my job a little easier, you'll be worth what I'm going to pay you." He did a quick calculation, converting the navigator's dollars into lire, and told her what he'd pay.

Maria nodded. She would start on Monday. They shook hands and Brovyard held hers for a moment longer than he had intended to. *What the hell*, he thought, *it was better than patting her on the fanny.*

Maria walked quietly out of the office and took the elevator down to the street level. But when she was outside the building, she laughed, skipped once, and shook her hair so the soft autumn breeze could riffle through her curls.

The street, which had looked only busy and crowded with people when she came here, now was bright and full of promise. Somehow, God had reached out and done a nice thing for her for the first time in months.

But why? she wondered. Someone had told this Brovyard that she was looking for work and he had called her in. The interview had taken no time at all, and she had given all the wrong answers, but he still had hired her, as if he was intending to, no matter what she said. She suspected she knew what had happened.

"Oh joy!" she said out loud, and people on the street looked over at this attractive girl talking to herself. "What difference does it make? I'm happy!"

She looked at her reflection in the shop windows as she walked. *I've finally got a decent job where I'm not working on my back*, she told the reflection. *It doesn't pay that much, but we can live on it. Maybe I can get out of that lousy circle of whoring. Maybe I can find someone to take Anna and me out of here and start a life in America. Maybe my luck has changed.*

As she walked along the curb, a truck rolled through a puddle and spattered her skirt. *Well*, she thought, not unhappily, *maybe that was God telling me I'd better not be so sure.*

Gene Cowen

#

On her first day at *Life* magazine, Maria was at the office door at seven a.m., a difficult adjustment from the nocturnal life she had been leading. But Brovyard had said, "Get here early on Monday and make yourself useful."

She heard the click-click-click of typewriter keys and had to knock three times before the door was opened by a weary young man who stared, looked her over from head to toe, smiled, said, "Hello," and led her into the office.

She waited for him to tell her what to do, but he simply went back to his typewriter and continued plinking away on the keys.

She looked around and, since no one had told her what "useful" meant, decided that this pigsty needed a good cleaning. The office was one big room with five desks, each with a telephone, a Remington mechanical typewriter and ugly brown marks where cigarettes had been left to burn themselves out. One closed door said "Darkroom," and on the doorknob hung a hand-lettered sign that said, "Knock. Don't open unless you get permission. On pain of death."

Most of the ashtrays on the desks were full, and some cigarettes had been ground out on the floor. Teletype machines were running and the copy paper, which was supposed to stack automatically behind the machines, had backed up into unruly yellow curls that snaked their way into the room. Pages of paper with typewritten notes had been tossed generally in the direction of overflowing waste cans.

Maria cleaned, stacked, swept and dusted. When Brovyard came in, he looked around and smiled, so she decided she had done the right thing.

Then Maria found a chair in the corner and sat silently, waiting for Brovyard to tell her what she should do next. He sat at a old metal desk that rocked unsteadily on the uneven floor. At his elbows were three black telephones, one with red tape pasted over it, apparently to indicate that this was the hot line—probably the one connected to his New York office where people "pulled his chain."

My Life, A Novel

Brovyard talked alternately into the phones, usually trying to placate someone who had a problem, sometimes cajoling, sometimes barking an order. Whenever the hot phone rang, he put the other phones down immediately and picked up the red-taped one.

At one point, when he was in an animated conversation with someone on the red phone, he motioned to Maria to pick up one of the others that was ringing.

"*Pronto*," she said.

The caller was pleased that someone was speaking in Italian and began giving her a detail message.

"Please wait while I get a pencil," she said, and looked around.

Brovyard, recognizing her problem, put some paper and the stub of a pencil on the corner of his desk and made a sign that she should use them. He also motioned to the young man at the typewriter to bring Maria a chair so she wouldn't have to take notes crouching over his desk.

And that was the way her job shaped up. Over the weeks, she was eventually given a desk and chair in a corner and her own telephones to catch incoming calls. She cleaned in the mornings, answered telephones and delivered messages during the day, and usually left at five p.m.

Seemingly, everyone who came into the office was on one deadline or another. They talked fast, they walked fast and worked fast. This office operated on American time. No afternoon breaks for long lunches in the continental tradition. Maria usually brought a sandwich from home and ate at her desk.

She began practicing her English and, at home, she even started teaching her daughter to speak the Americans' language. *This is where the future is*, she thought, *I have to be part of it. My daughter has to be part of it.*

#

After several more weeks, Maria announced to her mother, "I like this job."

Her mother was stirring a thick soup over a gas fire. Her hands were wrinkled with age and cracked from all the years she had spent scrubbing floors. At her feet, Anna was playing with little wooden alphabet blocks.

"Why?" said her mother as she ladled out portions of the soup and put them on the table. "Anna, please wash and come to dinner."

"Because," said Maria, "they treat me nice. The hours are long, but the place is full of pleasant people who rush around doing interesting things."

"Like what?" said her mother.

"Oh, taking pictures and writing stories for an American magazine," Maria said. Then she spoke to the floor, "Anna, Grandma said dinner was ready. What are you doing?"

"I'm trying to spell with my blocks."

"Spell what?"

"Alligator."

"Why do you want to spell alligator?" said Maria.

"That's the name of the guy who put the ice cream in his melon."

Maria laughed. "He's 'Navigator,'" she said, and began arranging the blocks. "And then what are you going to do with the blocks with his name on them?"

"Maybe he'll come back and take us to America."

Maria changed the subject. "I'm not only learning English, I'm learning to type," she said to her mother as she swallowed some soup. It tasted of the fresh vegetables and the little bit of meat they could afford. "I went to the library and took out a book on typing. When things are quiet in the office, I go to a typewriter that isn't being used and I practice."

"That will help you on the job?" said her mother.

"If I get better at some things, I maybe will be given more professional things to do."

"So you can impress the American boss."

"So I can impress the American boss."

"Maria," said her mother, without looking up from the steaming pot, "the only thing you could do to impress an

My Life, A Novel

American man is to pull up your skirt, So you better not get too professional."

Maria slowly put her spoon into the soup bowl and walked silently out of the room.

#

On August 14, 1945, after Maria had been at the *Life* offices for several months, Lou Brovyard looked at the teletype machine and let out a whoop. "It's official, lady and gentlemen!"

Maria heard the "'lady'" and smiled.

"The whole goddam war is over! The Japs have thrown in the towel, and this is officially VJ Day. And, boy, do we have work to do!"

He shouted to the photographers to get out onto the streets and get some "celebration" pictures. He then looked at Maria and said, "Maria, do you think you could do a little reporting for me today?"

Maria looked up, startled. She'd love to, but report on what? she asked him.

"On anything that's happening on the streets of Rome," he said. "The photographers are going to get pictures, but I need copy. Do you know what 'color' is? I need notes on what people in the streets are saying or doing. Anything. Maybe someone will jump into a fountain. Maybe someone will climb a telephone pole and put up a flag. Anything."

So she went off to look for fountains and telephone poles. But there was a problem. Hardly anybody was celebrating. No flags, no bands, no marching. The people in Rome had lost their war months before, and this was an Allied celebration, with very few Yanks or Brits around to celebrate.

She finally found a couple of American GIs sitting at the edge of a fountain, idly running their hands through the water. She approached tentatively and said, "Can I ask you something for *Life* magazine?"

The shorter of the two, with a shaved head and handlebar mustache, laughed and said, "You, for *Life* magazine? Who are we kidding, *signorina*? If you're asking if we want to get laid, I don't have any money."

Maria flinched. But his buddy put a wet hand on the young man's arm and said, "Wait, Sam." (It came out "'Sham.'") "Let's see what she wants. I don't think this is a hustle. Miss, what can we do for you?" He was thin, with a drawn, sallow face, and he ran his hand through dark hair.

"I really am working for *Life*," she said. "I'm a researcher and we're gathering information about what is happening in Rome on VJ Day. I apologize if I'm intruding, but this is a very big story for us."

He wiped his hands on his trousers, took Maria by the arm and led her around the corner of the building. "Look," he said. "No one on these streets is celebrating and that probably will make as good a story as anything. 'War Ends, No One Happy in Rome.' How's that for a headline? Wars are funny things. A lot of bad things happen. Some good things happen. And then there are the fluky things, like no celebrations when they end. None of it makes sense, but that's war for you. War doesn't make sense, either."

He paused. "Besides," we don't want to be in *Life* magazine. Sam and I were celebrating earlier, and we've had too much to drink—that's what made him mouth off at you just now. And we're AWOL. Do you know what that means?" Then, almost as an afterthought he said, "You know, you're nice."

Maria said she knew what AWOL meant, and she looked more closely at this young soldier who was shaking his head as if to clear it. He reminded her of some of the airmen she had picked up at the Excelsior Hotel, drunk, homesick, and wanting compassion as much as they wanted sex.

"But don't worry about us," he said.

Maria wondered why he should think she would worry about them.

"We'll get back to the base and probably get confined to barracks for a week or so. No heavy penalties for being AWOL these days. Anyhow…" He had to stop and think how he'd gotten into this line of conversation. "…when I get out, can I look you up at *Life*?"

Maria smiled, shrugged and began to walk away.

"Hey," he shouted, "what's your name?"

"Maria," she said, and then added, "If you look me up, be sober."

He bowed low, straightened up, crossed his heart, and said, "I'll be sober. My name is John."

#

Three weeks later, when Maria was practicing her typing, she was startled to hear a soft "Hi!" from behind her. She had been alone in the office, but with the teletype machines clacking and its bells ringing periodically she hadn't heard anyone come in.

She turned to find the tall, thin soldier with the sallow complexion standing there. He was wearing a freshly-pressed uniform with corporal's stripes on the sleeve, and he stood with his thumbs in his side pockets.

"I'm sober," he said with a grin, trying to cover up the fact that he was very ill at ease.

"You're also out of jail, John," she said.

"Oh, I never went to jail" he said. "As I told you, I only got confined to barracks. How've you been, Maria, since VJ Day?"

"Fine," she said. "That was a good idea of yours that I should report that no one was celebrating. It got used in the magazine. Only one sentence, but that's something in a big magazine like this. And it was big for me, too. It was the first time anyone used anything I wrote."

That reassured John and he said, "Can I buy you lunch?"

A telephone rang, giving Maria a chance to think as she picked up the phone. *Do I want to know this guy?* she thought. *This skinny guy with a weak chin and big ears who is nervous about asking a girl to lunch. But he is sober now, and I haven't been asked out by anyone since I got this job.*

"I brought a sandwich and I can only get half an hour at around noon," she said.

"Oh, that's fine," he said. "I'll get one of my own and come for you at noon."

He shook her hand, waved, and left happily.

When he arrived at noon, Maria told Brovyard she'd be back after lunch and she and John walked out. John bought two coffees at a little shop, and they took them to a low concrete wall in front of a bank where they sat and began eating. Trucks rumbled by, and an occasional motorcycle roared and belched exhaust fumes at them. But Maria didn't mind. It was a cool fall day and she welcomed the warmth of the sun on her neck.

As John talked, Maria mostly nodded and listened. He already knew as much about her as she was willing to tell at the moment. It was his turn to do some revealing.

John was from Iowa and had been drafted right after he graduated high school. He had qualified as a cryptographer in the Signal Corps. This involved coding and decoding and a certain amount of "listening in." He didn't say what he was listening to, but he liked the work.

His family? Just a mom and a dad and a kid brother.

His social life? Well, he really didn't have much of one. But he'd like to.

Maria ate the cheese sandwich that her mother had prepared and sipped the bitter coffee. She would have preferred to have milk in it, but she had forgotten to ask. She also would have preferred to have someone more interesting to talk to. This guy was pleasant enough, but seemed a little strange. She couldn't quite put her finger on it, but he seemed to be one step removed from fully involved.

I bet he's not very good in bed, she thought, *and I ought to know about things like that*. But she erased the thought quickly from her mind. Her past life had to stay buried and it was probably dangerous even to think things like that.

"Well," she said, as she glanced at her watch, "this was very pleasant, John. I've enjoyed meeting you." She put the empty coffee cup and the sandwich crumbs into the paper sack, and offered her hand in farewell.

John's face fell. "Can't I see you again?" he said. "I'm sorry I sounded a little awkward, but I haven't had a date for a long time. There are some very interesting things to see in Rome. Maybe I could take you to dinner. There's a museum with an

My Life, A Novel

exhibit by the sculptor Giacometti. Would you like to see that, maybe on a Sunday?"

Maria had two thoughts. First, she really didn't have much interest in seeing this guy again. Second, his pleading made her feel embarrassed for him. But a third thought, dinner, crowded out the others. She'd really love to have a good meal in a nice restaurant.

"Okay," she said, mustering a smile. "Giacometti and dinner. Not next Sunday, but the one after that. Please pick me up at home at three o'clock."

He smiled and nodded. She wrote her name and address on a slip of paper and then, on an impulse, pinched his cheek lightly. John was startled and took a step back, then recovered himself, touched her cheek and waved goodbye.

Gene Cowen

A Novel: Chapter Seven

John knocked at the door at three o'clock on a chilly Sunday, his coat collar turned and one hand in his pocket to keep warm.

Mrs. Tedesco, squinting into the sun, opened the door and looked him over before stepping aside to let him come in.

He shifted uneasily, took off his hat, offered his other hand, and said, "I'm John, madam. I've come here for Maria."

Mrs. Tedesco disregarded his hand, led him into the parlor, pointed to a couch for him to sit down, and left him alone in the room.

He had barely enough time to look around, when Maria walked in briskly. She was dressed in a simple white blouse and long black skirt, and a headband held her dark curls away from her face.

"Hi! You made it," she said. "You look handsome in that coat. Are you sober?"

John was annoyed. *Where the hell does this babe get such a sharp tongue?* he thought. But the thought was interrupted when a little girl came around the corner of the room and rushed up close to Maria and hid her face in her mother's skirt.

"This is my daughter, Anna," said Maria.

"Hi," said John. "You are a pretty one. You're the spitting image of your mother."

"You bring things for me?" she said haltingly.

"Oh, I'm sorry," he said to Maria, "I didn't know you had a daughter."

Maria explained to Anna, who sat down on the floor at Maria's feet and stared fixedly at the visitor.

"Can I offer you something to eat or drink?" Maria asked.

"No," he said, "I had a big lunch. Why don't we just go?"

My Life, A Novel

Maria nodded, shouted something to her mother in the next room, bent down and kissed her daughter and headed for the door.

"Bye," said John. "What did you say her name was?" he asked Maria.

"Anna," she said.

"Bye, Anna," he said, then took Maria's arm and they left.

When the door closed, Anna stuck out her tongue.

#

As they climbed aboard a bus labeled "Villa Borghese" and settled into their seats, Maria said, "Well, now you know I have a daughter."

John nodded pleasantly and said, "And a husband?"

"He died during the war."

"I'm sorry to hear that. Any boyfriends?" he said, looking at the cameo pin she was wearing and guessing that she had gotten it from some guy.

She didn't answer, but sat primly with her hands in her lap, looking at the traffic as the bus worked its way through narrow streets. Pretty hands, he thought. Pretty girl with dark hair with the pleasant aroma of shampoo. He wondered why she had not remarried. It probably was because of her having a child. Most men hesitated to take on the responsibility of someone else's child. Well, that wouldn't matter that much to him.

"This is our stop," Maria announced and stood up. They walked along a gravel path in the Villa Borghese. A grove of pine trees broke the force of the wind. Maria brushed her hands lightly over the variegated yellow leaves of the broom bushes planted at their base.

As they walked into the museum, Maria said, "Cardinal Scipione Borghese started collecting these paintings in the sixteen hundreds. This was the summer house. The collection was bought by the state at the beginning of this century."

John looked at Maria. "You know all that?"

"I've been here before. When life gives me a kick in the ass, I come here and look for a while at a Raphael or a Rubens or a

Titian and I am reassured. Is that the right word? It feels good to know that human beings can make such beauty. And it puts me back on the sunny side of the street. Is my English funny?"

"No. Yes, it's funny, but I like it," he said. "You're quite a girl, Maria. But let me ask you. If you've been here before, why did you want to come again?"

"Because you promised to give me a nice dinner."

"Fair enough!" He laughed and led her to the Giacometti exhibition. The museum had seen better days. They walked along dusty marble floors through dim rooms. The light that worked its way through hazy windows picked up the dust motes that danced in the gloom. The Corinthian columns were majestic, and the frieze beneath the molding had a breathtaking beauty, but they were much in need of cleaning.

When they got to the Giacomettis, they saw that the curator had arranged for coin-operated lights to be focused on each piece of sculpture. *It costs to see*, thought John as he reached into his pocket.

As he lighted each sculpture, they walked slowly around the Surrealist piece, looking, circling, but not saying much to each other. They passed by an abbreviated stone carving of the face of the Swiss artist's father.

John looked over at Maria. She was deeply involved in the works. Tears welled in her eyes.

"Are you okay?" he said.

"I guess so."

"Don't you like these?"

"I love them."

"Then why are you crying?"

"Because they're so beautiful. There's something so alone about them," she said.

"Why alone?"

"I don't know why," she said, "But they're standing there alone. I know the feeling."

From the museum, they took a bus back to the center of Rome and John took her to a restaurant where they had to walk down a flight of stone steps. The floors were black-and-white tiles and the tablecloths were snowy white.

My Life, A Novel

The waiter promptly put bottled water and bread sticks before them and took their drink orders. Maria said she'd like Asti Spumante and John motioned that he'd have the same. Then he was surprised to see that what he had ordered was a sparkling white wine.

Waiters swung by with large trays of antipasti, beet-red hard-boiled eggs and sardines. Whenever Maria pointed, John did, too, and before long, his plate was loaded with things he had seldom eaten before. He tasted each dish gingerly.

They ate and drank quietly for a while before John said, "I'm leaving soon."

"I haven't finished eating yet," Maria said.

"No, I mean I'm leaving Italy soon," John said.

Maria said nothing.

"And I'd like to marry you," John said.

Maria looked at him, smiled and said, "That's nice."

"That's all you can say?"

"What else would you like me to say? You just met me a few weeks ago. I ate one sandwich with you and now this dinner. I don't think you're serious."

"Well, I am."

"Why are you leaving Italy?" Maria said.

"Because I'm being shipped out."

"And where will you go?"

"Probably home. The war's over."

"To America? Where in America?"

"It depends on what opens up. I have to make a life."

Maria stared down at her food and thought, *Damn! This guy's serious.*

#

When Maria came home, 'her mother looked up from the pale pink nightgown she had been sewing. Little Anna had been watching her intently, imitating the motion of her grandmother's hand as if she too were sewing. When she saw her mother, she jumped up, threw her arms around her mother's skirt and waited to be lifted into a warm, nuzzling hug.

"Why are you still up, little one?"

"Grandma said I could wait until she finished sewing," Anna said.

"That was only the last of it," said Mrs. Tedesco. "I asked her to get ready for bed, and then she had to eat a cookie and drink some milk, and she couldn't find her toothbrush, and when she finally got her nightgown on, it had a ripped seam. So I'm sewing it now, and Anna is trying to think of a few more things to keep from going to bed."

Maria said, "Why should this night be any different?" She put the repaired nightgown on the child and carted her off to the bedroom they shared and tucked her in. In a soft voice, she told Anna a story.

"There was once a beautiful princess who was walking in a forest when she came upon a wicked witch."

"What was her name?"

"Mrs. Wicked Witch."

"And what did she do?" said Anna.

"She put a curse on the little princess and said she had to live in a tower that was damp and drafty and far away from any people."

"Was it also cold?" said Anna.

"Very. And she said that the princess would have to stay in that tower until a handsome prince came along and freed her and married her."

"And took her to America," said Anna.

"That, too. So one day, a handsome prince came riding up on a horse."

"A white horse?"

"Of course. And the little princess called to him and he saved her and carried her off and they were happy ever after."

"When did they get married?" said Anna.

"Later. Now it's time we give each other the special goodnight kiss and you close your eyes and go to sleep."

"Don't close the door all the way," said Anna.

They snuggled for a moment and Maria left, leaving the door ajar. She walked into the next room and sat down in front of her mother and said nothing.

Mrs. Tedesco said, "You're home early." What Maria had been doing nights in the recent past was unspoken between them. "Did he give you a decent meal?"

"Yes."

"Do you like him?"

Maria said nothing for a moment, and then, "It's more than that."

"He proposed?"

"Yes."

"And he will take you to America?"

"Yes."

"And what about Anna?" Mrs. Tedesco asked.

"Her, too."

"And you're wondering what will happen to me."

"Yes," said Maria, and stood up and put her arms around her mother.

Mrs. Tedesco kissed her on the cheek. "I could see this coming for a long time. You're a beautiful girl who wants to go to America, and I knew that sooner or later, someone would find you. Don't worry about me. I can go back to living with my brother again." She paused. "But do you love this man? How long have you known him?" "Not very long," said Maria. "When you met him tonight, what did you think?"

"You mean when I opened the door? That was quite an interview to decide whether your daughter should marry a man." Then, lifting one hand, she said, "All I could see was that he has a pinched face and eyes that dart around. But he's young and looks healthy and, since you've already made up your mind, I suppose he'll do."

"Mamma, I need to get away from here and you know why. John seems okay and treats me nice, and he'll give Anna and me a home in America. And if things don't work out," she said, running her fingers through her hair, "well, I can always look around. It's a big country."

"What a way to find a husband," said Mrs. Tedesco. "But God bless you and protect you in America."

And a voice from the bedroom said softly, "I liked the alligator better."

Gene Cowen

My Life: Chapter Seven

I left Italy in August, 1946, happy to be out of service, but happy also for the year I had spent on occupation duty in a country that really didn't need occupying. The war had left many Italians desperately poor, but everyone I ever met was warm and welcoming, in part because of the aid that the U. S. dispensed so freely, but also because it seemed that everyone had a relative in America. Never in my time over there did we have a problem more serious than one Foggia resident's complaining rather plaintively that we could have come up with a nicer name for our newspaper than the *Occupator*.

We had good working relationships with the several Italians who worked for us on the newspaper and many GIs married local girls. When I came home and went to college, I made sure that one of my courses was Italian, just for old times' sake.

PART TWO: 1925

Gene Cowen

My Life: Chapter Eight

<u>Born</u>

I was born in 1925, the year Charlie Chaplin was packing them in to see *The Gold Rush*, the *New Yorker* magazine began publication, 40,000 white-hooded Ku Klux Klanners marched in Washington, President Coolidge said, "The business of America is business," Lou Gehrig signed on with the New York Yankees, a Model-T Ford was selling for $350, U.S. refrigerator sales reached 75,000, and the U.S. population was 106 million, of which 54,000 were urban dwellers.

Our family was among those urbanites—with a car, but without a refrigerator.

We lived in a six-story apartment building on Cruger Avenue in the Bronx, the place to which immigrants graduated, after starting out on the Lower East Side of New York. My father, Jacob Moses Cohen, the immigrant son of a Russian tailor and his wife, finished only grade school, got a job in the garment industry and eventually became a tiny manufacturer of neckwear, with himself as the only salesman (hence, the car).

He was short, with a bulbous nose and a ready smile. We saw him only on weekends and holidays because he spent his life making and selling neckties. He would go to fabric houses and pick out the colors and patterns that he thought would sell. Then he'd take them to cutters and stitchers who made them into neckties, and he added labels that read, "J.M. Cohen Co., Style-Bilt." (I asked him once why he used "Style-Bilt" when he could have picked a more descriptive term, and he got annoyed at me for suggesting that he change a slogan that had worked for years.)

He then would make up necktie samples, pack them into big leather "grips" and take them "on the road," to small haberdashery shops in upstate New York, New Jersey and Pennsylvania. He would visit stores that had been his customers for years, take what orders he could get, come home, go to a loft in lower Manhattan, pack the merchandise into corrugated boxes, and tie, label and ship them to his customers.

Dad was proud of what he did. He never made very much money, but through good times and bad, he said he was (shrug) "making a living." That living, meager though it was at times, managed to feed and clothe a wife and two sons, help support his widowed mother and his widowed mother-in-law, and put away a little money for his wife before he died when his car hit a tree in 1957.

During the 1930s, we would read the New York *World-Telegram*, a Scripps-Howard newspaper. Those were the days when President Roosevelt shocked a lot of the more affluent in America by imposing an income tax that really bit. So the *Telegram,* in editorials and editorial cartoons, would often inveigh against the unwelcome levy.

I must have been nine or ten when I asked Dad what he thought of this hated tax. He said, "I wish I made enough money to have to pay an income tax."

The year he died, Mother said it had been one of his best. He had earned $5,000. Dad considered himself a neckwear manufacturer. As far as I knew, he never had anybody working for him. He was the first and smallest small businessman I ever knew.

#

Mother, Shirley Sherman, was the daughter also of a tailor and his wife (there weren't too many other jobs open to immigrant Jews in those days). Shortly after the turn of the century, as a young child with her mother, she had arrived in the United States from Russia. They joined her father, a deserter from the Russian army, who had sneaked in earlier.

The Aaron and Bessie Sherman family was eventually made up of Shirley, the oldest, then Eleanor, Lee, Belle and Harold. They lived first in Providence, Rhode Island, and then, as did many other immigrants, in the Bronx, on Bathgate Avenue. Living conditions were harsh. When she was dating, she never wanted to have a young man come to her apartment because the family had to use a toilet down the hall and wash their hands in the kitchen sink. She had graduated from high school and was very proud of that.

My Life, A Novel

The four sisters were very close, but jealous of their brother because he was apparently favored by their father. Harold was the only child to attend college. He graduated from the City College of New York and then got a degree in dentistry at Tufts.

Mother was often bitter about her childhood, because of poverty, an imperious father, a cold and self-centered mother, and the rivalries that churned through the family. Dad, however, looked back on his childhood more cheerily, even though his living conditions had been very similar. That was probably because his family life was happier. His mother, our Bubbie, was a prototypical Jewish grandmother, short, moon-faced and wearing a *sheitl*, a wig prescribed for orthodox married women to cover their shaved heads. But she was a bright, warm and loving person—so much so that young people like my cousin, Julius, who was having problems with his father, came to live with Bubbie and our grandfather, Zadie, for many years. But Dad's devotion to his mother also had the unintended effect of alienating his wife, who felt he spent entirely too much time at Bubbie's house.

In recent years, I asked Mother about the Great Depression of the 1930s and I said, "Things must have gotten much worse for you."

She said, "No, things were the same—bad before the Depression and bad during it."

My first awareness of how tough those times were came during the 1930s, when I was about eight or nine years old and I was carrying around a little collection box (*pushkie*) for the Jewish National Fund. I was systematically knocking on our neighbors' doors, collecting small coins. I remember telling Mother that I had solicited Aunt Eleanor, who lived in a neighboring apartment building. I said that she first told me she was sorry but she didn't have any pennies to give me, and I said, thinking at the time that it was a smart remark, "Well, then, give me a nickel!"

Mother was shocked. "How could you say a thing like that?"

A nickel was a lot of money in those Depression times.

Shirley Sherman married Jacob M. Cohen in 1924. Mother and Dad "moved up in the world" to live in the west Bronx, which was then a pleasant lower-middle-class part of New York City.

Gene Cowen

Milk Bottles and Icemen

In those days, milk was delivered in glass bottles. It wasn't homogenized, so the cream floated to the top—which made me realize that "heavy cream" wasn't so heavy, after all. When you wanted to pour milk out of the bottle, you shook it first, unless you wanted some cream for your coffee. In that case, you just poured some off the top, then shook up the rest. The bottles were capped with a cardboard disk that fit inside the rim and was covered by a crimped hood that resembled today's shower cap.

A milkman carried his bottles in metal carriers, which you could hear rattling their way up to your door early in the morning. He'd know how many bottles you usually took. But if you wanted more or less you'd leave him a note—which led to the cartoon of a milkman at the door and a puzzled woman in a house coat looking incredulously at him, as he asked, "Does 'no milk' mean you have no milk or you want no milk?"

His wagon was hauled by a horse who knew all the stops. After the milkman left the wagon to carry the bottles to one house, the horse dutifully plodded on to the next stop and waited while the milkman completed his rounds.

Those were also the days when burly men delivered ice. Few people could afford refrigerators. They had iceboxes that used blocks of ice on top. Cool air dropped and chilled the contents of the box below. They were messy affairs, because the ice melted and the water had to be hauled away and poured off several times a day.

The icemen came by in big wagons, loaded with huge blocks of ice. They would take your order, then work at the big block with an ice pick, put it into a canvas carrier and deliver it to your door. Lifting that ice gave you muscles and those guys had builds like the men today who deliver big barrels of beer. Between their muscles and the fact that they carried a pick, they looked dangerous. Actually, most of the ones I met were fairly cheerful fellows and often would offer us kids big chips of ice to suck on.

Growing Up

My earliest recollection of childhood is an incident that occurred when I must have been five or six years old. It was of Mother slapping another child. I don't know what he did to deserve that—and let me tell you that when Mother slapped, it hurt—but I remember being very pleased. I assume he was picking on me.

Finding money was always fun. The older boys had a clubroom of sorts in the basement of our apartment building. One day, they bought a new second-hand sofa and burned the old one in the back lot. When the ashes cooled down, I poked around and found loose change. What a thrill! Years later, one of my associates would refer to the tiny appropriations that we sought from Congress as "loose change that drops into the sofa cushions," and each time, I would think fondly of my discovery in the ashes of the back lot.

The back lot was a multipurpose play area. We occasionally built bonfires there and even did some primitive outdoor cooking. When we cooked potatoes, which we called "mickeys," we just threw them into the fire and waited until everything burned down. Shades of Charles Lamb's *A Dissertation Upon Roast Pig*. Then, juggling the hot black spuds in our hands, we would break them open and eat the baked potatoes—thick, blackened skin and a little surviving potato inside.

Saturdays were kids' days at the movies—just the way television is today. But our time to howl was in the afternoon and we'd watch cliff-hanger two-reelers. Soon, I realized that no matter what peril Pauline was in at the end of one episode, she would manage to escape by next Saturday.

Most of us in the family had allergies. Mother sneezed through most of the summer; I did part of the time. We were told that goldenrod, that beautiful weed that gave a touch of color to vacant lots, caused the sneezing. When Dad was driving us through the countryside on a sunny Sunday, whenever someone spotted a goldenrod field, great shouts went up. All of us in the car held our breath for as long as we could, then exhaled and inhaled very carefully. It didn't do much for the respiratory allergy. But then again, neither does a great deal of modern allergy medicine today.

As children, we also believed that the feathery dandelion tufts that floated through the air ate nickels—yes, the kind that you spent for a Popsicle. But since, as kids, we had darn few nickels at any time, there really wasn't much we had to do about it, except shout warnings to the other kids.

The Farm

Uncle Sam and Dad's sister, Aunt Ida, lived on a farm outside of Albany. They were the only Jewish farmers I ever heard of. I thought all Jews lived in big cities, worked in the garment trades and drank sweet Concord wine.

We'd drive up from New York to find this simple farmhouse where, for many years, until plumbing finally came to the area, the pump atop the well was the source of water. The farm had lots of chickens, six or eight, cows and a kitchen garden.

Sam and Ida's son Julius, a few years older than I, was fun to be with. He was old enough to fire a .22 rifle and was good with repairs on a place that was always being repaired. To this day, I remember his admonition: "Having the right tool is very important. It might not be expensive, but when you need it, you need it badly and you can't do the job without it."

At sundown, Uncle Sam would let me walk with him through the meadow calling "Ca-bass, Ca-bass!" to bring the friendly, passive animals in.

If you stepped into some cow-flop, it was considered lucky. All the members of our family, whenever they had a stroke of luck, would say, "I must have stepped in something."

Cousin Julius tried mightily to teach me how to milk a cow, but I was not able to master the art. Partly, I just couldn't get the hang of it; partly, I felt squeamish about handling the teats of a living, breathing animal. But Julius would let me drink some of the newly squeezed milk. I didn't know if I liked the warm, bubbly stuff. But Mother, when she found out that I had been drinking unpasteurized milk, forbade it in the future.

A bovine highlight came after we had eaten corn-on-the-cob. When we finished, we'd bring the warm, buttery, salty cobs to the cows, who gobbled them up and looked around plaintively for more.

Uncle Sam made a living from eggs, but he hated the chickens. They were dirty, tended to run outside whenever they could find a hole in the rough fencing and were often invaded at night by predators. This created a strange paradox when he fed them. Sam sold milk and cream, which he made by running the milk through a separator, which left him cream in one container and skim milk in another. But no one in those days would buy milk that had been skimmed of its cream, so it had to be used somewhere else. A splash of it was often used to "baptize" the cream, but the rest went to the chickens. As he poured it into feeders for them he would curse, "You dirty little bastards, this stuff is too good for you, but what else can I do with it?"

The farm was the place where we ate raw turnips, brown eggs (they didn't sell as well as white ones), and watched Farmer Sam eat stale cheese with green edges. He'd whack off a piece with his knife and announce that it was better for you when it was aged.

We also toasted marshmallows over an open fire. That was fun and delicious, except that I'd often get distracted during the toasting process and end up with sweet black ash.

Cousin Julius was a rebel. He and his father fought constantly and eventually he left home in his late teens. He moved into New York and lived with Bubbie, who gave him the affection he apparently didn't get at home and tried to keep him from getting into too much trouble.

The trouble included his declaration that he was a "Communist sympathizer." I assume that meant he was wedded to the philosophy, just short of becoming a card-carrying member of the party, but it worried the hell out of the rest of the family.

Remember now, this was in the mid-1930s, the depths of the Great Depression that was ravaging the nation and most of the rest of the world. In 1932, there were 34 million Americans who had no income of any kind, and those who did work averaged $16 a week. Banks were closing by the thousands and bread lines formed in many cities. Influential intellectuals like Sherwood Anderson, Erskine Caldwell, John Dos Passos, and Theodore Dreiser said that only the

Communist Party proposed a real solution to the nation's agony. So it should be no surprise that my cousin Julius joined those ranks.

Actually, he didn't do anything more radical than wear black turtle-neck sweaters and talk glowingly of the dictatorship of the proletariat. He could be a little much at a time when anti-Communism was still the prevailing feeling in the United States. Mother nervously didn't want to have anything to do with him.

But Aunt Dora, Dad's sister, did. Her husband was a successful businessman and the envy of the rest of the family. When Aunt Dora invited Julius for lunch at their apartment on Central Park West, she noticed that he was spending a lot of time in the kitchen, talking to her black maid.

"What was he talking about?" Aunt Dora asked after he left.

"He told me I was being grossly underpaid, that I should revolt. Only under Communism would I get a decent wage," said the embarrassed woman, who had no intention of leaving a job that she liked just fine.

Aunt Dora never invited Julius to lunch again.

The Bronx

Cruger Avenue in the Bronx formed a triangle with Mace Avenue, and the Boston Post Road, old Route 1, the first north-south federal highway in the United States. In the center of that triangle stood a big billboard, which advertised beer, soap and automobiles to the traffic on the Post Road, which was distinguished principally by its cobblestones, the leftover ballast from some ships—maybe the same ones that had brought my family from Europe. As kids, we would play on the struts of the billboard and watch the cars, trucks and busses as they bounced, rattled and clanked on the cobbles.

That was in front of our apartment house. In the back was more noise: an elevated subway about a block away. If you grow up with an "El" in your backyard, you get inured to the sound of the trains rumbling by every few minutes. I first realized how noisy it really was when some relatives spent the night and reported in the morning that they hadn't gotten a wink of sleep.

Our Gang

When I grew up in the Bronx, it was a different and more livable place than *Bonfires of the Vanities* says it is today. We had clubs that we called "gangs," but were really more like the *Our Gang Comedy*. We were just a bunch of guys who hung around together, smoked cigarettes surreptitiously in the alleyways of our apartment buildings and played some ball games in the back lot.

I might have saved someone's life once in that back lot. We were playing football that morning. I was probably around nine or ten. We were too tough to play a soft game like touch football, in which any contact with a defender stopped the ball carrier. We played full-blown tackle football in that undeveloped lot of weeds, stones, discarded building debris and empty tin cans. One of the ball carriers was tackled hard and must have hit something sharp, because he began bleeding profusely from his right wrist. He got up crying and walked away, trailing a lot of blood.

I caught up with him. I wasn't sure how to stop the bleeding, but I knew we had to do something, so I pulled a handkerchief from my hip pocket, tied it very tightly around the wound, and walked with him until we could hail a passing car, which took him to nearby Fordham Hospital. I was told later that the attending physician said he would have bled to death if that handkerchief hadn't stanched the flow. My fame lasted only about a day until a member of our gang said that the proper way to stop bleeding was with a tourniquet, not by tying a dirty handkerchief over the wound.

We also played stickball, a kind of softball for paved streets, with a broomstick for a bat and a "spaldeen" (Spalding) pink rubber ball about two inches in diameter. One parked car was first base, another was second, and a sewer cover was third. I was no better at stickball than I was at other sports, and hitting a two-inch ball with a broomstick was an achievement for anybody.

That same alley was a hangout for some of the older boys. One day, I stood watching some of them shooting craps. A policeman suddenly appeared, broke up the "illegal gambling" and scooped up the dice. He motioned to the small change on the ground and said, "Kid, that's for you. Spend it."

Gene Cowen

I took the stash to a nearby candy store and bought some chewing gum for Mother, which I knew she liked. She was upset that I was hanging around a crap game, but touched that I'd buy her a gift.

She was less touched when, one day, alone in the apartment, I climbed out the window onto some scaffolding that window washers had left hanging there. When I saw my mother come back into the apartment, I waved to her and she nearly fainted. She couldn't see the scaffolding, only her trouble-prone son standing like an apparition outside the sixth-floor window.

When my father came home that Friday, he hit me with a strap across the backside. It was the only time he ever used a strap on me and he didn't seem to have his heart in it.

#

When I was five or six and living in the Bronx, we would see aircraft overhead from time to time because of the nearby airport—later named LaGuardia for our popular and wonderfully loony mayor. We'd call out, "Hi, Lindy!" in recognition of the only pilot whose name we knew.

We had a different response when we saw aircraft with other markings. By the middle 1930s, the hated Nazi swastikas, emblazoned on the tail of aircraft, began flying above our apartment house. We'd shake our fists in the air, spit, and curse: "Get out of our country, you bastards. May God shoot you down!" or something like that.

On May 6, 1937, I was standing in our vacant back lot when a German dirigible flaunted its swastika in the skies above the Bronx. I waved my fists, spit, cursed, and then went back to whatever I had been doing in the lot. Later that day the *Hindenburg*, coming in for a landing at nearby Lakehurst, New Jersey, caught fire, exploded and crashed. I was convinced that God had heard my curses and with a mighty hand and outstretched arm smote it from the sky.

A Novel: Chapter Eight

Wasn't that amazing! Something worked, he thought. He wondered how it had happened. Was it the fists in the air? Was it the spitting? No, it had to be the curses. Now, just what had he said?

He couldn't remember. Something about God shooting it down. He didn't point or anything, just shot it down. Gosh, if there was an American plane up there, he could have shot it down instead. Or a bird, or some kid up in a tree.

He pondered the miracle as he lay in bed, staring at the ceiling. Wouldn't it be nice if that curse would work on the kids who called him Fairy? He was lousy at ballgames. He seemed so awkward, and when the gang chose up sides, they always picked him last. He was usually assigned to the outfield where he'd do the least damage, be involved in the fewest plays. Once when a ball was hit his way, an easy fly, he had dropped it. Groans from the sidelines. His throw toward home plate usually dropped way short. More groans.

"Oh, there goes Fairy again," they'd laugh. The next time, they wouldn't even pick him.

Fairy. He hated that name. Be nice to use that curse on those smart-alecks in the gang. But how to make it work? He'd try at the right moment.

The next week, the gang got a game of stickball going. When they chose up sides, the heads of each team agreed they didn't want Fairy on their teams.

He stood off to the side and spat. Nothing happened. He importuned God. Still nothing. He moved off to an alley, looked to make sure no one was looking and shook his fists in the air. When he looked carefully around the corner, the ballgame was going well and someone had just scored. *Shit!*

Back in bed, he decided he might have been asking for too much. After all, he had brought down the *Hindenburg*. That was a lot. Maybe he should try something easier. So he tried to get Cecilia, a well-developed young charmer, to smile at him when he passed her in the corridor at school. Nothing. He was doing poorly in French and took a shot at asking for a decent grade on the midterm exam. He got a "D." He asked that his mother not yell at him so much. She still did.

So he decided there was no God. He had brought down the *Hindenburg* himself. Something about him was special. He had a power peculiar to himself. As he stared at the city lights that played on the bedroom ceiling, he realized what it had to be.

Until he was born, there was no world, no universe. When he was born, the world began. Everything that happened, he could see through his eyes. No one else saw the world through those eyes. And when he was no longer able to see something or hear something, there would be nothing. There would be no one left to see the sun shine, hear the car horns, laugh at something funny, feel the pain of insults. If he died, the world would end.

But if everything started when he was born in 1925, how could he explain all of history before then? The stars and the sun and moon? The dinosaurs, the cave drawings, the American Revolution? The archeological sites and the shards of ancient pottery?

It had to be the creation of an instant universe. Not God's mighty hand and outstretched arm that worked for six days. But a world created with the stars already in the sky, the pyramids already standing in the arid wastes of Egypt, the history books already written, Mother and Dad already married and him, he thought, crying at birth. An instant off-the-shelf universe. When he'd opened his eyes, it had all begun.

And God pity all of you, he thought. *When I close my eyes at the end, it will be the end of me and the end of you and all the world.* Frightening, but thrilling.

By now, the sounds from the street were muted. He could hear the horse's hooves and the milkman's rattling bottles. He smiled and fell asleep.

My Life: Chapter Nine

Dad's Car

We always had an automobile, which was unusual in our neighborhood, because it was usually the mark of the wealthy. We were not; but Dad, despite his description of himself as a neckwear manufacturer, was also his own salesman and needed a car. He usually bought a boxy four-door Essex and traded it in every couple of years.

That was in the days before automatic drives. His cars had three-speed transmissions (depress the clutch, move the gear shift lever into first, drive faster, depress the clutch again, etc.). When parked, the driver was supposed to engage the handbrake, but Dad preferred instead to leave the transmission in first gear, which worked as a brake of sorts as long as the clutch was not depressed.

One day, we were visiting Bubbie. The adults were upstairs. The car was parked on the hill in front of her house. Some of us were outside and I decided—at age seven or eight—to take the wheel of the car. I remember turning the wheel authoritatively but I don't remember shifting out of first gear, which I must have done because the car suddenly started to move. All of us scrambled out of the car and I ran away and locked myself in Bubbie's bathroom.

Miraculously, no one was hurt. The car had rolled a few feet and rammed another car that was parked below it. The only damage done was to my backside later.

Elliott

I was five when my brother Elliott was born. He was a chubby, healthy baby and grew up to be a personable, smiling kid. He was generally a happier child than I was, played sports easily, and got along well with the other kids. Naturally, I was jealous. We weren't as close as brothers really should be until both of us married. In more recent years, we have had a warm and loving relationship. Although we live in different cities, we try to get together every few months with our spouses, and sometimes with cousins, in places that are halfway between his home in Nyack, New York, and ours in Washington, DC.

Seders at Passover

We spent a lot of time at the apartment of Dad's parents (our Bubbie and Zadie), which was a walk-up tenement in the east Bronx. Dad would visit them every Saturday, much to Mother's consternation, because weekends were often the only time when Dad was not traveling on business. And we had our seders—the ceremonial meals on the first two nights of Passover—there every year.

The annual seders were the only times I can remember all of Dad's family getting together with regularity: Mother and Dad; Elliott and me; wealthy Uncle Moe and Aunt Dora and their two sons, Ray (five years my senior) and Jerry (five years older still); Aunt Rosie, whom I remember as severely hunchbacked, and her three children; and Aunt Jenny who never married and lived with Bubbie, because Jenny was considered too incompetent to manage on her own.

I think back on the seders as fine family gatherings, suffused with the smell of traditional Jewish food and the flickering light of candles on the table. Everyone sat around the one long dining room table. At the head was Zadie and, after he died, Dad sat there because he was the only son. The man at the head had a bedroom pillow between his back and the back of the chair because, officially, he was supposed to be reclining. The ceremony was almost entirely in Hebrew, which we read from books. But the older men knew many of the chants by heart.

I, when I was the youngest male who could read Hebrew, would open the proceedings by reading the traditional "Four Questions." Why is this night different from all other nights? Why do we eat matzo, bitter herbs, dip them in salt water and dine with special ceremony? Because it gives the man leaning against the pillow a

My Life, A Novel

chance to tell an important story about the history of the Jews, because it gives a family a chance to get together, even if it doesn't most of the rest of the year, and because it gives the kids a chance to have some fun—some planned, some not.

Planned was the ceremony. Passover is observed at home and the seders are designed largely to instruct the children. So it is interesting, explained in simple terms, and has built-in incentives for the kids. For instance, Zadie would break a piece of the unleavened bread and hide the half of matzo under a pillow, fully expecting us to "steal" and secrete it where the adults couldn't find it. Then the ceremony would continue, then we'd eat, then more ceremony. That piece of matzo is necessary for the conclusion of the service and after a perfunctory search, Zadie would reward us with some pennies for us to forfeit the hidden matzo.

Unplanned was the effect of the wine on us kids. Bubbie's house was the only place we were ever given wine, mostly at the seders where wine is an integral part of the ceremony. We weren't given much, but even so, it could be an intoxicating experience.

You have to understand something here about how men's trousers were made in the 1920s and 1930s. The trouser fly did not have today's state-of-the-art zippers. The fly closed with several buttons. They were sometimes tough to close in a hurry, and a well-placed swipe at your victim's trousers could rip them open. All anyone could see was underwear. But that didn't matter; it caused uproarious laughter by most little boys in the audience. At the seders, when the boys started "ripping flys," our parents knew we had had enough wine.

Photography

When I was about twelve, I learned from a patient gray-haired janitor how to develop film. It led to my fascination with photography and convinced me that you can appreciate photography best if you follow it through in the darkroom. Not color, which is very difficult to process at home and which is often done well by commercial establishments, but black-and-white—which can capture images in

Gene Cowen

delicate shadings of gray that can express both realism and impressionism with great force.

There are few things more discouraging to a photographer than getting back from a drugstore murky, blotchy images, often flecked with specks of dust. And there are few things more exciting than sliding a piece of just-exposed photographic paper into a tray of developer and watching in the pale yellow light of a darkroom lamp as the outline of the face emerges, then the fullness of the lips spreading into a smile, and suddenly the head glowing with the sheen of blond hair, more beautiful even than you can remember its being when your finger clicked the shutter button the day before.

But that excitement of fulfillment came more than twenty years later. Now, in 1937, I was developing film taken with a camera that Uncle Harold had given me for my twelfth birthday. It was a little plastic Kodak with a folding bellows that took 120-size roll film.

I carried the camera to nearby Bronx Park and found a squirrel that looked like a likely subject. To him, I must have looked like a likely predator as he sat on his haunches blinking at me while I raised the camera to my face. As the distance between us closed, he reopened it, stopped running, turned, sat, and blinked again. I clicked away. That was about what the camera got: trees, sky, leaves under the trees, and somewhere in all that foliage, a blinking squirrel. Now the film had to be processed.

Mr. Bellins was the patient man who taught me how to process film. (He was an Englishman and because he spoke with an accent, I didn't realize for years that he was Jewish. At twelve, I had never heard Jews speak like that. Many years later, I thought of Mr. Bellins with a smile when I heard Oxford-educated Abba Eban, the Israeli Ambassador, speak in Washington.)

Mr. Bellins was the janitor in our Bronx apartment building, but he was always referred to by the more prestigious title of "superintendent"—or more familiarly as "the super." He took the garbage pails we sent down dumbwaiters and dumped them into big corrugated metal cans for the city collectors to pick up, and then sent the pails back up the dumbwaiter. He shoveled coal into the furnace that heated our radiator pipes and tap water. He fixed things. And he had a love for photography which he shared with me, offering to teach me how to develop the film that I had exposed.

All we needed, he said, was a darkened room, three bowls, two chemicals and a red light. (Today's films use the same two chemicals, but must have absolute darkness. In 1937, however, black-and-white film was orthochromatic—insensitive to red light—and much less sensitive to all light than are today's. So developing could be done by the light of a dim red bulb.) Mr. Bellins painted a fifteen-watt bulb with red nail polish, and we were ready to go.

At night in our apartment, we closed the bedroom door, drew the shades and drapes and poured some developer powder into a bowl of water and stirred gently. The soup had a sharp, alkaline smell. The second bowl got cool tap water, and the third, a powder that, when mixed with water, smelled acrid and irritated the linings of the nose. It was a fixative, called "fix." Every time I think of hypo I can smell it. Then, by the dim light of the nail-polished little bulb, we carefully removed the film from its metal spool and discarded the opaque paper backing that had prevented it from being exposed to unwanted light.

Next came the hard part. Mr. Bellins held the ends of the film in each hand and dunked the middle of it into the developer. The right hand went down as the left went up, then left down and right up. I found all that up-and-down tough on my arms, which were not very long.

Photographic film is coated with an emulsion that is sensitive to light, as are plants and flowers. I am not sure what happens to the plants or to the coating on the film when light strikes them, but it causes a chemical reaction. The surface of the film looks no different after it has been light-struck than it did before, but when it is bathed in a developing compound, the exposed portions of the emulsion turn to shades of gray. More light, more gray. A lot of light and they turn full black and that portion of the film is opaque. No light, no gray, and that portion of the film is virtually transparent. Please remember that.

So if a bright point of light put a twinkle into your sweetie's eye as you pressed the shutter button, it passes through the glass lens (magical, isn't it?) and strikes the film, to show up as a tiny point of black as the film is sliding in and out of the developer. If she was also wearing a black dress which reflected virtually no light, the dress made no impression on the film at all, and that part of this negative is transparent. That's why, at that stage, the film is called a negative.

Gene Cowen

What's bright in life comes up black on the film and vice versa. That's what you had to remember.

After the film sloshed around in the developer long enough (determined in those days by squinting at it in the dim red light, and today by time and temperature), out it came, then into the bowl of water for a few ups and downs, then into the fix, which washed away the unexposed silver salts, and finally into a bath of running water, and hung to air dry.

Printing the negative is the same process, but produced by shining light on a negative that is pressed up against a sheet of photo-sensitive paper. The negative's black spot in your girl's eye transmits no light and the paper restores the twinkle, and the dress—transparent in the negative—regains its familiar blackness.

I printed my pictures of the worried squirrel by sandwiching the 2 1/4-inch square negatives against printing paper in a small frame which, in the darkened room, was pointed at a bright light bulb; then I developed, fixed, washed and dried the paper. The result—although a long way and forty-four years from the luminous enlargements I made in 1981 at the Corcoran School of Art—was still wondrous…and mine, all mine.

World's Fair

I was fourteen when the World's Fair opened in New York City in 1939. The regular admission price would have been entirely too expensive in that year of the lingering Great Depression. But as a student in DeWitt Clinton High School I was able to buy a book of twenty tickets for the wonderfully low price of two dollars. I used every ticket that summer.

The fair was located at Flushing Meadows, in a remote section of Queens, a long subway ride from my home in the Bronx. Twenty times during the summer of '39, I put two homemade sandwiches into a paper bag and fifteen cents of my allowance money into my pocket—one nickel for each way on the subway and the third for a Coke. Also with me sometimes was a friend, but always my Voightlander Baby Bessa folding camera, a tiny primitive light meter and as much film as I could afford.

My Life, A Novel

It's only by looking back to that great World's Fair that I can realize how much has changed since those days. The exhibits predicted that in the future, machines would actually wash clothes and dishes! Hard to imagine that when Mother washed pieces of clothing by dunking them into the kitchen sink and scrubbing away at them with an accordion-pleated wash board that rumbled each time she pushed the garment down and up. Back-breaking work.

The rinsed clothes were hand-wrung, also good for developing muscles, and hung out on a line that stretched outside our apartment windows. As for dishes, it was silly to think of a machine doing the clean-up. Mother did the washing, and when Dad was home, he dried.

Symbolized by its white obelisk trylon and billiard-ball perisphere—designed by Wallace K. Harrison, the architect for Rockefeller Center and later the United Nations—the fair divided itself into free national or corporate exhibits and commercial entertainment. Obviously, I spent almost all my time at the free parts.

Some exhibits were regular ports of call as soon as I got through the gates: Beechnut, which gave away single sticks of chewing gum; Maxwell House, where we could get enough free coffee for about two swallows; and Life Savers, for a few candies nicely wrapped.

But the real magnet that drew me was Kodak's fascinating exhibit. There, in a small dark auditorium, I would look up at enormous flowers blooming on the screen in vivid reds and yellows. Kodak was promoting its newly-developed Kodachrome slide film, which it sells to this day. It was there that Kodak demonstrated how the brain plays tricks with the eyes when they see colors. The audience was shown a peculiar American flag, black stars on a lemon-yellow field and stripes of alternating blue and black. Everyone was told to stare fixedly at a marked spot for some seconds, then the flag was replaced quickly by a blank white space and—wow!—up came a proper red-white-and-blue Stars and Stripes.

Outside the auditorium, Kodak had a little kiosk that attracted both amateur photographers and people who just liked to smash glass. Kodak was demonstrating the wonders of electronic flash, today a part of almost every little camera, but then used only by scientists. A sheet of window glass was mounted on a metal frame and a few feet away a baseball-pitching machine—the kind batters use for practice hitting—was aimed at the glass. Then the lights went out in the kiosk

Gene Cowen

and we, on the outside, smiling in anticipation, were told to press our camera lenses against the peephole windows that looked into the darkened kiosk.

"Set your shutter for 'time' or 'bulb'," said the attendant and then he pressed a button. Pitching Machine fired a strike at Glass and, at the moment of impact, off went the flash. That was it. A crash and a fantastically brief and bright light and I had something magical on my film.

When I got home and developed and printed the film, there was a perfectly sharp picture of a baseball hammering through a sheet of glass that was being shattered into a fascinating pattern of shards. I had on photographic paper and would show to the family and friends an image that the human eye could not see when it happened.

At times like that, Mother would often accept my handiwork with a bland, "That's a nice snapshot."

Snapshot, indeed! With a little help from Kodak, I had duplicated in 1939 the same optical miracle that scientist Dr. Harold Edgerton had published in *Life* magazine just a few years earlier. Forty-two years later, when I was studying art photography at the Corcoran Gallery of Art and printing pictures 16-by-20 inches in size, Mother again admired my "snapshots."

Only occasionally would my parents go to the World's Fair because it was too expensive. But Mother went once to see the famous light display. At dusk, at the center fountain, with piped-in music from a symphony orchestra, lights traced the churning water, gas jets shot flames, the lights changed colors and the water danced, all the while the orchestra was playing Sibelius' stirring "Finlandia."

At the end, Mother, who was rarely given to displays of emotion, said, "I can die now. I've seen everything."

And there were other things to see at the World's Fair that were wondrous to a fourteen-year-old: pressure cookers and nylon fabric; frightening simulated lightning in the General Electric building; hearing my recorded voice—for the first time—in the Bell Telephone exhibit. (I sounded awfully high-pitched.)

One day, a popcorn machine in a curbside booth caught fire, and I snapped my first live-action picture of the vendor spraying a fire extinguisher into the smoking booth. But the final print showed hardly any of the smoke that I remembered from the excitement of the moment.

At the end of the wonderful summer of '39, I compared what I had seen and photographed with a tourist map of the fair, and I was able to check off about half of the exhibits listed at the fairgrounds. So I then set about the task of seeing all the others. I returned in 1940, and by the end of the fair's second year, I had walked every foot of that place and could check off every building.

If there had been a Guinness Book of Records back then, I might have qualified for a mention in the Teen-Age-Boy-With-Cheap-Camera category. In 1940, I made up an album of my World's Fair pictures, which I still have—some little 2 1/4-by-2 1/4-inch contact prints, a few 5-by-7 enlargements. I looked at them just recently and, although they wouldn't win any prizes, the prints held up well, hardly showing their age after sixty years. I wish I could say the same for myself.

Smoking

I first started smoking when I was about thirteen, just before the '39 World's Fair. The guys in our "gang" would find a remote corner of an alleyway and puff furtively on one cigarette that someone had been able to buy. Single cigarettes were sold over the counter in those days for a penny or two. My Aunt Eleanor, something of a non-conformist in the family, asked me if I smoked, and I admitted, "Sometimes."

She said cigarettes were not too good for you, but a pipe was fine, "and you look better smoking a pipe." So I took up a pipe when I was fourteen.

Dad was a serious smoker of cheap cigars. He'd light up about four Murials a day, and the stink of the saliva-soaked tobacco would drive Mother crazy. So, around the house, he'd often substitute a pipe. His favorite tobacco was Half & Half, and the standing joke was, "Half is tobacco and you know what the other half is." I settled on Walnut tobacco.

I thoroughly enjoyed smoking a pipe. Never mind that some people couldn't stand the smell or that stray ashes would burn holes in my clothes. I found it relaxing, a comfort to have the pipe stem in my mouth, soothing to draw the warm smoke into my lungs and to smell the aromatic fumes that curled up from the hot bowl. One writer said that it was also useful when you want to point with the stem when giving advice to a younger person.

Pipe tobacco was a lot less expensive than cigarettes, especially when I was in service. In Italy, during and immediately following the war, American cigarettes were much prized by the civilians, who were willing to pay what we considered fabulous amounts of money for them. The Army rationed us to one carton a week at the PX, for which we paid only fifty cents. But that same carton would sell for twenty-five dollars on the black market.

The market was black only in the sense that it was technically illegal to be trafficking in cigarettes. But everyone did, and as long as he was selling only his own one-carton-per-week ration, no one cared; and if there was a law, it was never enforced.

But think about the arithmetic. If you sold, instead of smoked, your weekly carton, you could have twenty-five dollars, which went far in a soldier situation, in which all your food, lodgings and equipment were provided by Uncle Sam. So, in the two years that I spent in Italy, I smoked my pipe, spent only my "black market" cigarette money and was able to save a couple of thousand dollars of military pay.

I gave up smoking cigarettes in the 1960s when the first cancer warnings began appearing. But I smoked a pipe until 1972, when a doctor—disagreeing with Aunt Eleanor's advice—persuaded me to give it up. To this day, I miss it so much that at times, I dream about smoking a pipe.

Politics & Friends

At about age sixteen, I found politics. It became obvious that there was more to life than school (hard work) and photography (fun).

I had never had a very satisfying social life. I didn't really get along well with boys, which I blamed on my not being good at sports, a lame excuse. And with girls, I was awkward to the point of embarrassment. I attended an all-boys' school and the girls in our

My Life, A Novel

neighborhood who were my age were not really interested in immature kids with pimply faces. At sixteen, I still hadn't had my first date and hadn't even tried to get one.

But politics was different. Election campaigns needed teenagers to hand out leaflets, knock on doors, and do all the other kinds of exciting street activity. (Once I even went into a Metropolitan Life Insurance Company local office, took a fistful of brochures with a promise to distribute them, and then dutifully handed them out to crowds coming off the local subway stop. Why? Because it was fun.) So I frequently found myself folding political-issue papers that I had hardly read and becoming involved in organizations whose policies I only vaguely understood.

Early in 1941, World War II had been raging for two years, and the Allies were at the edge of collapse. France, Belgium, Holland and Poland had fallen to the German armies. Some 200,000 English and 140,000 French troops tried to evacuate the continent at Dunkirk, and 30,000 were killed or taken prisoner. The British stood alone as the Germans prepared an invasion fleet.

"England alone stood between the Germans and their aim of full European conquest," Dorothy Rabinowitz recently wrote in the *Wall Street Journal*. "The British adamantly refused, thanks to Winston Churchill, all offers of a negotiated peace with Hitler. They refused, even as a threatened German invasion seemed ever more imminent, and as the arch-appeaser, Lord Halifax, went about trying to arrange one, and while the U.S. ambassador in England, Joseph Kennedy, spent his days transmitting assurances that the British were finished...[Churchill said] in perhaps his most famous speech, 'We shall defend our island whatever the cost may be, we shall fight on the beaches...we shall never surrender.'"

At that time, I joined the Student Defenders of Democracy, whose main objective was to get the U.S. into the war on the side of Britain. I wasn't aware of all the global implications but I knew that Hitler had to be stopped. The SDD, and other organizations like it, were attempting to influence U.S. public opinion over the opposition of most Americans, who didn't want the U.S. to get into another European war only 23 years after 115,000 Americans had died in World War I. SDD was also very liberal, a staunch admirer of Eleanor Roosevelt, against Westbrook Pegler, in favor of freer trade, against

Gene Cowen

farm subsidies and in favor of Carmen Miranda, who sang at our rallies.

One early fall day in 1941, SDD asked for volunteers to distribute to shopkeepers in downtown Manhattan posters announcing an Eleanor Roosevelt rally. The adults matched one boy with every girl because we boys were strong and girls were weak and needed protection.

I volunteered and found myself teamed up with a pretty brunette with very pale skin and lively blue-green eyes. Phyllis Wallach was the kind of person I instinctively wanted to protect. But our task was pretty tame. Most shopkeepers were gracious and many accepted the posters for their windows. The day went by pretty routinely. I reminded myself to hold doors open for her. She always said thanks. We talked about the organization and its causes. She seemed to know a lot about everything. And I screwed up my courage and asked her if she'd like to join me when my high school football team played its traditional rival the next week. And she said yes!

My Life: Chapter Ten

Phyllis

In 1948, two years after I got out of service, I married the pretty brunette with the blue-green eyes who had stood atop her apartment building, crying and waving a towel for the Flying Fortress that never appeared. I knew that I wanted to marry her from the time we went on that first date in 1941. But before I could take her to my high school's football game, I had to run the gauntlet of a family gathering in a Manhattan apartment. I don't remember much about the Inspection of Eugene, except that I felt like the skinny, pimply teenager that I was, and I was mentally flinching at all those eyes in the heads of a mother, grandmother, aunts and uncles that had me triangulated in their radar beams.

Phyllis and I dated frequently after that but—a sign of how times have changed from 1941 to today—I did not kiss her until she was sixteen. After that first kiss, I was not so much elated as worried. Had I done it right? Was I clumsy? Was that the way they kissed in the movies? Apparently, I passed the kiss test because she agreed to see me again.

I proposed marriage shortly after I got my notice to report to active duty,. But Phyllis said she thought we were too young at eighteen and nineteen. We waited until the war ended and were married in 1948. It has been a love affair from the beginning, and today, we are so much involved in each other that when one is hurt, the other one aches.

Phyllis has changed a little since then. Her hair is blonde now, not brunette. Today, she no longer subscribes to the Robert Benchley theory of exercise that "when I feel the need for exercise, I lie down until the feeling passes away," and she has become a serious aerobic walker.

But some things have not changed. She still has her black-belt in shopping and, since she still diets too hard, she weighs about what she did half a century ago. She is still passionately devoted to her family and to its moral values. She still bowls me over. When I see her approaching from a distance, my heart still skips a beat. We can still look at one another and, without saying a word, we can both hear, "I love you."

From New York to Syracuse

I got out of service in 1946, one of thousands of veterans who were anxious to make up for all that lost time. I knew one thing that I wanted to do and one that I didn't. I wanted to get an education so I could work on a newspaper, which I had learned to love while I was in service. And I didn't want to stay in New York.

I had rarely traveled as a child, but the Air Corps had showed me that there was a whole 'nother world out there. People looked different, they ate different foods and they spoke differently. Strangers actually said, "Good morning!" when they passed you in the street, rather than looking blankly ahead. I thought that only happened in the movies. People lived, not in apartment buildings, but in single-family houses with gardens in the back and grass lawns in the front where dogs barked from behind fences. People ate "dinner" as the main meal of their day, not "supper," and sometimes it was in the middle of the day. I liked all that, not just because it seemed better, but because it was different.

So, when I got out of service, I returned to the City College of New York for one semester, while I applied feverishly to lots of schools, all outside of the big city. I was accepted at Syracuse University in 1946 and quickly packed a bag and was off.

I liked S.U. It was outside of New York City, it had a first-rate school of journalism and although its buildings were a potpourri of different architectural styles, to my eyes it looked like a university ought to look: a grassy, tree-lined campus and some of the buildings actually had ivy on their walls!

When I got there, the university was seventy-six years old, having been founded as a Methodist Church institution. Although it was by then non-sectarian, some of the puritanical influences remained. No alcoholic beverages were allowed in any of the dorms and, until

My Life, A Novel

shortly before I got there, men and women students still had to sit in different parts of the football stadium.

I liked the years I spent at the university. Living conditions were difficult because the school had expanded its enrollment greatly to accommodate veterans. For a while, I lived in barracks set up outside the city. Then, after Phyllis and I married, we got housing that was a little prefabricated military-surplus bungalow. It was hardly luxury living, but having recently lived in an Army barracks, it didn't really bother me that much.

The faculty was generally pretty good. I especially enjoyed the School of Journalism (which later changed its name to the Newhouse School after S. I. Newhouse donated fifteen million dollars to the school). The instructors were no-nonsense folks who knew they were training the students to become journalists. But the university, to prevent the place from becoming a trade school, required students to qualify for a bachelor of arts or science degree and have a full major in another subject. Then, the School of Journalism substituted for the minors that we would otherwise have been required to carry. So a graduate, who learned to write, at least had an academic background underpinning his writing.

The one exception I found to the good faculty was in a disappointing course I took later when I pursued a masters degree in history.

I was taking a course in the history of science. As I leafed through the book that had been assigned for the course, I noticed that there was no reference to Albert Einstein. It had chapters on Archimedes, Galileo, Pasteur, Watt and others, but no Einstein. So I asked the instructor, how come.

He answered, "Well, you know, Einstein's theories are pretty controversial, so he really doesn't qualify to be rated with the masters."

Controversial in 1950? That was forty-five years after he had published his special theory of relativity and thirty-five years after his general theory of relativity and, incidentally, years after his work had been tested, confirmed and used in the development of the atomic bomb.

It makes no difference today, because Einstein is widely revered and even *Time Magazine*, for instance, named him "The Man of the

Century." But it's an interesting sidelight on how some books and some academics—even at a good school—could be pretty dorky.

The *Daily Orange*

School of Journalism students polished their skills on the school's daily newspaper. I joined the *Daily Orange* (orange was the school's official color) and in the semester before I graduated, I became editor.

Having been editor of the *Foggia Occupator* in Italy when I was in service taught me that journalism was power. So I looked around for a way to make waves. One summer day, a few of us on the *Daily Orange* staff gathered in the paper's hot, crowded prefab, picking our way around such obstacles as a Great Dane sleeping in the walk area ("Get the elephant out of the news room!" some one shouted.), and discussed how we could leave our mark on the history of the university's newspaper.

We decided to target the little shops just outside of campus where students bought sandwiches and coffee and played pinball machines. If pinball players scored high enough, the shopkeepers would pay a nickel or a dime in winnings. "Gambling Alongside the Campus!" was a headline we could visualize. Never mind that the little shopkeepers were innocent of anything heinous; it was still gambling and we were going to reveal all. These days it would be called investigative journalism. For us, it was just a stunt.

So off we went, investing our own nickels, losing most of them, but finally hitting a winner or two at each of several off-campus stores. I wrote the story, which appeared alongside a quote in boldface type from the New York Penal Code.

Then the fur flew. The police were disgusted with what those smart-assed students had cooked up, but the law was the law and they dutifully arrested and charged several shopkeepers. They booked us agitators as material witnesses. I was angry and upset, sure that I'd spend the rest of my life with a criminal record.

Four of us were hauled down to the police station one morning and sat forlornly and interminably on a corridor bench, waiting to be booked.

A Novel: Chapter Nine

The grimy corridor walls were an institutional brown. Overhead fluorescent bulbs flickered erratically. An odd assortment of the debris of the local population sat on benches alongside the four glum university students. A man in a tattered overcoat kept insisting he wasn't drunk. A black man in coveralls was telling a white lawyer in a shiny business suit, "The son-of-a-bitch fell on my knife." Two weary prostitutes were comparing bruises on their arms and one muttered that "the cops are rougher than the johns."

Navigator's elbows were on his knees and his head was in his hands.

"*I'm the guy who brought down the* Hindenburg," he thought, "*took riot pictures in Italy that ended up in* Life *magazine, and set up Maria Tedesco to get a real job—and now they've got me sitting in a police station as if I was arrested on campus for conducting a panty raid on the women's dorm. Something has got to be wrong here.*"

As if echoing his thoughts, a voice said, "Is this the best you can do with your life?"

Navigator looked across the corridor and saw Lou Brovyard, the *Life* magazine bureau chief. Navigator's angst faded a degree as he focused on the familiar face. "Lou! What the hell are you doing here?"

Brovyard had aged. His shoulders stooped a little. His stomach rolled a bit over his beltline. But his blue eyes still had the flash of a newsman looking for another story.

"I got transferred back from Rome. Europe is quieter now. No war. No food riots for the *Life* cover. They've got me on special assignments. '*Life* Goes to the Races,' this month. You've got an auto race just outside of Syracuse on Saturday. Dirt track. Lots of color. Maybe some crashes. Good pictures.

But the question really is what the hell are you doing here with all these other criminals?"

Navigator told him. Brovyard thought it was all very funny. "Atta boy! When you can't find a story you create one," Brovyard said. "Come on, let me buy you some coffee."

"Lou, you seem to forget that I'm the guest of the Syracuse police department."

"Let me work that out. I've become good friends with your police chief in the course of working out our coverage of the auto race. He's a guy with an appetite for personal publicity. Let me talk to him about paroling you into my custody long enough so we can get some coffee."

Five minutes later Brovyard came back, handed a piece of paper to the policeman in charge, and then walked out. He put his big hand on the nape of Navigator's neck, as if he were arresting him and laughed all the way out of the building and across the street. He said they had thirty minutes before Navigator and his buddies were needed.

They walked into a greasy-spoon diner opposite the police station. It was after breakfast and before lunch, so they had the place to themselves. They squeezed into brown wooden booths with black plastic tables and cracked maroon plastic seats. A chunky waiter in a spotted apron, probably the proprietor, asked them what was their pleasure.

"Fried cakes and black coffee," said Navigator.

"What's fried cakes?" asked Brovyard.

"Doughnuts," said Navigator. "All us Syracusans call them that." He smiled for the first time that morning.

Brovyard pulled a notebook out of his pocket, made a note of the localism, and ordered the same. They looked at each other silently until the waiter brought the food.

"What ever happened to Maria Tedesco?" asked Navigator.

"She left after about a year."

"Only a year? Did something go wrong?"

"Naw. She got married."

"To who?"

"Some GI. Why did you ever give that girl up? She was a beaut—smart, hard-working, did a good job for me. And she

My Life, A Novel

was Anglo-Sexual," Brovyard said with a grin, "a magnet for men around her. But she behaved herself, as far as I could tell. Can't see what she saw in that guy she married. He came around a few times. Skinny, pinched face, kind of withdrawn. But I guess she wanted someone to marry her and take her and her little kid to the States."

Navigator just nodded.

"She invited me over to her house for dinner one day," said Brovyard, through a mouthful of doughnut, "so I could see how Italians really lived. They lived not so hot. Her mother, by the way, was a piece of work. Did you ever meet her? She hated Americans. We killed her husband and Maria's first husband. But that little girl was cute—Maria's daughter. She asked me if I knew 'the Alligator'. Funny question for an Italian kid to ask.

A ripple of sadness rolled over Navigator. He hadn't touched his coffee or doughnut.

"Say, was that you?" Brovyard said, waggling a forefinger at Navigator and laughing. "Alligator! I bet that's what Maria called you in bed. Boy, you dynamite lover. Alligator! I love it."

"Lou, lay off," said Navigator. "I'm depressed enough as it is and now you're going to drive me over the edge."

"What are you so depressed about?"

"Lou, I've spent the last several years trying to get a good education at a good school. I'm now a senior. I'm Phi Beta Kappa. I'm editor of the college daily. All that should add up to decent references to get a job. But now I'm going to be booked as a material witness and I'll have a criminal record for the rest of my life. That's why I'm depressed."

"Come on, Navigator. Stop crying in your fried cakes," said Brovyard, motioning to the waiter for more coffee and a check. "You're a magnet for trouble and you parlay it into something good every time. You're like Joe Bfstplk in *'Li'l Abner'*. I think that's the way he pronounces his name. You know, the character who always has a dark cloud over his head that's raining on him."

Brovyard motioned with his fingers over his head. "He attracts trouble wherever he goes. That's you. You get shot down and get away with only a broken ankle and an Air Medal.

You run into a riot in Italy and you grab a camera. When you're driving the pictures back from Bari, a firefight starts near you and you get away without a scratch. Now you're editing the university paper and you trigger off an investigation of gambling near the campus—I still can't believe it. Nickels and dimes!—and the police make arrests and you get a hell of a story out of it.

"Go back to that police station, buddy. Being booked as a material witness doesn't mean you're going to have a criminal record. It just means you have to show up at a trial. Now, you don't stand a chance of a fart in a thunderstorm of getting a local jury to convict those mom-and-pop merchants. But what you will get is a first-class paragraph to add to a job resume. You fell into a pile of shit and you're going to come up smelling like a rose again."

Brovyard looked at his watch, swallowed the last of his coffee, left money on the table and said, "Your parole has expired. Let's go. But do me one favor, Joe Bfstplk. Come to the auto races on Saturday. I need a few good crashes for my story."

My Life: Chapter Eleven

A bemused photographer from the Syracuse *Herald-Journal* saw the four forlorn students on the police station bench, pointed his Speed Graphic at us, and took a picture. When you fire a flash gun into people's faces, even if they are happy, they often look pasty-faced and grim. We weren't happy and that picture made us look like sad and angry young men being treated as criminals.

The case itself, when it finally came to trial, was a joke. After a half-day's trial, a bored judge acquitted all four shopkeepers who had been harassed by out-of-town students who kept inadequate records of their bets and winnings.

That was the end of a bright idea that had seemed to go sour. But a few months later, when I went looking for a job at the same *Herald-Journal*, the editor said, "Weren't you one of those students in that picture at the police station?"

I said I was and was trying to explain my way out of the situation, when he said, "That was pretty enterprising. I think we can find a place for you here."

Oh joy sublime! I was now a real reporter.

Syracuse *Herald-Journal*

The *Herald-Journal* was owned by S. I. Newhouse and still part of that family's chain. I was a classmate of S. I. Jr., the present head of the media conglomerate. He distinguished himself at Syracuse University by the number of parking tickets he amassed on campus. S. I. Newhouse also owned the other daily paper, as well as a television and radio station in Syracuse. So the small size of Syracuse and the lack of real competition meant that it could sell papers without reaching for any journalistic heights. There was nothing really wrong with the *Herald-Journal,* and it was a good place for a starting reporter to learn his trade. But it also never won any Pulitzer Prizes.

Gene Cowen

In the late 1940s and early 1950s, when I worked on the newspaper, the Iron Curtain had descended on Eastern Europe and the Cold War closed in on most of the world. We rarely reported on any of that, the editors being content to run stories verbatim as they came in over the national news wire services.

In 1949, a new Ford four-door sedan sold for $1,236 F.O.B. Detroit; Phyllis and I owned a dilapidated pre-war Chrysler coupe. Although several million U.S. homes had television sets, we were not one of them.

The North Atlantic Treaty Organization came into being. The Communists took over China. *South Pacific* opened on Broadway. President Truman escaped an assassination attempt. (Which caused a fellow reporter to tell me the story of his visit shortly afterwards to the National Press Club in Washington. He said he noticed that when a club member at the bar ordered Scotch with soda on the side, he gulped down the whiskey and then slowly drank the soda. "Why do you do that?" my friend asked. "Because," said the other reporter, "when they tried to shoot Truman, I rushed out to cover the story and left my drink on the bar. I'll never do that again.") The Federal Reserve estimated that four out of ten families were worth $5,000; I started working at the newspaper at $1,820 a year. And Senator Joseph McCarthy began getting headlines for his Red-baiting campaign. That resonated in central New York State. One city official told me that "where there's all that smoke, there must be some fire."

But the *Herald-Journal*, as most newspapers did then and still do today, focused on local stories, such as those involving the mayor and the police force, and, especially, on the weather.

Syracuse winters were bitter cold and snowy. The hostile weather influenced almost everything we did, including Phyllis's and my decision to leave five years later. When I discussed with Phyllis where we should go next, she said, "Any place that's warmer."

We used to call the city that had been built on the Erie Canal in the nineteenth century the "funnel of the universe," because if snow fell anywhere, it would hit Syracuse. Once, while we were still students, Phyllis and I attended a traditional university spring weekend event, where the women wore Easter bonnets, the men straw boaters, and we ate strawberries and cream on the steps of Syracuse University's Maxwell Hall. It was May, and it was snowing.

My Life, A Novel

The city editor was Ken Sparrow, a man who resembled his name, and was pleasant, inoffensive, and plump. The only thing I learned from Ken in my five years there was his technique for dealing with papers that cascade upon you until you think you'll never dig out: make one huge pile of them and then just methodically work your way down from the top.

The assistant city editor was something else again. A. Brohmann Roth (he used his first initial and full middle name because he "didn't want to be known as Abie Roth") was an alumnus of Hearst's defunct Syracuse *Journal*. Brohmann thought of himself as a character out of Ben Hecht's "The Front Page" and talked longingly of the wild, swinging, no-holds-barred school of Hearst journalism.

He once sent me on assignment to get from a mother a picture of her son, whom she did not know had just been arrested for murder. I hated those sneaky assignments, when you could never admit why you wanted the picture and had to contrive a story. When I got to the house, a couple of plainclothes cops in a car outside the house motioned me over and said I was not to go to the front door. I called in and told Brohmann my predicament. He said, "Gene, who the hell are you working for, the cops or me?" I got the picture.

Brohmann liked me, in part because I could write fast and sometimes funny. And I liked him because, when he gave me an assignment, I knew if I did it well, he'd praise me openly. Often he'd say shortly before press time, "Gene, I need about eight inches of 'funny' for page one." I'd hunt around, find a story, and usually give him what he wanted.

Brohmann also knew something else about my writing. After reading my copy, he would often shout across the city room, "Gene can't spell shit!"

I'd stand up solemnly and recite, "S-H-I-T."

I also learned from him the expression, "I'd rather be in the room with a thief than a liar, because you can keep your eyes on a thief."

Probably the most talented man in that city room was Alan Jacks, a sharp-tongued Associated Press correspondent, who had a desk in the *Herald-Journal* office. I noticed that when he took one of his rare trips outside the office to cover an event (most of his work was done by phone), he dictated the story into his main office in Albany by referring only to scratch notes that he had written on a folded sheet of paper. Wow! That was really professional stuff. I visualized myself wearing a trench coat and shouting over the phone, "Millie, give me rewrite!"

So I tried that out when I was assigned to cover a bank fraud case. The Syracuse Trust Company case was the biggest story to hit that little city in years. The city editor told me to cover the series of trials in Federal Court, come back to the office, type the story and turn in the copy, just the way most stories were covered. When I asked if I could call it in to a rewrite person on the city desk, I was told they couldn't spare one. So I said, just give me a typist and I'd take it from there. I was ready to try what I had learned from the AP correspondent.

Before leaving the office, I'd write what had happened the day before, then leave to cover the opening of court. At each recess in the trial, since we were an afternoon newspaper with changing deadlines throughout the morning, I'd call in, get my pleasant little typist on the phone and, largely from memory, dictate changes in the first paragraph lead and add some current data. I'd then tell her where to drop the new data into the story, what to delete and so forth. After about a week, I was delighted to see that the editor had begun putting my byline on my stories. I thought I'd come of age. But another reporter laughed and said, "Gene, a byline is in place of a five dollar raise."

#

For this twenty-five-year-old, newspaper reporting was very exciting. I was occasionally assigned to stories off of my regular Federal Building beat. Once a year, the N.Y. State Fairgrounds was the site of a one-hundred-mile Indy-car auto race. It was on a dirt track and the cars would churn around it, tossing dirt like brown waves into the audience. The event itself was covered by the sports department, but the city desk would send a reporter and photographer to stand at each turn, waiting for crashes (news people are fundamentally ghouls), while being covered by layer after layer of dirt. We dressed in coveralls and periodically throughout the race, we'd have to scrape the dirt out of our eye sockets. Most of the regular reporters hated the assignment, but I loved it. I'd never seen a car move so fast and with so much noise.

In 1951, the sports department was shorthanded and asked the city desk to assign someone to report the event. Brohmann Roth looked up at me and said, "Gene, you're the crazy bastard who likes to get dirty at the racetrack. Do you want to actually cover the race?"

I quickly said I did.

"You can sit upstairs in the press box and stay clean," he mumbled.

The race was exciting, was held right near our deadline, and was full of the kind of crashes that make the blood sport of motor racing popular. That year I invited Joie Chitwood, the American Indian former race driver, to join Phyllis and me for dinner. He was running an auto stunt show that appeared at the New York State Fairgrounds. He said he had raced at seven Indy 500s, but had never placed better than fifth.

Phyllis asked him, "Weren't you ever frightened?"

He thought about that for a moment and said, "No, not frightened. But the real money in racing is in owning a car. So I began investing in my own car. Then I began to worry. I noticed that the larger the piece of the car I owned, the more I worried. But, no, I've never been really frightened."

Race drivers are a strange breed of cat. They go into a profession in which the injury and death rates exceed that of any other sport. A recent study showed that 260 people, both drivers and spectators, have died at race tracks from 1990 to 2001. But the drivers somehow seem inured to the perils that ride in the cockpit with them. Some tests have shown that a racer's blood pressure rises more when another car passes him than when his car spins out of control. Their attitude is, well, when you're spinning, you're just a passenger, so you might just as well relax and hope you don't hit something hard.

Some drivers who are both smart and lucky retire while their bodies are still in one piece—such as Mario Andretti, the brothers Bobby and Al Unser, and A.J. Foyt. But unfortunately, most others depart the profession in an ambulance or a hearse.

News reporting, like auto racing, should be confined to the young: it's exciting and sometimes rewarding, but after a while, you find yourself going over the same old ground again and again. Except for the lucky few who move up to more responsible positions in journalism or become a talking head on television, you're smart to get out while you have your health and sanity. Otherwise you end up being one of the old crocks of the business, honored more for your past victories than your present achievements.

Going to Washington

So I asked the *Herald-Journal*'s executive editor if he could arrange to transfer me to the Newhouse newspaper chain's Washington bureau, which he did in 1952. Phyllis and I and our infant son Jamie moved to Washington. But after six months on the job, I was fired. Apparently, the bureau chief resented having been told that he had to hire someone whom he had not picked himself.

We never got along well, but when he gave me two weeks' notice, I was stunned. I'd never been fired before; I really didn't know what I had done wrong, and I was worried sick about having to support a wife and child and look for work in a town where hardly anyone knew me.

The day of my notice, I sat on a park bench, thought about my predicament and felt like a homeless person. I called the Syracuse newspaper's executive editor, the same one who had arranged to get me into the Washington bureau, and told him I'd been fired. He said he was sorry to hear that.

I asked if I could have my old job back and he said bluntly, "No. I don't need someone who's going to stay here for his coffee and cakes and then take off again."

It was the "coffee and cakes" that felt as if the knife had been turned in the wound.

I didn't have the courage to tell Phyllis that I'd been fired. So each morning, I left for work at the same time and went about my job search. Capitol Hill, then and now, was a place with a lot of staff turnover and a need for writers, so it was a good place for job-hunting. In about a week, I struck it lucky. A woman Member of Congress was looking for someone with just my background, and I was promptly back at work.

But the fact of being fired was shattering and I didn't recover from the trauma for years. It led later to my need for psychiatric counseling. Even long afterwards, whenever I had to fill out a government security clearance form and confronted the question, "Have you ever been fired or asked to resign?" it brought back the anguish and humiliation. But on one positive note, my own experience helped a number of times when close friends were fired from their jobs and I could offer some solace, a sympathetic ear, and the assurance that, with time, the wounds eventually heal.

The Gentlewoman from Ohio

I got my job with Congresswoman Frances Bolton (who was referred to officially on the House floor as "the Gentlewoman from Ohio") in 1953 because she had recently hired a publicist and she needed someone to implement his ideas. When I met the famous Edward L. Bernays, who was Sigmund Freud's nephew, he was a short and graying and had a little mustache and a huge ego. But he was also the most brilliant public-relations strategist I have ever known.

In Bernays' office in a Manhattan brownstone, the walls were lined with books, most of whose jackets were well-worn, maybe by design more than by use. His business letters were typed on a heavy, magazine-grade, slick white paper, so that if you ran a finger over the words, they sometimes smeared. He used a huge desk pad to take notes, then cut the notes out of the top sheet in jagged patterns.

In the recently-published biography of Bernays, *The Father of Spin*, Larry Tye slapped him around pretty badly. But, as I read the book, Bernays' principal offense seemed to be only that he had committed the crime of public relations. With me as a disciple, we brought off a bell-ringer of an event for Mrs. Bolton.

The Congresswoman, who had endowed a nursing school, was always looking for activities that would further her reputation as a nursing leader. So, in 1954, when the U.S. Army announced a new head of its nurse corps, Mrs. Bolton asked me to write a congratulatory statement. Being a good publicist-in-training, I focused on the news stories about a French nurse who had been captured in the fortress at Dien Bien Phu as the French were being driven out of Indochina by the Viet Minh. The news media tagged her the "Angel of Dien Bien Phu." I called Bernays and told him I thought it would be appropriate if Mrs. Bolton said good things about the valor of military nurses and then pointed to the "Angel." What did he think?

"Gene," he said, "if you're ever going to be good at public relations, you have to learn to think bigger than that."

"How much bigger?"

"Mrs. Bolton should get that nurse into the United States."

"To the United States?" I said. "Mr. Bernays, she's a prisoner of war!"

"That doesn't matter," he answered. "Prisoners get released. Draft legislation and let's see what happens."

I did. After the "whereas" clauses which referred to Lafayette and to famous heroines, the concurrent resolution said that Lieutenant. Genevieve De Gallard Terraube was respectfully invited to be a guest of and to be honored by the people of the United States. The resolution passed unanimously. Meanwhile, the Angel and some other prisoners were indeed released.

When I told Bernays of our legislative victory, I could almost hear his mouth watering on the telephone. "First," he said, "set up a meeting at the State Department for you and me. We're going to get a foreign service officer assigned to this case (which he did). Then, write a letter to the following officials in the New York City government and arrange for a Broadway parade."

"A Broadway parade?" I asked incredulously. "She didn't fly solo across the Atlantic or win a World Series. Why would they give her a parade?"

"They do, for a lot of people," he answered impatiently. "When you call the city officials, don't say Edward L. Bernays asked you to get in touch. Say Eddie Bernays; that's how they know me. Now, let's move on. If Mrs. Bolton is really going to benefit from this, we also have to be sure that one of the nurse's appearances is in Cleveland (the Congresswoman's Congressional District)."

I did as he said, and then, for the next several weeks, I was in something of an awe-struck daze as the plot unfolded. I attended a meeting of New York City parade planners, for whom this was all matter-of-fact. The police commissioner was to maintain order; the fire commissioner was to make sure no fires broke out from the confetti on the streets; and the sanitation commissioner was to clean it all up. I was told that all Broadway parades take place around noontime, so they have built-in crowds while people wait to cross the street to get to lunch.

The police assigned one male and one female detective to protect the celebrity nurse. Her hotel phone calls were routed through their room so they could screen calls from "nuts who always attach themselves to these events." One such character was a dowager who made a far-fetched claim of being related to the nurse and wanted to arrange a lunch for her with the then-Cardinal of New York. That never took place, but at one point, the dowager offered me money if I could persuade the Angel that all this was legitimate. I couldn't and wouldn't.

The parade, which was fun, was something of an anti-climax. The Angel rode in the top-down convertible lead car; alongside her sat a regal Mrs. Bolton. A few handfuls of confetti were thrown from above. Some people let toilet paper unroll from office windows. The crowd was respectful, but quiet, probably having no idea what this parade was all about, and being anxious about getting to lunch.

Genevieve de Gallard was an attractive, serious young woman, who considered herself a representative of her comrades in arms, many of whom never made it back alive. She was devoted to the French army nurse corps and very proud of the fact that she was only the most recent member of her family in a long line of decorated military officers. She also let it be known that she had an uncomfortable feeling that she was being used. But the U.S. and French governments were enthusiastic.

President Eisenhower invited her to the White House to receive the Medal of Freedom. Mrs. Bolton and I accompanied her. There is a vibrant sense of power in that famous Oval Office, which I have felt every time I've been there. For my first visit, there was nothing quite like having the President of the United States, the victorious commander of the Allied troops in World War II, shake my hand and look into my eyes for just a moment.

"The only complaint I ever had about military nurses," he said, with the glowing Ike smile, "was that they insisted on getting too close to the fighting."

After that, Mrs. Bolton and the Angel made a victorious appearance in her Congressional District in Cleveland, and then the nurse said her good-byes and went back to France.

Mrs. Bolton, a very mercurial character, liked the publicity she got, but apparently had had enough of famous publicists and released Bernays. The French government awarded Mrs. Bolton the Legion of Honor for her effort.

PART THREE: 1954

Gene Cowen

A Novel: Chapter Ten

"Hey, Navigator, you hard to find."

He had picked up the phone in the apartment in suburban Maryland and heard this voice from his past. It brought back nine-year-old memories of the pretty Italian girl with sexy hips who had brushed the curls out of her eyes with the back of her hand.

"Where are you calling from?"

"Nearby Virginia," she said.

He laughed, even though he didn't think anything was funny. A small muscle in his right temple began to twitch.

"Be calm, baby. I'm married," she said. Her English, now with a soft, warm accent, had improved a lot in nine years.

"It's really good to hear your voice," he said very quietly. "Um, we have some catching up to do, and I don't think we should do it on the phone. Maybe I can buy you lunch. How about next Wednesday? I know a nice quiet restaurant in Washington where we can talk and get caught up."

#

Cantina d'Italia was below street level in downtown Washington. At lunchtime in 1954, well-dressed young people—who would be called yuppies in later years—strode by in the bright sunlight outside. But no daylight penetrated the cave-like atmosphere of the restaurant. It had plastic flowers in its faux windows and Italian operas wafted over the scratchy sound system. But the food was good and not expensive. The owner-chef lovingly described the daily specials with such emotion that it made your mouth water just to listen.

When he got there on Wednesday, Navigator could barely see her sitting in one of the dim booths, looking anxiously into the daylight of the doorway. When she recognized him, her face lit up. She wore a headband to keep the curls in place. Her red-striped blouse was more colorful than the clothes he remembered her wearing in the bad old days. Around her neck she wore a black velvet ribbon with his cameo in front. She had put on some weight, which was becoming, and he wondered if any of it had gone to those inviting Mediterranean hips that were now hidden by the table.

When he sat down, she put an arm around him and kissed his cheek.

"Maria, it's really good to see you," he said. "I'm sorry I couldn't talk on the phone at home. I'm also married now, and I didn't think it would be such a good idea."

She smiled, nodded, and said nothing. But she was thinking, *And you didn't want a reformed whore screwing up your life.*

"Tell me how you got from there to here, and how you found me, and how is little Anna," he said.

"I found you because you wrote to Lou Brovyard, the *Life* magazine bureau chief in Rome, to tell him where you were living, and he spilled the beans," she said. "I knew all along that me getting that job was no accident. So I asked him and he told me. While I was on that *Life* job, I met this nice American GI. He's a cryptographer. John agreed to marry me and take my daughter and me to America. He's got a job in your government, and that's why we're living near Washington. My name is now Mrs. John Alden. I'm a real American lady. I even go to PTA meetings."

"Mrs. John Alden," he said. "You can't get much more American than that."

"And Anna is fine and she's not so little anymore. She's twelve and in school. Phew, some of the schools in this country—is a foreigner allowed to say this?—are pretty awful."

He said he was pleased for her and hoped she was happy. He fidgeted with his silverware, putting one fork atop the other and lining up the tongs, as if that mattered. And he waited for the shoe to drop.

"I know what you're thinking." She brushed an imaginary curl out of her eyes, and her face turned somber. "So let me say this now. I owe you, Navigator, and I must repay the debt. You got me out of the gutter—where people use language you don't like—and gave me a chance to make a person of myself and give my daughter a decent life. So I owe you. So I must pay back. I have only one request in exchange."

He moved the forks back to the left side of his plate and put his spoon atop his knife to see if it could balance. He really needed a drink right now.

"For as long as I live, I'm available for anything you need," she said. "No, I don't mean sex, so you can stop looking around as if you're about to run out of this restaurant. Sex is cheap. You can buy it two blocks from here in front of the Statler Hotel. I mean a '*compare*,' in Italian, a buddy, who you can turn to when there is no one else. You understand? I know how important it is to have someone. If you need money, you can have whatever I have. If someone hurts you and you need me to even the score, I'll…"

Then she started to cry. This girl confounded him, showing up like this after nine years, crying alongside him in a restaurant. And then there was still that one request.

"And my one request is simple," she said into her handkerchief. It was spooky the way she could read his mind. "It is that you never tell anyone where you found me in Rome and what I was doing at the Excelsior Hotel. Not anybody. Not your wife, not your rabbi, not anybody. Certainly not my daughter."

He leaned back in the booth. Desire welled up inside him; he fought it back, put his arm around her and said quietly, "Well, I met you in the USO in Rome. You remember that. You were good at serving coffee and would cheer up lonely GIs like me. But if you don't want me to talk about that, that's fine.

"As to your other offer, I'm speechless. I've never had anyone give me such a gift. You know what you are? You're a fantasy, my fantasy. I don't know how to deal with a fantasy as pretty as you who comes into my life. But I'm going to accept your gift in the tender spirit in which you offered it. I will, as they say, put it in my pocket and take it out if I need it. Now, let's order lunch and I think we should have a bottle of wine to celebrate our meeting again, while you tell me more about your life as an American lady who goes to PTA meetings and what your husband does in the government."

Then Joseph, the owner, smiled at the happy couple and recommended the endive salad with a light vinaigrette dressing and the restaurant's signature veal, which they ate slowly, while drinking a bottle of Chianti. Her husband, she said, was in some kind of hush service in the government.

My Life: Chapter Twelve

<u>United Nations</u>

In the fall of 1954, Congresswoman Bolton was made a member of the U.S. Delegation for one session of the United Nations General Assembly. She asked two of us on the staff to accompany her. The session was uneventful, except for one lunch. Mrs. Bolton offered to host a traditional American Thanksgiving luncheon for the other women delegates.

Mrs. Bolton told us to go to find tablecloths, napkins and ornaments that would illustrate the holiday. She particularly wanted three dried corn kernels to be placed on each plate. We got the materials, hurried back to the delegate dining room, and set the tables with colorful tablecloths and napkins in fall themes, corn kernels on each plate and little cardboard figures of Puritans, Indians and turkeys around the table.

Then Mrs. Bolton spoke to her luncheon guests. She described the significance of each of the ornaments, the long tradition in America of giving thanks to the Almighty at this time of the year, and the importance of corn to the observance.

"Therefore, I've given each of you three kernels of corn which I hope you will plant when you get back to your native lands, and when the corn grows, I want you to remember what America stands for," she said, or words to that effect.

The problem was, the stuff was never going to grow. In our rush, we hadn't been able to locate dried corn, so instead, we'd gotten a can of popcorn and decorated the plates with the kernels from the can.

Primate Filing

One day, Mrs. Bolton threw her hands up and said, "We must do something about these files. I can't find things I want. Let's change the filing system. Find somebody!"

The Library of Congress sent us a specialist, who looked over our files and said, "What you now have is unnecessarily complex and, frankly, some of it doesn't make sense.

"Let me tell you about the Primate Filing System. If you give a piece of paper to a monkey, he drops it on the floor. Give him another piece and he'll drop that also. Pretty soon you've got a pile of papers stacked up in the order that the monkey dropped them. That's one good way to file. It's called a chronological file and everything is in date-order. There are lots of other ways to file: alphabetical by last name, by subject, and so forth. But in addition to all those, you should always have a Primate File, a chron file. When you can't find something and when all else fails, you can always say, 'Well, I know I wrote that letter sometime last month,' and you dig through a month's Primate File and there it is!"

I've used one ever since.

Puerto Ricans

When the House of Representatives calls its members to the floor, it rings bells in the House chamber and lights go on in the offices around the Capitol. In those days, two lights indicated a recorded vote, three a call for a quorum, and five a recess. Early one day in 1954, I noticed five lights go up on the clock in Congresswoman Bolton's office. That seemed strange because the House had just convened a short time before. In moments, we learned that there had just been a shooting.

"Free Puerto Rico!" shouted four armed confederates from the House gallery, and they began firing at the Congressmen. The shooters were likely part of the same group that had fired at the White House in 1949, in an attempt to assassinate President Truman.

Most Congressmen, especially those who had seen combat in World War II, immediately dropped to the floor and sought cover. We found out later that Mrs. Bolton was standing up, looking around, when a colleague shouted at her, "Frances, get the hell down here!"

She hesitated because it was beneath her dignity, but he reached up and hauled her down to the floor and under a desk. Eight Congressmen were wounded in the attack. The shooters were sentenced to more than twenty years in prison and, ever since, the Capitol galleries have had metal detectors and tightened security.

Changing name

About that time, I changed the spelling of our last name. My family's name was Cohen and for many years, I had been sensitive about thinly veiled anti-Semitic sniggering and slights. I decided that changing the spelling to Cowen would cure all that. I don't know if it did or not, but the fact of changing the name had a devastating effect on me. I began having guilt pangs about not wanting to admit that I was Jewish. The result was long months of therapy that had the beneficial side effect of telling me a lot of interesting things that I never had never known about myself.

By 1969, when I was in the White House and someone approached me to be the honorary chairman of the United Jewish Appeal for the U.S. government, I took the job, knowing that every so often, you have to stand up to be counted.

African Newsletter

In Congresswoman Bolton's office, I did a lot of writing—something I had done all my adult life and which I still love to do. One of my assignments was to draft a monthly newsletter for the Congresswoman to mail to several thousand constituents.

In 1955, as the ranking Republican on the Foreign Affairs Committee, she arranged to take a long tour of Africa. A very wealthy woman, she paid a specialist on Africa and a doctor to accompany her. I suggested she send material back that I could incorporate into her newsletter and she agreed.

But the letters that came back were largely chatty, mentioned various high government officials whom she had met and whom her constituents had never heard of, and were all very much in need of editing. I then remembered that during World War II, the *New Yorker* magazine had published thumbnail profiles of the countries where American troops were fighting. Each article had a little map and fascinating minutiae about how the locals lived and sights people could have seen if the war had not been on.

So I asked a researcher at the Library of Congress legislative reference service to give me background material on each country the Congresswoman planned to visit. He did, and I began stitching together whatever was usable from Mrs. Bolton with local background color—how there were immense piles of peanuts waiting to be shipped in Lagos, Nigeria, what the people ate for breakfast in Ghana, and how Rhodesia got its name. Each time, I wrapped it all around a sketch map and then stepped back and admired my work.

The newsletters got some complimentary letters from Mrs. Bolton's constituents, but when she returned, she was visibly annoyed that those stories were really not what she had written. Then the New York *Herald-Tribune* carried a brief editorial commending her on her literary ability and that mollified her somewhat.

But then I made a mistake. She heard that I was showing some of my friends the editorial and saying that I had had something to do with the newsletters. Shortly thereafter, I was asked to look for another job.

Senator Scott

I first met Hugh Scott in 1957 when he was a Philadelphia Congressman. He had been chairman of the Republican National Committee in 1948. In his career, he went on from the House of Representatives to serve for eighteen years in the U.S. Senate and was for several years Republican Leader of the Senate. I met him through a public-relations stunt.

My Life, A Novel

When I left Congresswoman Frances Bolton, I signed on with L. (for Louis) Richard Guylay, a New York publicist, and became vice president of his Washington office. One of the firm's clients was All America Rose Selections, the rose growers' trade association. Guylay thought it would help his client if there were a campaign to make the rose the U.S. national flower. He persuaded Congressman Scott, who had rose growers in his state, to introduce a bill to do that. Guylay also contrived a ceremony to crown the "national rose queen." We acknowledged that the queen and her court were just chosen by us—no contest, just a lot of fun. So Scott, the sponsor of the bill, presided over what was essentially a photo-op with pretty girls, a Congressman who wanted to become a Senator, and a bit of hoopla. (Scott's bill never passed, but a later one did in 1986.)

Scott was a fascinating and lovable guy. He was overweight, had a sporty little mustache, was an excellent speaker, a chain pipe smoker, and had a huge ambition. He told Guylay that he was planning to run for the Senate and asked if Lou would do some polling for him. Lou agreed and assigned me to handle it.

The first poll we conducted was designed to establish the fact that Scott was popular and could win the Senate seat. It went out by mail to selected people in Pennsylvania and was one of the least scientific polls I had ever seen, in a business that even today is pretty darned unscientific.

The problem we faced, however, was that the Pennsylvania Republican Committee, which had endorsed Scott, would only give him lukewarm support, and they refused to pay for the poll. I finally went to the Congressman's office and told him that we couldn't continue to work for him unless we got three thousand dollars for the poll. Scott agreed to pay for it himself, reached back behind his desk, and unlocked a big footlocker that stood against the wall. He rummaged around through various things he had stored there, and then brought out some bills and paid me in cash.

I thanked him and gathered up the money, but wasn't sure were to put it. I was thirty-two years old and had never handled that much cash in my life, and in 1958, three thousand dollars was an awful lot of money. So I stuffed the bills into my jacket pockets, got into a cab, and headed for the Riggs National Bank. I didn't feel safe from pickpockets and other marauders until I had the money converted into a cashier's check.

Scott's first campaign

In the course of the polling, I spent a lot of time in Scott's office and began giving his small staff pointers on what I thought was needed to conduct public relations for a political campaign. The Congressman, desperately in need of campaign help and very short of money, asked if I would work on his campaign.

"I'd love to," I said, "but I can't go to Pennsylvania and leave my other work behind."

"Work from Washington," said Scott. "Besides, I can't afford to pay you to live in Pennsylvania for several months."

Run a public relations campaign in Pennsylvania from Washington, DC? It was absurd. But it also was a challenge, so I agreed and Scott worked out a financial arrangement with Guylay. I studied the Congressman's campaign literature, read Pennsylvania newspapers, and came up with this formula: Once a week, I would sit down with Scott and he would sketch out where he would be speaking and roughly what he might say in the area. "And from there on, it's up to you, Gene," he'd said.

He didn't need speeches because he was facile on the stump. But he needed publicity. So I contrived a simple device, which was basically to write a few paragraphs, mail them well in advance to newspapers and other media, urge them to hold the story for release on the day Scott was to speak, and then caution Scott to be sure to say those words in his speech.

It looked something like this (a paraphrase of one press release I actually did):

Advance for Release After 6:00 p.m., Oct. 9, 1958

SCOTT SAYS CHRISTOPHER COLUMBUS

MIGHT NOT BE ADMITTED INTO THE U.S. TODAY

My Life, A Novel

"If Christopher Columbus came to the United States today, they might not let him in," said Congressman Hugh Scott (R-PA) at a Columbus Day celebration in Philadelphia today.

Scott, candidate for the U.S. Senate, told the Italian American Society:

"It's ironic that today, with the restrictive U.S. immigration laws that discriminate against many people because of their national origin, race or religion, we honor a great man who has the 'wrong' national origin, as far as those laws are concerned.

"If I am elected to the Senate, I would propose amendments to the McCarran-Walter immigration law to lower the barriers..."

The technique worked. Often those releases would appear in the Pennsylvania papers, giving Scott the coverage that he would not otherwise have gotten, since news organizations often will not send reporters to cover such speeches, certainly not early in a campaign. Sending releases out well in advance was the technique that made all the difference.

The Columbus release especially hit home. Since it was timely for a national holiday, newswire services picked it up. The following day, Scott went to New York to raise money at a Wall Street meeting, and a couple of paragraphs appeared on the front page of the New York *Herald-Tribune*. Scott was a minor celebrity at the fund-raiser and became an admirer of my writing.

I should point out that, as far as I know, I was the first to use the phrase about Columbus. I've seen it in print many times since, but without attribution—the price of being a ghost-writer.

Scott won the 1958 election in an upset. He was running against the incumbent governor of Pennsylvania in a year when Republicans elsewhere did poorly.

I was in Washington on election night. As soon as Scott's victory was announced, I sent him an exuberant one-word telegram: "*Banzai!*" Later that night, equally exuberant, he phoned me at home and began chattering in pidgin Japanese.

Gene Cowen

Working for Senator Scott

I was with Scott from the 1958 campaign through mid-1969. These were some of the best working years of my life and were also a time of considerable political and social turmoil throughout the world. Early in 1958, Nikita Krushchev took over as premier of the Soviet Union and, in July, U.S. Vice President Richard Nixon engaged him in a highly-publicized debate in a model kitchen. Fidel Castro overthrew the Batista government in Cuba and became dictator. In the United States, Americans owned 41 million television sets in 1958, up from 5-to-8 million in 1950. But the number of daily newspapers stood at 357, down from 2,600 in 1909, indicating the shift in where people got their news, sports and entertainment.

In 1959, Postmaster General Arthur Summerfield attempted to ban *Lady Chatterley's Lover* from the mails, but the courts held against him. Summerfield subsequently intensified his anti-pornography campaign and invited Members of Congress and *male* staff members to view hard-core porn movies. I went to one showing and recommended it to my colleagues. One of the women on our staff wanted a detailed description of the show which she had not been allowed to see.

In 1960, Senator John F. Kennedy defeated Vice President Richard Nixon for President, a campaign in which Scott played a role, both stumping for Nixon and sending him suggestions from Washington.

Scott was buoyant, politically adept and personally close to his senior staff. Often, in the evenings after a Senate session, he would invite us to have drinks with him, review what had transpired in the previous twenty-four hours, and often accept our suggestions for what to do next. Sadly, his own personal life was not as satisfying. When his difficult daughter, an over-aged flower-child, got into serious legal trouble, he said sadly to me, "So much for the downward mobility of American life." So he transferred many of those familial emotions to his staff, and even to our spouses. In 1964, in the midst of a bruising re-election campaign, when Phyllis came down with pneumonia, Scott called her to find out how she was doing.

Whenever he traveled, which was often, he invariably brought back small gifts for the whole staff. He would lay out the wallets, earrings, bracelets and pins in neat rows on his desk and invite each of us in, in order of rank, to pick one. I was so impressed by this gifting of staff that I did it for people on my staff in every other job I had. In 1959, shortly after I came to work for him, he went off on a long Senate Commerce Committee trip (otherwise known as a junket) to the Far East. On November 11, his birthday, Edie Skinner, his confidential assistant, said, "We really should send him a birthday cable. Gene, you're the writer; think of something."

The relationship with him was always easy, so I felt comfortable writing, "Roses are red/ violets are blue/ we're all working/ how about you?/ Happy Birthday."

Edie liked it, so did I, so off it went to Indonesia. About two weeks later, we got a letter from the Senator. He wasn't really angry, but probably a little hurt at the smart-assed ditty, and he felt the need to justify himself. His letter was long, detailing all the burdensome visits he had to make, all the self-important people he had to meet, and including a little about the food not being so hot either.

Scott was an avid, enthusiastic Republican with a good sense of humor. He said he had met President Truman at a reception sometime after Truman left office. "I introduced myself to him," Scott told me, "and said, 'Mr. President, I wonder if you know that I made a major contribution to your election in 1948 when you beat Governor Dewey.' Truman said, 'How so?' I said, 'I was chairman of the Republican National Committee.'" Scott laughed and added, "The Old Man just turned on his heel and walked away."

King

"I have a dream," said Reverend Martin Luther King, Jr. "I have a dream that one day, on the red hills of Georgia, sons of former slaves and the sons of former slave owners will be able to sit down together at the table of brotherhood."

As he spoke on the steps of the Lincoln Memorial in 1962, Scott and I were there to hear him. President Kennedy, for his own reasons, did not attend, and Senator Scott didn't want to either. He was a firm civil rights supporter, but the crowds and some threats of violence made him nervous and he had told me that he thought he should skip that event.

I disagreed, checked around, and found out that Senators Javits and Keating would be going, and told Scott. So they provided some political cover for each other and went as a group, and I grabbed a camera and went along. (The following day, the *Washington Post* carried a picture of the singer Marian Anderson and there I was, camera at the ready, on the steps below her.)

I was able to get an excellent picture of Scott in the foreground of the sea of humanity at the monument, and we used it in a special newsletter that we distributed to several thousand Scott constituents. It got mixed reviews. Some of our mail reminded us forcefully that the people in Pennsylvania wanted nothing to do with a Senator who "pandered to blacks." But both Scott and I knew what we were doing. There was a goodly block of black voters in the state, and in the very close election of 1964, they probably were the margin of Scott's narrow victory for re-election.

Kennedy

Almost everyone who was alive on November 22, 1963, remembers what he was doing when he learned that President John F. Kennedy had been shot in Dallas. I was in Scott's offices and we were stunned at the news.

The Senator, his face stricken, walked into his private office, dropped to his knees and began praying. But not everyone mourned. One of the Scott senior staff members, a political animal if there ever was one, stood up on a chair and addressed the staff. He urged everyone to be calm and think of the brighter side of the tragedy. "Remember now," he said, "Lyndon Johnson is going to be President and when he runs for re-election, he won't stand a chance. No southerner has been elected President in recent times."

I was so shocked that I just shook my head and left for home.

1964 Republican Convention

Despite what that political animal had said, there was no doubt in anyone's mind that President Lyndon Johnson was going to be elected in 1964. It was the year when Senator Scott was also running for re-election, and our task was to try to help him get elected as a Republican when this huge Democratic tide was running.

Scott first tried to get a moderate candidate for President on the Republican ticket, and threw his support to Nelson Rockefeller. But the New York governor, who had been running strongly in the polls before his divorce, suddenly bottomed out when his second wife gave birth to a child. Then Scott helped persuade Pennsylvania Governor William Scranton to run for the Republican nomination.

Several of us on the Scott staff joined him at the Republican Convention in San Francisco. The convention was tumultuous. Barry Goldwater's supporters, under the management of the able Clif White, had firm control of a majority of the delegates. Scranton didn't stand the chance of a snowball in hell of breaking through, but he and Scott hoped to do something to soften the very conservative platform. Scott met frequently with moderate Republicans to get their ideas for platform plank language that was softer than the harsh words of the conservative platform. We gathered in hotel rooms that were hot, crowded and smoky.

But an added touch was the bodyguard. Because of the violence at the 1960 presidential nominating conventions and the threat of more of the same in 1964 (it turned out there was little in 1964), we arranged for the police to assign a detective to Scott, who was Scranton's campaign manager. Nothing ever happened in the hotel to require the services of a policeman, but he persisted in sitting in the warm room with his jacket off and his pistol very visible in a shoulder holster. Whenever anyone entered the room, the first thing he saw was that man with a gun. It so distracted everybody that we eventually thanked him and asked him to leave.

But if there was no violence in the hotel, we did have a problem in our trailer office just outside the convention in the Cow Palace. One day, as I was writing a speech for Scott, I smelled smoke. I looked out the window and discovered that the rear of the trailer was burning. I shouted, "Fire!" and the staff stampeded out through the small trailer door. We never found out who had set the fire, but obviously suspected our opponents in the Goldwater camp.

The situation inside the convention hall was contentious. Both sides were angry and both were probably guilty of excesses. Scranton's managers distributed gallery tickets and encouraged us to use them so they would have a favorable audience in the stands. I gave one to Phyllis, who took her seat, but was later told by an usher that it was counterfeit. Hers and the other tickets that had been handed out by the Scranton people had identical serial numbers.

The political issues were joined when the delegates voted on amendments to the platform. I sat alongside Senator Scott in a limousine as we headed for the Cow Palace. He held index cards in his hands, some with the names of prominent delegates who had agreed to be speakers, and some with convention plank language. He kept shuffling the cards like Casey Stengel mulling over batting orders in the New York Yankees' dugout. "We'll be allowed votes only on three issues. Civil rights, the finger-on-the-trigger [of atomic weapons] and Social Security," he said. "Our best shot at getting any platform language changed is on civil rights. I've got to decide who should offer that amendment."

"Well," I said, with the assurance of a political novice, "you certainly ought to let Governor Rockefeller offer the civil rights amendment. He's the best-known speaker you have."

"No, Gene," said wily old Scott. "I don't think those folks in that convention floor think very highly of Nelson. I'm going to let someone else handle that one."

When it came time for the delegates to vote, I learned how right Scott was. I was standing in the press section just in front of the speakers' platform, alongside columnist Stewart Alsop. When Nelson Rockefeller got up to speak on a different amendment, the booing and catcalls were overwhelming. You could feel the hate pouring out of the stands at this man who stood for everything the Goldwater delegates were trying to eliminate from the Republican Party. Murray Kempton later described the scene as "the ravening fury of Goldwater delegates envenomed by victory as they had never before been in defeat."

My Life, A Novel

Stewart Alsop looked at me in dismay and said, "Gene, I think we are attending the last Republican National Convention."

It didn't turn out that way, but when Barry Goldwater said during his acceptance speech, "I would remind you that extremism in the defense of liberty is no vice! And let me remind you that moderation in the pursuit of justice is no virtue!" I also thought it was the end of the party.

Scranton lost and we went off to lick our wounds. On the day after the convention, Phyllis drove the two of us along the beautiful California coastline, but I was so drained that I slept in my seat on the whole trip.

1964 Scott Campaign

When Hugh Scott sought re-election to the Senate in 1964, he had a huge problem: How do you win as a Republican when Barry Goldwater, at the top of the ticket, is certain to lose badly in Pennsylvania?

We decided early on that Scott would run on his record as a moderate, and reach across to try to pick up Democratic and independent votes, which was possible because of his good record with Jewish, black and other ethnic voters. We underscored his appeal to non-Republicans by letting it be known that he was being "dragged kicking and screaming" into supporting the whole Republican ticket.

The campaign was tough. A few of us from the Scott staff moved to Harrisburg and opened a headquarters there. Bob Kunzig, Scott's administrative assistant, was the campaign manager, and I was in charge of press, public relations and advertising.

We worked from just after breakfast to dinner each evening, then usually went as a group to eat—usually to a spaghetti joint nearby, where the service was fast and the food cheap—and then went back to work until nine or ten at night. Campaigning is not only hard work, but often very lonely. Phyllis would come to Harrisburg on weekends with our two children, so that we would have some semblance of a family life.

Scott's opponent was Genevieve Blatt, a Pennsylvania state office holder. In her primary campaign, something happened that played into our hands, contrasting her with Scott, who was well liked by Italian-Americans (note the Christopher Columbus story in his 1958 campaign) because of his position in favor of amending the then-tough immigration laws. Blatt's opponent in the primary was Judge Michael Musmanno. The incumbent Democratic Senator from Pennsylvania, Joseph Clark, campaigned for Blatt and, in nativist central Pennsylvania, he made disparaging remarks about Musmanno—such as the allegation that he had once practiced law under the name Musmann so he would be perceived as a Jewish lawyer, rather than as an Italian lawyer. That understandably infuriated many Italian-Americans.

So I wrote a television commercial in which Scott spoke of the strength of ethnic diversity in the state and ended with, "And as your Senator, I represent *all* the people in Pennsylvania, not just those whose names don't end with A or E or I or O."

The commercial played well, and later, one of Senator Clark's assistants said to me with a laugh, "You sonovabitch, you got not only the Italians angry with us, but also all the Poles in the state."

Finally, our own polls confirmed our fears that Goldwater was going to lose Pennsylvania very badly. We had a long conference with the Senator and decided that we had to contrive a television commercial that urged people to split their tickets. We went through Jackie Robinson, the former baseball star and a friend of Scott's, to an advertising agency and explained that we had a special problem. In Pennsylvania in those days, the ballots had "party levers"—if you pulled the one political party's lever, instead of the separate levers for each candidate, you voted for all that party's candidates But you could, alternatively, pull separate levers for each candidate of any party.

The agency handled the problem cleverly. The twenty-second commercial opened with a man, his back to the television camera, facing a voting machine. As he reached up to vote, an off-screen voice said, "Don't touch that party lever!"

He turned to face the camera and said, "Why not?"

The other voice said, "Because in this campaign we're going to vote for every candidate on his own record," and went on briefly to extol Senator Scott and his record on key issues.

At that point, the man turned his back to camera and reached up to pull a lever, saying, "Right! Scott for Senate and then for President, I'll vote for…" and his voice trailed off without another word and the commercial ended.

When I played the commercial for Senator Scott in his office, he said, "That's pretty good. But I couldn't hear what the man said at the end. Play it one more time." I did and Scott roared his approval.

We kept the how-to-split tape under wraps until about three weeks before the end of the campaign. At that point, the Pennsylvania Republican State Chairman called and, almost in a whisper, said, "We're facing a potential disaster with Goldwater. I'm telling all candidates to save themselves any way they can."

We rushed our tapes to televisions stations in the state. The commercials played well and got lots of attention, including a few angry calls from Goldwater supporters.

Scott won the campaign by less than half of one percentage point in the face of President Lyndon Johnson's winning with about sixty-four percent of the vote and carrying most other Pennsylvania Democratic candidates in with him.

A Novel: Chapter Eleven

Maria stayed in touch with Navigator by exchanging letters every few months. It was 1961, and they had not actually seen each other in seven years. Maria discreetly wrote to him at his office, typing the addresses on a business envelope so they would not look personal. He appreciated her discretion, but every so often, he had to laugh to himself, because, despite the occasional wave of desire that would roll over Navigator, nothing was going on between them that his wife would care about anyhow.

Maria and her husband lived in Reston; Anna was nineteen and a lovely girl, but Maria was not too happy about Anna's American companions, who were caught up in the '60s agitation. John was still doing his cryptography in some sort of secret government job.

Navigator learned all this by reading her flowery Italian script, but an unease echoed through like a muffled whimper. Recently, her letters had been signaling an undertone of unhappiness, an unwritten sigh. So he called her one afternoon when he assumed her husband would be at work.

"It's so good to hear your voice," Maria said.

"Same here," he said. "I wondered whether we could get together. Should we have lunch?"

"No," she said.

That surprised him.

"Do you go to church?"

That surprised him even more. "We don't call it church," he said. "For Jews, it's a synagogue. Why do you ask?"

"I'd like you to take me there," she said.

"To a synagogue? What on earth for?"

"Never mind. I'll tell you when we're together," she said.

This was going to take some planning. The rendezvous would have to be at a Reform Jewish congregation because that was the branch of Judaism he was most familiar with, but it certainly couldn't be the one that he and his wife attended. He shuddered at the thought of what some of their friends would say if he walked into their temple with a good-looking, dark-haired Italian woman. So he located a temple in the suburbs and told Maria to meet him there for Friday evening services.

He arrived first, climbed a flight of wooden stairs, and asked if it would be possible for him and a friend to attend services. A pleasant plump woman at the door of the wooden building said they welcomed anyone who wanted to pray.

This was going to be something other than a praying session, he thought, but he didn't explain.

Then he walked back down the stairs and saw Maria's car pull up. As she swung out of the driver's seat, he could see attractive legs leading up to a simple black dress. She wore his cameo as a pin, and had a black lace shawl over her head. She walked purposefully toward him.

They kissed each other's cheeks, and he said, "Babe, this isn't a funeral. You don't need the shawl."

"I thought it would be best if my head was covered, since yours will be."

"Mine won't be," he said. "In a Reform congregation, you don't have to cover your head."

"Some of those men have those little things on their heads," she said.

"They're called *yarmulkes*. And it's hard to explain, but you can wear one or not, as you wish."

"I don't understand," she said, looking at him seriously.

"Actually, I don't either. Let's just say it's optional. But more important, why on earth do you want to go to a Jewish place of worship?"

"Because mine isn't working."

He looked into her dark eyes to see if she was being funny. But before he could pursue that, the plump woman at the door said that the service was about to start, and they hurried inside and took seats in the back of the small sanctuary.

There were rows of folding chairs arranged in a semi-circle around a center platform. Many of the people in the seats were young adults and some had children with them. The older kids squirmed a lot, and the youngest munched crackers or cookies that their parents gave them to keep them quiet.

As he and Maria sat down, she crossed herself.

"We don't do that in a synagogue," he said in a gentle whisper.

"I do before I pray. I don't care where I am," she said very quietly. Then she smiled and added, "You can say it's optional."

Two unlighted candles in silver candlesticks stood on a small table in front of the center platform. A woman walked up, put a match to the candles and said a prayer in both Hebrew and English.

Behind her on the platform, the rabbi stood at a lectern. Behind him was an ark, inside which there was a Torah—a covered scroll of the first five books of the Old Testament, hand-lettered on parchment—and, alongside the ark, two wall-mounted candelabra with lighted candles. Suspended from the ceiling, a lamp flickered with the "eternal flame."

The rabbi was young, with a neat beard, a black robe, a prayer shawl around his shoulders and a worried look on his face. He welcomed all the congregants, reminded them that this was the start of the Sabbath, a holy day of rest and prayer, and then motioned to an equally young woman cantor to sing.

"We usually have a choir and an organ," whispered Maria.

"Different religion," he said.

The prayers were alternately in Hebrew and in English, and some were read responsively. After the rabbi said something in Hebrew, the congregation responded with:" And yet, within us abides a measure of Your spirit. You are remote, but oh how near! Ordering the stars in the vast solitudes of the dark, yet whispering in our minds that You are closer than the air we breathe. For You have made us little less than divine, and crowned us with glory and honor!"

As Maria leaned her head against his, her hair brushed his cheek. She took his hand and whispered, "I believe that."

"Which part?" he said.

"All of it, but especially the part that says we're a little less than divine. Don't you?"

My Life, A Novel

"Not really," he said.

"Why not?"

"Well, for one thing, I think I'm the one who ordered the stars in the vast solitudes of the dark."

"Oh, my God!" she said, much too loud.

A woman in the row in front of them turned around and glared. A child with a cookie in her mouth stopped eating and looked at Maria.

Navigator motioned to Maria and they left as quietly as they could, excusing themselves as they scrunched in front of the people seated between them and the aisle.

When they got to the door Maria fumbled in her purse.

"What are you doing?" he said.

"I'm looking for some money to leave," she said.

"We don't do that," he said.

"Well, you're so blasphemous that I feel I have to. You're just terrible!" she said, as they walked to his car. "Here I come to see if I can find some solace in another religion and you just piss all over it." Then, after a pause, she added: "I'm sorry, you don't like dirty words. I don't want to get into an argument with you. But I'm looking for something spiritual, and it would be nice of you to help me find it."

They got into his car and just sat looking at each other. He didn't turn on any lights, preferring to have the night engulf them. He pushed her dark curls back, put his hand on her face and kissed her lightly on the cheek.

"I accept your apology and I apologize to you for talking like a cynic. But you remember, I told you that I believe that the universe was created when I was born and stars moved into their places at that moment and so forth. It may not make sense to anybody else, but that's what I believe. It's no more farfetched than what a lot of other people believe."

"I don't understand you, Navigator," she said. "You're smart. You got a good education. You're an achiever. You write speeches for a U.S. Senator. But you talk like a child. Every child thinks the world revolves around him. The world started when he was born and the world aches when he is hurt. And everything feels better when Mommy kisses the sore knee. So what's so different about your grand theory? And I'm angry with you, because I have real problems and I want to talk to you about them, but I don't want to talk to a *stupido*."

"Does that mean what I think it means?"

"It sure does."

"Well, there was the *Hindenburg*..." he said.

"You think that balloon wouldn't have gone down without your curses?" she said, looking out the car window at the evening sky. "Look at those beautiful stars. God put them there. Can you move them? Can you get one star to go somewhere else? Come on, show me. Move something."

"Okay, I can't," he said. "But nobody sees the world through my eyes."

"Or my eyes, unless he's an eye doctor," she said.

"This conversation is getting pretty silly."

"If it wasn't so sad."

"Okay, I give up," he said. "I promise not to bring this up again unless I can get a star to move. Now, tell me what's wrong and what you're searching for that you can't find in Catholicism. I don't know if I can help, but you know I'm a good listener."

"You're more than that. You're not God because you can't get stars to move, but you're a good friend, a *compare*, and I will tell you." Maria said. "You know how desperate I was to get out of what I was doing in Italy, to come to America with my daughter and have a different life. And I love you, Navigator, for helping me do that. Then I married John and it seemed that my dream was about to come true. We'd come to this wonderful new country, be a family, make new friends and—I don't know exactly, but be happy, decent people. Well, it didn't work out that way. We came here and we live in a house, but we're hardly a family. There's none of the love and warmth that I remember from my own life with my mother and father. Hardly any friends because John mixes with strange, unpleasant people who look at me suspiciously, and...and...I'm really not happy with John. We don't...well, let me say it this way...I occasionally see other men."

Maria's hands were clasped tightly in her lap as she spoke. He listened and said nothing.

"I know you don't like to hear things like this," she said, watching him for some reaction. "You're such a prude about things like that. You can afford to be. You're happily married, dammit. I wish you weren't. No, I shouldn't say that. I love you too much to wish you any unhappiness. Anyhow, I talked to my priest and, well, he was not much help. We don't permit divorces in our religion, and we don't encourage sleeping around. So I decided to look around to see if maybe another religion would give me something."

"I'm hardly the one to come to for spiritual advice. As you said yourself, I'm pretty irreverent." He rubbed his chin and stared out into the night. "I'm terribly sorry to hear about what's happening to your marriage. I wish I were a doctor who could write a prescription to cure your ailment. But you don't have anything a doctor could cure. And you don't have anything a change of religion could cure, either.

"You're having marital problems. A lot people have them and they do one of several things. They sit down with their partners and have a heartfelt discussion and try to work out the problems. Or they consult a marriage counselor. Or they get divorced. That's not terribly good advice, but it's the best that I have."

Gene Cowen

My Life: Chapter Thirteen

Campaigns

Let me digress at this point, as I did during my years with Hugh Scott, when I went off temporarily to work on other political campaigns.

During my political life, I worked on ten election campaigns. In some, I just helped out; in others, I was a principal in the effort; on one, I was the campaign manager. From that banging around with the elective masses, I came up with some conclusions. First, most voters are a hell of a lot more intelligent than the intellectual elite gives them credit for. They are motivated by such fundamental non-political problems as: how to make a living; are they going to be able to afford the mortgage payments on their houses; will their children have good schools; and are their streets safe. So when they vote—or if they vote, which is in itself a political statement—they seek candidates who they believe will further their being able to make a living, pay the mortgage, and so forth. You may not like whom they voted for or the issues that seemed to motivate them. But, rest assured, the voters in general know very well why they went into the polling place and chose one name on the ballot instead of another.

Then there are those who don't vote. They are, in the words of the political scientist Walter Dean Burnham, "the largest political party in America." They are those who are more or less satisfied with their lives, those who feel no threat to those lives, or those who are just fed up with the system.

Many campaigns I worked on were facilitated by an informal arrangement some of us on the staff had with Senator Scott, whereby he would offer our services to a candidate for office and then ask us if we'd like to work on the campaign. I often accepted those assignments, going off his payroll and onto to the campaign's payroll, and worked in some interesting campaigns.

Arlen Specter

One was for Arlen Specter, now a U.S. Senator, then a Philadelphia lawyer. In 1965, Philadelphia, the city where the Declaration of Independence had been signed, had long been under Democratic Party control. Just as in any one-party city, the municipal bureaucracy was encrusted with layers of employees who owed their jobs not to their competence but rather to their party affiliation. The Philadelphia Republican Party sensed the discontent in the city and reached out to Specter.

The young Democratic lawyer agreed to run for district attorney on the Republican ticket if Meehan's organization would give him adequate financing and professional assistance. Bob Kunzig, Scott's administrative assistant, agreed to come on as campaign manager, and I took the job of press secretary.

Specter, today a U.S. Senator, was a very bright, very intense man who decided to start his political career by taking on the rough-and-tumble politics of Philadelphia. His platform was tough-on-crime-but-equal-justice-for-all. In addition to the votes from Republicans, who were a small minority, he picked up votes from Democrats and independents who were desperate for someone to make the streets safe. He even got the support of the liberal Americans for Democratic Action.

Specter worked the crowds, speaking from the back of flatbed trucks. We got him radio and television interviews, and ferreted out some unique issues. One was a peculiarity in the way the voting machine levers operated—almost a precursor to the notorious "butterfly ballots" in Florida during the 2000 Presidential election. We discovered that, if a voter pulled the Specter lever, although it started out alongside his name, it ended up down near the name of his opponent. Specter challenged the election commission, threatened lawsuits and generally created a brouhaha. He got no satisfaction from the election commission, but the dispute got a lot of media attention.

Our advertising helped the campaign. The ADA paid for a "rolling billboard," one that was mounted on a flatbed truck. It had a long, message that said something like, "Had enough of crime in the streets and corruption in City Hall? Then vote for Arlen Specter for District Attorney."

It was much too wordy for a conventional mounted-by-the-side-of-the-road billboard. But since the truck rolled slowly through congested downtown traffic, we figured that drivers and pedestrians would have time to read all those words. Since it was novel for that election, it got a lot of comments and a few chuckles.

We also created what we called in-house the "attack commercial." Without saying the word "rape," it alluded to an attack on a woman, and had to be handled very delicately. The camera showed a woman from the waist down, walking down a dark, menacing-looking street. The only sounds were her footsteps. The woman suddenly stopped, turned her body around as if to look back, then quickened her steps. And finally, she was in a dead run. As the screen went dark, a voice-over said, "Arlen Specter, as district attorney, will fight street crime in Philadelphia."

The commercial caused a lot of comment in the city and the Democrats railed that it was subtly racist. But it was credited with helping to win the campaign, and afterwards, I was asked to show it at the Kennedy School of Government at Harvard.

The campaign had its lighter moments. Since Kunzig and I were from Senator Scott's office, we asked some of the interns in the Scott office if they'd like to work on the Philadelphia campaign. One who volunteered was Janet Bond, a very bright student from Mt. Holyoke College, slim and attractive with long blond hair tumbling down her back. In later years, Janet went on to a successful political career of her own, and today, under her married name, Janet B. Arterton, she is a U.S. District Judge. But this was her first campaign; she was about nineteen years old, and she worked very hard at the gofer jobs that the interns inherited.

Our offices were hotel rooms, and one day, when Campaign Manager Bob Kunzig and I were working in one room, Janet, who was not feeling too well, asked if she could take a short nap in one of the adjoining rooms. We said, sure, and forgot about her until Arlen Specter came in. He entered the suite through the adjoining room, looked at Janet asleep in the bed, her long hair tousled around the rumpled sheets, and snapped, "Kunzig, Cowen, just what the hell kind of campaign are we running here?"

My Life, A Novel

We introduced him to the startled Janet and he seemed mollified.

A couple of weeks later, my wife Phyllis came up to Philadelphia for the weekend. Early one morning, the phone rang in our room and Phyllis answered it with a sleepy, "Hello?"

"Excuse me, I must have the wrong room," said a flustered Specter, and hung up.

A moment later, after Phyllis guessed what had thrown him, the phone rang again and she said, "Arlen, darn you, this is Phyllis and I'm his wife!"

Specter won that campaign handily. We all congratulated one another and he began musing about the new job, especially what he would do with the hold-over staff in the district attorney's office. One remark stands out: "Gene, I'm a sore winner," he said with a growl.

It was the only thing he ever said that reminds me of my later employer, Richard Nixon.

Ray Shafer

Probably because I had worked on several successful campaigns in the early 1960s, I was invited to work on Pennsylvania Lieutenant Governor Raymond Shafer's campaign for the Republican nomination for Governor in 1966. It was a real downer for me.

For one thing, Shafer's regular Harrisburg staff looked at those of us from Washington as interlopers. Among that xenophobic group, we were known as "the men in black," partly because of the dark clothing we wore, partly because of something "sinister" they surmised about our working in "their" campaign. They met separately from us, kept their plans secret, and occasionally gave us wrong information just to keep us confused. Worst of all, a tragedy struck in the midst of the primary.

Walter Alessandroni, then the Pennsylvania Attorney General, was running for the Lieutenant Governor nomination. Walter was a short, outgoing, and feisty rooster of a guy. I can never erase from my mind a meeting we had in a Harrisburg hotel suite as we planned for the candidates' transportation. Walter paced the floor while he described how he thought things should go. "There is one thing I have to insist on," he said. "We must use a twin-engine plane. Single engines are too damned dangerous, especially when you're flying over the mountains." So the campaign arranged to have a twin-engine Piper Aztec.

Later, during the campaign, I was assigned to that plane for a trip that Ray Shafer was to make. We flew from Harrisburg west, "puddle-jumping" from one little airport to another. I was seated in the six-passenger plane alongside the pilot, and I noticed that he seemed a little unsure of himself. He asked to me watch for clearances from time to time and needed help spotting runway guidance lights.

When we got to Pittsburgh, the weather closed in, and we spent the night in a hotel. Early the next morning I had breakfast with the pilot, a pleasant man, about thirty-five years old, and by way of conversation, I told him I had been a combat navigator about two decades earlier and hoped I had been of some help to him in spotting things from the co-pilot's seat on the Piper. I also asked how long he'd been flying.

"Three years," he said.

"Three years!" I said incredulously. "You've only been flying three years, and you're flying passengers commercially?"

"Oh, yes," he said. "I always wanted to fly. But my mother, while she was still alive, thought it was too dangerous."

His inexperience bothered me, and I was happy to get off the plane later that day. About a week later, that pilot in that plane, transporting Lieutenant Governor candidate Walter Alessandroni and two other people, apparently lost his bearings in heavy clouds while trying to find a tiny airport in Western Pennsylvania and hit the side of a mountain, killing all on board.

When the primary ended, with Shafer and another candidate for Lieutenant Governor as the Republican nominees, Shafer asked me to stay on for the general election. I declined. Everything about that election seemed star-crossed and I went back to Washington.

A Novel: Chapter Twelve

The call was from Francis X. McElroy. You always take a call from McElroy, one of Senator Scott's principal contributors, the head of the campaign finance committee, a close personal friend of the Senator's, and a thoroughly decent guy.

"Hi, Frank. I haven't heard from you since you got Hugh Scott elected to the Senate two years ago."

"Flattery will get you everywhere," said McElroy. "But what will it get me?"

"Anything you want, my friend," Navigator said.

"How far advanced is the Senator in picking interns for the office this year?" said McElroy. Interns were bright young college students who worked without pay in Congressional offices (and then listed the experience on their resumes for the rest of their lives).

"We closed out the list for this year."

"Do you think the Senator would open it up for one more?" said McElroy. "I've got a candidate that someone in former Vice President Nixon's entourage would like to have placed in a Senate office. Your office is the only one where I have any clout. Dick Nixon is going to make another run for President in 1968, and I'd very much like to do this for his guy."

Without hesitation, he said, "You've got it, Frank."

"Would you talk to the Senator and let me know what he says?"

"I said, you've got it, Frank." Navigator knew very well that if McElroy asked for something as simple as that, there was no question that Scott would agree. And, besides, as chief of staff in the office, he was the one who picked most of the interns for Scott anyway.

"Thanks," said McElroy. "It's a pleasure doing business with you. She's the stepdaughter of a John Alden, who did some sort of intelligence-gathering for Nixon when he was Vice

President. He's a strange, almost spooky guy, but his stepdaughter is lovely. Her name is Anna, about twenty-four, and a graduate student at Columbia University. I had lunch with her in Philadelphia yesterday. I think she's technically a native Italian, came over here as a child, and she doesn't live in Pennsylvania. I hope that won't interfere with your rule that all your interns have to be from the state."

That wasn't going to interfere with anything. But he did have to pause a moment while he caught his breath.

"Frank, I told you, you've got it." Pause.

"Could you ask the Senator to send me a confirming letter?" said McElroy, with a smile in his voice. One thing you learn in politics is to get written confirmations.

"The next envelope you open will be from the Honorable Hugh Scott," Navigator said.

#

He knew the moment he looked at Anna Tedesco Alden that she was Maria's daughter. She had the same sparkling Italian eyes that lit up when she smiled, which was often. She wore a becoming flowered blouse and matching short skirt and had the same dark curly hair he remembered ruffling when she was a child. He knew she could not remember him, since she had been only three in 1945, but he watched to see if her mother had said anything.

With Senator Scott in a committee meeting, Navigator used the Senator's private office to introduce himself to the new interns. Seven youngsters arranged themselves in the leather couches and armchairs against the wall. They were casually dressed and looked bright and nervous.

He walked up to each one of them, shook hands, and thanked the intern for coming. He thought what he thought every time he did this: *When I was their age, I wouldn't have been smart enough or politically well-connected enough to qualify for a job like this.*

When he got to Anna, she smiled politely and said she was pleased to be here.

My Life, A Novel

Then he leaned back against the front edge of the Senator's desk and began his usual indoctrination lecture for new interns. Anna furrowed her brow a bit, listened intently, and took notes on a yellow legal pad.

"We're delighted all of you could come. I hope you're going to have some fun in the next six weeks, get some exposure to the legislative process, and learn a bit about how the Senate works—and if you can figure that out, please tell me."

Polite laughter.

"You're also probably going to see some famous people in the corridors—people you may have read about in the newspapers and seen on television. But you very likely won't actually meet them because they're busy people. You will, however, be able to meet a lot of interns from the other Senate offices, and they can be a lot of fun because they organize parties and meetings and God-knows-what-else that goes on at night. As far as the work you'll do, please don't expect to write speeches for the Senator or draft legislation or brief him for an appearance on '*Meet the Press*.'"

Solemn nods. One boy scratched his ear; another shifted his weight. Anna crossed her legs. Nice legs, which brought back memories of her mother at about that age.

"If you're good at research, we'll ask you to do some of that. Same for drafting letters to constituents. But, unfortunately, we're also going to ask you to do some of the grunt work of this office. Sorry, but the trade-off for your being here is that you have to help us answer phones, open envelopes, sort the tons of mail that come into this office and—dare I say it?—get me a cup of coffee once in a while. One caveat, however. And if you're taking notes, caveat is spelled W-A-R-N-I-N-G. You will be, in reality, a Senate staff member for six weeks, and, as you know, that gives you bragging rights. But it also comes with a curse. The curse is that you must comport yourselves like professionals and, please, *please* try to stay out of trouble—even what you'd call minor trouble. For instance, back home, if you're stopped for speeding, nothing terrible happens, except that you may have to pay a fine and maybe you get some points on your driving record. But while you are working in this office, if you get that same ticket, you're very likely to read a story in the *Philadelphia Bulletin* that says, 'Senate Aide Stopped For Speeding.' As a result, your family is embarrassed, Senator Scott is embarrassed even more, and I'm sore as hell.

"But enough of this grim stuff. You're going to have an exciting six weeks and we're happy you're here. Just to give you some idea of who preceded you in these internships in past years, two former Scott interns are today in the Pennsylvania state legislature, one man and one woman have published books, another former Scott intern is the Washington correspondent for *The Atlantic Monthly*, and three are assistants to CEOs in the private sector.

"All of you will be assigned to one of our regular staffers." He looked at a list. "Anna Alden to me, William Beveridge to our case worker, Mary Brockowitz to the executive assistant, Jerry Hedrich to the scheduler, Beverly Passman to the receptionist, Joe Wasiliewski to our legislative assistant, and Dorothy Wooten to the assistant in charge of the machines that answer most of our mail. Can I answer any questions?"

He pulled a pipe out of his pocket and filled it from the humidor on the Senator's desk. Show off. But he had forgotten that the Senator was currently smoking American Indian tobacco, a gift from a Pennsylvania tribe. It was harsh stuff, mixed with bits of twigs and leaves, and tasted as if there might also be some chopped pale-face scalps in there. Navigator began coughing and his eyes teared, ruining his attempt to look cool.

The interns' questions were routine. What are the working hours? ("Whenever the Senate is in session.") Is there is a dress code? ("No, but be neat.") Can we smoke on the job? ("Only pipes." Laughter.) Then the interns dispersed to their assignments.

The next six weeks were a joy. Anna was older than the other interns and more mature. She had gotten a good undergraduate education at Columbia, so he started by giving her the job of editing some of the material he was writing for the

My Life, A Novel

Senator. She caught the typographical errors and then discreetly made suggestions about his grammar.

"No fair," he said. "You're not supposed to know more than I do."

Then he advanced her to doing research for the speeches he was writing. Finally, he let her write a brief statement and told the Senator she had done it. The Senator wrote a congratulatory thank-you to her across the top of the page and she glowed.

"Anna," he said one morning, "you've been here five weeks and have earned a lunch. Are you free today?"

"I'm not free, but I'm cheap," she said.

"Very funny. But we're not going to eat cheap in the Senate staff cafeteria. I'd like to take you to a little restaurant called La Colline, just across the Capitol grounds, where lobbyists ply me with nice continental food."

They walked along Delaware Avenue under the delicate white petals of the dogwood trees. It was early spring, and the sun was pleasantly warm, the birds were carefully selecting the right twigs for their nests, cars honked, and he was happy. They turned left before Union Station and arrived at La Colline about noon.

This was the informal headquarters for low-key lobbying of the Senate. Serious-faced men leaned over tables and talked intently to male Senate staff members, who tried to look older than they were. Some lobbyists sat alongside young women in the booths and got close, but not too close, because the target was legislation, not sex.

Jean Michel greeted him by name, glanced at the pretty brunette, but said nothing because liaisons are not noticed by a good maitre d'. He seated them at the quiet corner table which Navigator had asked for when he made his reservation.

Anna studied the long menu and then asked if she could have a salad.

"Is that all? You've done such a good job, the sky's the limit," he said.

"I'm trying to watch my weight," she said, motioning in the direction of her hips.

"You don't have a weight problem," he said.

"Oh, I do. Like my mother, whom I think you know," she said.

He smiled and went quickly over in his mind how much of what had happened in the past this girl might know." Yes," he said, "we met briefly when I was in the Army Air Corps and she was serving coffee and doughnuts in the USO. But why did you wait so long to say something about that?"

"I was embarrassed," she said. "I knew my stepfather contacted someone to get me this internship, and you were in this office and you knew my mother in wartime…It took me a bit of time to screw up my courage to bring this up."

"And how did you know that I knew your mother?" he said.

"She told me as soon as I told her where I'd be working."

"And what did she say about me?"

"She thinks highly of you," she said.

"That makes two of us on my side."

"I'm the third," Anna said, blushing slightly. When she smiled, her face lit up, and it brought back the memory of that little, dark-haired three-year-old who had peeked at him from behind her mother's skirt.

"Thank you," he said. He tried to decide whether to tell her what he'd been considering for the past week, nodded to himself, and plunged ahead." Anna, a couple of us from Senator Scott's staff have been invited to work on Lieutenant Governor Ray Shafer's campaign for governor of Pennsylvania. My associate will be the campaign manager, and I'll be the press secretary for the campaign. We've been told that we can hire our own assistants. I've been impressed with your work, and you seem to like legislation and politics. So I wonder whether you'd like to join the campaign staff. You and the other intern we're taking can share a room in Harrisburg. If you like legislation, you'll love politics. Campaigns are really hectic, and you can learn more by working in one campaign than you'd learn in several years of studying political science at Columbia."

Anna's forehead furrowed while she thought. She had to decide a lot of things. Should she tell him about her plan to change careers? Did she want to go to Harrisburg with a man

My Life, A Novel

old enough to be her father? Should she tell him about her stepfather?

"Your offer is very appealing," she said. "And this may sound funny coming from someone my age, but I really must discuss this first with my mother. We're very close, you know."

He just nodded.

"I probably can't stay for the whole campaign, because I'm planning to change careers and go to law school. You see, I want to help my stepfather in his work."

"What is his work?"

"He's in surveillance, sort of a private detective," she said. "You know, padding around finding things out, using listening devices, things like that."

"Listening devices? Is that legal?"

"I guess. Oh well, let me tell you the other thing that's bothering me," she said. "I want to help him. I think he's entitled to that because he helped get my mother and me out of Italy right after World War II. He seems to need some guidance. John really doesn't have very good judgment. I'm not sure how legal that surveillance is. And he seems to hang out with funny friends."

"You mean funny ha-ha or funny oh-oh."

"They're a very rough crew," she said. "They make me nervous."

"What kind of rough crew?"

"It's a group that wants to get Richard Nixon elected president," she said.

"Nothing wrong with that. He tried once and got beaten by Jack Kennedy."

"John says Nixon is almost certainly going to run again," she said. "And that's fine. He seems like a very able man and, after all, he was Vice President of the United States. But this rough crowd, they're sort of a splinter group of the John Birch Society. They collect automatic weapons and march around a lot. They spend a lot of time at target practice. I think some of them were explosives experts during the war, and my mother told me they wanted to store gunpowder in our basement."

"In your basement?" he said. This was unbelievable. "What are they going to blow up?"

"I don't know" she said. "But that's not the point. I'm just trying to get my stepfather redirected into some less dangerous form of political action."

"Lots of luck on that that," he said. "But, as far as this Shafer campaign for governor is concerned, talk to your mother, tell her I'll take care of you in Harrisburg, and let me know what she says."

The next day, Anna came up to him in the office. "I'd like to accept your offer."

"Your mother approved?"

"Yes. She said you were a nice guy and I could trust your judgment, but not about ice cream in a melon. What did that mean?"

"I haven't the faintest idea," he said.

#

All political campaigns are turbulent and most come up with their own surprises. The surprise in the Pennsylvania campaign was one he had not confronted in the several previous campaigns he'd worked on. Ray Shafer's Harrisburg staff treated the staff from Washington with suspicion bordering on xenophobia. Whenever the Scott people entered a room, the Shafer staff stopped talking. So his assignment was a busy but lonely one.

He and Anna got adjoining offices in a far corner of campaign headquarters and labored in isolation. Which was not so bad when you are writing. Fewer interruptions. He drafted speeches and gave them to Anna to edit. The speeches would often be accepted happily by the candidates, occasionally returned for revision. No problem. That's what happens with speech drafts.

As Anna got better at the work, he began giving her the first draft to do, and he did the editing. At first, he spent more time editing than it would have taken him to write the draft in the first place. But eventually, she caught on to the system; her writing was in good, simple declarative sentences, and she developed a flair for making political points. Increasing numbers of her drafts made it right to the candidates.

The four Scott staff, since they were being treated like lepers anyway, stayed pretty much to themselves. They started work in early morning, ate lunch at their desks, then went out to dinner together in early evening. Harrisburg was no gourmet paradise, so they usually ate at the spaghetti joint where the food was cheap and the service fast. After dinner it was back to work again until about ten p.m.

He would take Anna to the room she shared with another young woman from the Scott staff, and then go to his own room to try to sleep. But sleep came slowly. He spent lots of time mulling over what had gone well and what had gone not so well. He decided early on that he was going to sweat this one out for a few weeks and, because of the stifling hostility in campaign headquarters, probably quit at the end of the primary. He didn't know that the decision would be taken out of his hands.

The candidates traveled the state by car, Winnebago van, or by plane when they had long distances to cover in one day. He and Anna got an assignment to board the plane for a trip around Pennsylvania with Walter Alessandroni, the candidate for lieutenant governor. That was exhausting. Although they used the same core speech for each stop, each needed a different emphasis, special language for the area, and prominent mention of the local Republican county officials. But they liked the work and worked well together.

After a week of that flying circus, he told Anna, "I'm so tired I'm beginning to make three tracks in the sand."

"This trip will end in another week," she said.

In Erie, the plane was met by the Republican county chairman whom he had dutifully mentioned in the speech draft. But he was surprised to see him there with his wife and that both were carrying overnight bags.

The county chairman took Alessandroni aside, and they huddled for a few minutes. Then Alessandroni came over and

Gene Cowen

said quietly, "You and Anna are going to have to leave the plane at this point."

Navigator was puzzled, but happy that his job writing for the swing around the state had ended sooner than he had expected. "What happened?" he said.

"I'm not sure myself," said Alessandroni, "but apparently the chairman got a call this morning, saying he and his wife were invited to fly with me to Pittsburgh. I hate to do this to you, but you know this plane can't seat that many of us, and I can't offend the county chairman. Would you two mind driving back to Harrisburg?"

"Not at all. But who called him?" he said.

"He didn't get the name, and I have no idea. Thanks for all the help both of you have given me in the past couple of weeks," said Alessandroni, clapping him warmly on the shoulder and looking sad and apologetic about the whole thing.

Navigator and Anna got a rental car and drove through the Pennsylvania hills toward Harrisburg. The foliage was lovely in its fall colors and even the heavily overcast skies did not dampen his spirits. He was delighted to get out of the turmoil for a few hours. He and Anna relaxed, admired the scenery and chatted about nothing in particular. He didn't even turn on the radio.

When they got back to the Harrisburg headquarters, they were met by somber faces. No one would talk to them. That was nothing unusual, but some people were crying. He took aside his Scott associate who said, "You haven't heard?"

"No," he said, "we've been driving for the last four hours."

The Scott associate said, "The plane went down in the mountains."

"What plane?"

"The one with Walter Alessandroni, the country chairman and his wife."

"Oh, my God. The plane we just got off?"

"Yes, you've got some kind of luck, pal."

"Did any one get out alive?"

"No."

He and Anna walked away in a daze. He went back to his desk, shuffled papers, and checked old messages. One was from the Governor, inviting him to a reception; another from Alessandroni, thanking him for a recent speech draft; another telling him to call a friend in Washington. He dropped them into a wastebasket. One note was for Anna, which he gave to her unread.

He put his elbows on the desk and his head in his hands. *What a tragedy. What a close call. Sometimes life stinks.*

Anna came back into the room, ashen-faced, and silently showed him the note he had given to her. It was typed and not signed. It said:

"That was no accident. It was just a warning. Tell your father that next time, you won't be bumped from the plane."

#

Maria's voice quavered on the phone. "I can't stand this, Navigator. My daughter came within a hair's breadth of being killed. So did you. I would die if anything happened to her."

"I let you down, babe," he said. "I was supposed to be taking care of your daughter, and then she gets into something crazy like this."

"It's not your fault, Navigator. It's that idiot husband of mine. He's been hanging around with those loonies again."

He looked at the note again. "Tell me what the hell that's all about."

"John is trying to help Richard Nixon get elected President," she said. "So are a lot of people, I guess. Most of them are just plain political activists, but there are some extremists who want take over Nixon's campaign and remake the world in the image of Benito Mussolini."

"Listen," he said. "Nixon's no fool. And he's no loony either. I can't imagine him letting those people take over."

"Well, I don't know your Nixon," she said, "but I do know about politicians. I learned two good words in English about politicians. They are avaricious for money and insatiable for votes. So they take support wherever they can get it. Your

Nixon may be running his own campaign, but he won't admit knowing anything about the loonies, and he's accepting their help sub rosa."

"But what has that to do with the plane that went down and this awful note?" he said.

"John won't tell me everything," she said. "But I understand that the loonies wanted him to do something bad and he refused. He also threatened to go to the police if they went ahead with their plan. They said he'd live to regret it, and then they mentioned that they knew he had a wife and stepdaughter."

"Listen, babe, this is not funny," he said. "We're dealing with killers here."

"I talked to John, Navigator, and told him that if he doesn't break with that crowd, it'll be the last he ever sees of me," she said. "I also told him something else that focused his attention. But I don't want to get into that now. He agreed to disassociate from the worst of them."

My Life: Chapter Fourteen

<u>Scott-Thornburgh-Watergate</u>

When I left the Shafer campaign after the 1966 primary, I switched to working for Richard Thornburgh, a young lawyer who ran for Congress in Pittsburgh. Thornburgh didn't stand a snowball's chance in hell of winning as a Republican in the heavily-Democratic district, and lost badly. But the race had two interesting byproducts. First, because he ran a good campaign, Thornburgh came to the attention of Republican leaders and subsequently was appointed to various jobs, one of them being Deputy Attorney General of the United States. Second, he and I developed a nice personal relationship. When he was in Washington, he would invite Phyllis and me to his home at Christmas to drink eggnog and admire the gingerbread-and-candy houses that his family had constructed.

So I shouldn't have been surprised that, eight years later, when Hugh Scott got into something of a jam, he turned to me for help with Thornburgh. Scott, whom I loved dearly, had a few weaknesses. He ate too much, smoked too much, and dipped too enthusiastically into the pools of money that surround American politics. Running for office in this country is very expensive and the process is lubricated with dollars. Many of the political contributions are legal, some are not, and there is often a very fine line between the two. Scott considered some of us on his staff to be pretty straight-arrow and usually kept from us those things that he knew would raise our eyebrows. During his 1964 re-election campaign, none of us knew until much later that he'd had a bundle of cash delivered to the head of a minority group who had set a price for the group's support. Scott also was very secretive about the fact that the Washington representative of a major oil company was regularly giving him money.

By 1974, I had become Washington Vice President of ABC. The Justice Department was probing the Watergate scandal and the investigators apparently turned over some rocks that revealed other smelly items. One of those involved the oil company's payments to Hugh Scott. At a meeting in his Senate office, he told me about the investigation and said that the funds were political contributions that had been given to him as Senate Leader for him to pass on to other Republicans who were running for office.

That would have been legal. But, since some of the candidates denied to the investigators that they ever gotten the money from Scott, it looked very bad. So Scott, who was getting desperate, asked me to "talk to your friend, Dick Thornburgh," about the matter.

We were now at a point at which I wondered whether I was going to have to skate pretty close to the edge of legality. But since I felt a very close kinship to Scott and would do almost anything for him, and since I was certain that Thornburgh himself would keep everything entirely kosher, I agreed to make an inquiry. I briefly spoke to the Deputy Attorney General, asking if it was proper for him to tell me anything abut the investigation of Scott. Thornburgh said that, since he knew Scott personally, he had recused himself from that investigation and knew nothing about it.

I was relieved and reported that to Scott. Then we had the following conversation.

"Senator," I said, "from what you tell me about this case, can I offer some advice as a friend? You're an attorney and I'm not, but I think you really need a good criminal lawyer."

"I've got a lawyer," he said, "a very good tax lawyer in New York."

"No, Senator," I said. "You need, not a tax lawyer, but a *criminal* lawyer—someone who knows that branch of the law, who can meet with the investigators, and if he thinks what they are asking for is reasonable, he can tell you to provide it to them. But if he thinks they are asking for something you should not provide, he can say, 'Screw you!' and that would be the end of it."

"Who do you suggest?" Scott said.

"Somebody like Edward Bennett Williams?" I said.

"If your lawyer is Edward Bennett Williams," he said, "it's tantamount to an admission of guilt."

"I said someone *like* Williams. I'm sure there are other first-rate criminal lawyers," I said.

Scott agreed, hired a good criminal lawyer, and managed to get out from under.

Eastern Privilege

Larry McMurtry, in his traveling memoir *Roads*, wrote that in the twenty years he lived in Washington "...I was shocked and still am by the desperate ambition of Washington's social elite, or at least by the part of it I was exposed to..." It gnawed at him that he somehow never became part of the black-tie dinner circuit; nor was he even accepted by the journalistic elite.

That's a grievance I've heard from a lot of people: not being able to break into the upper strata of something or another; or, once your job changed, being evicted from the charmed circle. I've always thought the complaint was just silly. Although Phyllis and I have lived in Washington for half a century and have been exposed to many self-important people with world-class egos, we never have thought it worth our while to elbow our way into someone else's level of exclusivity.

When I was on a Congressional staff, I always considered it just another job—challenging and exciting, but no more. I was scrambling to get ahead, not for prestige, but rather to get jobs with more responsibility which paid a little more, or were more satisfying. We only occasionally accepted dinner invitations from lobbyists, pleasant as their restaurants might be, because I usually got sleepy early into those long evenings.

At the White House, I was proud of my rank, but I was more conscious that the "White House is a good place to be from," rather than taking too seriously the fact that, because of my rank, I was forever after entitled to the title of "Honorable." (That generated an occasional question from fellow passengers on ocean cruises we have taken in the years since. Phyllis always insists on listing me as "The Honorable Eugene S. Cowen," and often I've been asked if that meant I was a judge.)

The rank of Deputy Assistant to the President of the United States also got us listed in the Washington Social Register (wow!). But in the thirty years since we were first listed in the Social Register, we have gotten invitations to buy various things and to contribute to various charities, but not one invitation to dine with then *Washington Post* Publisher Katherine Graham and only rarely to attend a function at an embassy.

However, when I worked at the White House, I was aware of the cachet that people attach to being invited to eat there, and I had no hesitation about using it. The White House dining room was literally a Navy mess, with a naval officer in charge and mess boys doing the work. (On the first day I worked there, Bryce Harlow asked me if I wanted to see "the other mess at the White House.") It was an unprepossessing place with adequate service and the kind of food you'd expect at a Navy officers' mess. But it was the White House. So, every day of the two and a half years I worked there, I tried to invite some Senator's senior staff assistant to lunch. I knew full well that on that evening, the staff assistant would say to his wife, not, "Who do you think I had lunch with today?" but rather, "*Where* do you think I had lunch today?"

As to embassies, Phyllis and I were invited to occasional functions at the Israeli Embassy, but not after I left the White House. We have, however, been at a number of very disappointing embassy functions when there was a business reason to be there. Once, Saudi Arabia invited to dinner all of us who were members of a Congressional club I belonged to, and they chatted us up on the joys of living in that country. But the food at our local, inexpensive Lebanese restaurant in Bethesda was really much better.

At another time, our taste buds were numbed by a dinner at the French Embassy. It was a function run by Women in Sports. It seems that most embassies, apparently to make ends meet, become rent-a-hall places for an evening, so that some group can boast of the surroundings. They don't use embassy chefs, and that night, they used a particularly poor caterer who had the unique distinction of serving both lousy food and second-rate wine—at the French Embassy!

At ABC, I got the ultimate status symbol, a chauffeured car. It came with the job. Since NBC and CBS had chauffeured cars, ABC, the runt network in 1970, was not going to be without one. James (yes, that really was his name, wonderful fellow that he was) Royster would drive me to and from work and wait for me at Congressional fund-raising functions. It was a great convenience, especially not having to search for parking at the receptions. But hardly more than a convenience. It gave me a bad conscience not to drive, so I had a lamp installed on the back shelf, and then I had to think of work to bring along with me so I could read in the back while James drove me home.

When Capital Cities Communications, noted for its lack of ostentation, bought ABC in 1986 and asked for suggestions on how we could economize, I gave up the chauffeured car, rather than having to fire an employee. The chauffeur had earlier told me he planned to quit and become a taxi driver.

My Family

Phyllis and I have two children. Jamie was born in 1952. It was a turbulent year for us. I had transferred from Syracuse to Washington and then lost a job with a news bureau shortly thereafter. Jamie reflected the tensions that Phyllis and I both felt. He was a colicky infant and not too happy a youngster. Then, in his teens, he got involved with an evangelical organization. Shortly thereafter, he announced that he was deeply involved in Jews for Jesus.

It upset us because of the aggressive attempts the organization made at conversions, but we tolerated the differences in the hope of keeping the family together. Finally, in 1985, when we were visiting Jamie and his family, I saw a stack of leaflets that were clearly designed to encourage people to convert from Judaism. Shortly before, a relative and a neighbor had told us that Jamie had given them conversion literature.

Phyllis and I decided that we were close to a breaking point. I had a long meeting with him and told him that, while I didn't agree, if he wanted to belong to another religion, I could understand. But if he was actively seeking to convert Jews, we could not be in the same family with him. He declined to change the way he approached his religion. That caused an estrangement. We have not had any direct contact with him since then.

Stephanie was born in 1961. In contrast to the problems of nine years earlier, life for all of us was now much better and more serene. Steph became the little girl that Phyllis and I had always dreamed of having. She grew up to be a lovely young woman and, in 1991, married Glenn Orr. They have two children who are the center of our lives. We go to Annapolis every week to visit with the parents and Mallory, now ten, and Olivia, now seven. Or we take the girls to see children's shows at the Kennedy Center in Washington. For our fiftieth wedding anniversary, instead of holding a party for friends "who don't really need any more food or booze," we and the whole family took a wonderful cruise in the Caribbean.

My Life, A Novel

PART FOUR: 1969

Gene Cowen

My Life: Chapter Fifteen

<u>White House</u>

I got to the White House because Bryce Harlow, who had been newly designated Assistant to the President, said at the Nixon Inaugural Ball in January, 1969, "Gene, Uncle Sam needs you."

I had known Bryce for years. He was a speechwriter for President Eisenhower when I worked for Congresswoman Bolton in the 1950s; then he was Washington vice president for Proctor and Gamble when I worked for Senator Scott. He had just been put in charge of White House Congressional Relations and leaned over from his box at the ball as Phyllis and I danced by.

I said, "Uncle Hugh Scott needs me, too." We chatted for a few moments while the band played.

As Phyllis and I moved away, she said, "I think he was serious."

I said, "I think he was drunk." But the offer had me interested.

About two months later, the White House was having trouble with Uncle Hugh Scott. The Senator was blocking the nomination of an assistant Postmaster General in order to get the attention of the White House. Bryce called me and asked if I knew what the problem was and if I thought I could help unscramble things. I said yes and yes. So he invited me to lunch. Where? "How about here at the Inn?" he said.

In spite of myself, I was thrilled by my first invitation to eat at the White House, did some homework on the Philadelphia problem, and joined Bryce for lunch. I told him that the problem was that the Republican boss of Philadelphia needed some federal patronage, and Scott needed the boss.

Bryce said he thought he knew how to work things out. Then he said, "Gene, have you been thinking about what we discussed at the Inaugural Ball?"

"Yes," I said. "Where would you like me work?"

"How about here at the Inn?"

"At the White House? Doing what?" I said.

Gene Cowen

"Special Assistant to the President for Congressional Relations," he said.

That was an offer I couldn't turn down.

#

Bryce Harlow was an education to work with. He was bright, well respected by most Congressmen, knew legislative procedure like a parliamentarian, and had a wry sense of humor. He was short (he often referred to his confrontations with tall legislators as an "eyeball to kneecap") and a chain cigarette smoker. The first big vote we worked on was one to ratify the Antiballistic Missile Treaty (which was back in the news recently, since President George W. Bush decided to scrap it). We were in the Capitol until late on the night of the crucial vote and were scrambling to get enough votes to win, which we did by just one vote. In the chauffeur-driven car on the way back to the White House, I said, "Bryce, it's a shame we couldn't have won by a bigger majority."

"No, Gene," he said. "That vote was just right. When we win with big majorities, the President thinks it was very easy."

One day I accompanied him to the House of Representatives for the traditional State of the Union speech by President Nixon. We followed Senate Majority Leader Mike Mansfield. As Mansfield entered the chamber, Bryce stopped short at the threshold, held me back and waited. Mansfield looked back, smiled and motioned us forward. I gave Bryce a quizzical look. He said softly, "The King's men are not welcome on the floor of Parliament."

After Bryce had been in the White House for a year, a reporter said to him, "There's a rumor that you're going to resign soon and go back to private life. Is that true?"

"Yes, that's true, there is such a rumor," he said with a straight face. Then, as the reporter started to make notes, Bryce added, "But no, I'm not going to resign soon."

#

When I first went to the White House, Phyllis and I lived on Loxford Terrace in Silver Spring, Maryland. It was a pleasant front-to-back split-level three-bedroom house, two stories high, and we planted a lovely rose garden in the back. Each working day, in order to make the seven-thirty a.m. staff meeting, I'd get up before five and, while eating breakfast, I'd read the *Washington Post,* which I paid the delivery boy to bring extra early. Then, at about six-forty-five, I'd climb into my Chevy, drive east along University Boulevard, south down New Hampshire and North Capital Street and east across to the White House. In winter, it was dark when I left home and dark when I returned home.

I'd park on the White House grounds and walk through the basement past the barbershop, dining room, kitchens and photo darkroom to the East Wing of the building. No Marines gave me smart salutes. That was reserved for the formal north entrance, where a butler was also ready to take the coats of dignitaries. All I saw were uniformed Secret Service police, ever watchful, but always polite, as long as I had the proper identification tag around my neck.

The Nixon White House was an exciting and strange place to work in. William Safire, who mentioned me briefly in *Before the Fall*, wrote in that 1975 memoir of his old boss, "If you are in your mid-forties, you have been for or against Richard Nixon in national elections, with only one exception, ever since you have been able to vote. He is part of you: a backboard, a mirror, a stimulant, a palliative, an object of your hate or adoration, your grudging respect or mild distaste, but like it or not he is a presence, the presence of the adult postwar generation."

In the White House, there were as many inside rivalries as there were outside pressures, the length of the working hours could kill, and I always felt that there was paranoia in the drinking water. You contracted the disease shortly after you got there.

All White Houses are pretty much like that. Lyndon Johnson insisted on immediate access to his principal assistants. When one aide apologized, saying that Johnson had been unable to reach him because he had been down the hall in the bathroom, Johnson directed that a bathroom be built into the man's office and had a telephone installed there.

There is an apocryphal story of Joseph Califano, assistant to President Johnson, trying desperately to get away from the omnipresent White House telephones. He finally marched out of his office, got into his car and drove without thinking about where he was going. Finally, he got to Atlantic City, got out and began walking down the boardwalk. In a beach-side phone booth, a phone was ringing. He picked it up and the voice said, "Mr. Califano, please hold on; the President wants to talk to you."

Bryce Harlow told me that he was assigned to a prime office in the West Wing, complete with bathroom, which he used until Henry Kissinger was given an office on the other side of their common wall. The bathroom jutted into Kissinger's office, so, according to the Harlow version, Herr Henry had it removed, which straightened out that wall and Kissinger situated his desk against the new wall. Bryce laughed. "Henry refuses to acknowledge that he now sits where I used to sit."

I got my daily meeting assignment with the senior staff because Bryce Harlow asked me one day, "Are you a morning person?"

I said, yes, I supposed so.

"I'd like you to attend Ehrlichman's seven-thirty meetings. I'm a night person; I don't focus that well in the morning." Then he added what was probably his real reason, "Besides, I'm the same rank as John, and I'm not going to attend a meeting where he's presiding."

In order to report on what had happened in the Senate the day before, I was supposed to know what had really gone on. I kept track as best I could, but I had to sleep eventually, and sometimes things kept changing, late into the night. So I arranged with the Government Printing Office to get an early copy of the *Congressional Record*. That was harder to do than it sounds. The *Record*, a more-or-less verbatim account of what happens on the floor of the Senate and the House, is printed overnight and delivered early each morning, but not that early.

So the GPO agreed to deliver the unbound galley sheets to the East Wing by seven a.m. and Dick Cook—who handled the House of Representatives—and I would scan them as we loped to the Roosevelt Room in the West Wing for the meeting. That worked, and I've been told that in subsequent Presidential administrations, a package of *Congressional Record* galleys, marked for Gene Cowen, arrived at the East Wing promptly each morning at seven a.m. The staff was pleased to have them but wondered who this Gene Cowen was.

Dick Cook's and my fast walk to those seven-thirty a.m. meetings took us west across the White House, past the beautiful Rose Garden. Usually I was too busy scanning galleys to pay attention, but it finally struck me that everything blooming in the Rose Garden was always bright and fresh. I once asked one of the gardeners, "Why is everything blooming at its prime in your garden, while mine at home constantly needs care and cutting?"

"Ha!" he said. "At night, we take out everything that's the slightest bit faded and replant something fresh out of the nursery." That's one of the perks of being President of the United States that you seldom hear about.

Dick and I would then enter the center of the White House, working our way carefully through lines of yawning early-morning visitors who were waiting to see the public rooms. We were usually careful to excuse ourselves as we pushed through the crowds, but we were also rushing to make the meeting and reading galley sheets as we moved.

One day, during the Vietnam War when the Cambodian invasion was underway, Dick was looking down at an item in the *Record* about some legislative development and started telling me that there was a hell of a fight going on in the House. "Total war!" said Dick, forgetting who was listening, "Gene, it's total war!"

I looked up into the eyes of an ashen-faced tourist. "Total war? Total war!" echoed down the line.

I said, "Dick, smile. These people don't realize what you're talking about." He looked up, laughed, apologized, pointed to the benign *Congressional Record*, and then we hurried on our way to a different kind of war.

The seven-thirty a.m. senior staff meetings were brief and intense. They were in the beautiful, dark-paneled Roosevelt Room, with pictures of former Presidents of the United States looking over our shoulders. John Ehrlichman, fiddling with a pencil, presided. George Schultz, ever scholarly and unflappable, sat alongside him. Also around the long table at various times were Peter Flanigan, Donald Rumsfeld, Murray Chotiner, Harry Dent, Chris DeMuth, Richard Cheney, Caspar Weinberger and Frank Carlucci. I represented Congressional Relations for the Senate, Dick Cook for the House.

Gene Cowen

Ehrlichman started each meeting with a barely audible tap of his pencil on the long walnut conference table, made a brief statement about whatever was important for us to know that day, and then went around the room to hear reports. Dick and I used to refer to those meetings as "a roll in the snow before breakfast."

Most of the others in the room spoke only perfunctorily, presumably holding back anything that they considered too confidential to divulge to such a disparate audience. I spoke about the Senate, what it had done, mostly what it had done wrong from our point of view. This was a Congress with big Democratic majorities in both houses, and there were seldom any positive actions to report. The best news I could bring was when we managed, with the help of conservative Democratic Senators, to stop some initiative generated by the Democrat majority. We would occasionally think to ourselves, "Wouldn't it be nice if we were *for* something once in a while?"

Often, I had to explain away a defeat we had suffered. In order to soften the blow, I took to telling about a book I had read while in journalism school. It showed a drawing of a Hittite princess staring remorsefully over the parapets of a castle while behind her were the bloody bodies of two messengers. "Such is the fate of the bearers of ill tidings," said the caption. After a while, when I had some bad news to report, I would say simply, "Remember that princess...?" and everyone would know what was coming.

Bar Mitzvah List

Winning votes in Congress involves a lot of things, but many people don't recognize that, above all, you have to know how to count. Sounds easy. If there are a hundred Senators voting and you need a simple majority, which is the case in most instances, fifty-one wins. Simple. Suppose now that you need two-thirds, a super-majority, which is the requirement when Congress attempts to override a Presidential veto or break a filibuster. In that case, you need sixty-seven, if a hundred Senators are voting. Still not too hard.

But when you're in the White House, you want to *block* Congress from overriding the President's veto, so when a hundred Senators are voting, you need thirty-four to block, so the other side can't get sixty-

My Life, A Novel

seven. Are you still hanging in there? Good. However, often you have to calculate for fewer than a hundred Senators voting. And things really begin to get out of hand when the total number of Senators voting changes just as you're approaching the vote itself. ("I can't vote with you on this one, Leader, but if you find me a 'pair' with someone who is away, I won't cast a vote—if that will help you.") Those were the days before pocket calculators. Try counting that in your head. I couldn't. So I drew up a quick-and-dirty chart to cover most eventualities of two-thirds votes. It looked something like this (you can check my arithmetic):

Number of Senators voting	Number needed for two-thirds	Number needed to block two-thirds
100	67	34
99	66	34
98	66	33
97	65	33

…and so forth.

I labeled it "Vetoes, Ratifications and Confirmations." My associate Tom Korologos liked it and added "and Bar Mitzvahs" after "Confirmations." Eventually, it became known as the Bar Mitzvah List. When we needed two-thirds majorities, we whipped out the Bar Mitzvah list It helped us count.

Security

All White Houses are preoccupied with the security of the President. The security precautions have become much more vigorous since the September 11, 2001, terrorist attacks on New York and Washington, but even when I was there in 1969, security was tight. The main gates obviously were kept locked and were opened only by uniformed guards. As they entered, visitors were carefully cleared by uniformed guards or Secret Service agents. Additionally, there were mechanical and electronic surveillance devices throughout the building.

When I worked there, I was forever seeing or imagining glass eyes watching me everywhere. One, in a heating register in the corridor leading up to the President's Oval Office, stared openly back at you. I had the feeling that those devices were picking up my every movement and sound. It got so that I felt uncomfortable when I was in the men's room, zipping down my fly.

It was quite a contrast to my experience in the Congress in the 1950s, when the uniformed guards were all chosen by political patronage (it's changed now). At that time, I reported to a police lieutenant that the oldish-looking guard in the Cannon House Office Building had disconcerting palsy and his hands shook. "Oh, don't worry about Tiger," the lieutenant said with a smile, "We don't let him have any bullets in his gun."

Secret Service agents in the White House, however, are well trained, generally intelligent and built like Olympic medalists. They use their bodies a lot. White House staff who wore the requisite security-clearance pass around their necks were never stopped, but visitors were watched closely. When one showed up where he perhaps should not have been, the Secret Service agent would put his body in front of the visitor. No guns showed, no rough talk. Just a body. The agent would ask where you'd like to go and if he could help you (smile). But the body was always there between you and wherever the President happened to be.

Periodically, the Secret Service would lecture us on security, not just in the White House but everywhere. Don't open suspicious packages; they may contain bombs. When driving, be aware of the cars around you, and when you stop in traffic, stay at least a car length behind the car in front so that you are not pinned in. They also had some favorite catch phrases such as, "There is no such thing as a friendly foreign agent" and "Don't trust the char people; throw all papers into burn baskets."

This itchy suspicion led to an embarrassing incident that took place in 1972, shortly after I had left the White House. In the mail at home, we got a package, wrapped in plain brown paper, roughly tied with twine, and with French stamps on it. No return address, no idea who was sending us something from France.

I took it down to the Post Office and asked if their security folks could peer into the box and see what mysterious thing might be inside. They agreed, but warned that if things looked suspicious, they might have to destroy the package. I agreed.

A week later, I got a call from a postal security person who said, "We looked inside and saw vials of liquids, so we took it apart in a bomb-proof container, and it seems that someone was sending you little bottles of perfume." Only then did Phyllis and I remember that Steph, our nine-year-old daughter, had taken a school-guided tour of France six months earlier. She was the culprit, bless her heart.

High Jinks

In 1972, the Vietnam war was still raging, and the country was riven by increasingly strident protests. One night, protesters marched around the building, carrying lighted candles. Wild and crazy John Neidecker, noted mostly for arranging colorful balloon drops during political conventions, handed us each candles and told us to join the march. "We're for peace, too," said Rally John. I was embarrassed to learn later that one of those protesters was Rabbi Leon Adler, the religious leader of our own synagogue.

John was capable of lesser crimes. In the White House, no food meant for the President was to be consumed which had not passed Secret Service inspection. Frequently Congressional and other VIP visitors presented the President with prize turkeys, huge ripe tomatoes, lobsters still twitching and other prime produce from their home communities. After the presentation ceremony, the Secret Service discreetly removed the offending food and destroyed it.

Periodically, Rally John would come to our offices in the East Wing of the White House with a canary-swallowing smile and a package tucked under his coat jacket. "Food," he would say, "Delicious food. Have some. Nothing wrong with it. It was just going to be destroyed and I couldn't see it go to waste." I usually turned it down, just as a matter of principle.)

Gene Cowen

Advice

Over the years, I've given career advice to some people. It's lucky they didn't take it. In the White House, I worked with a fellow by the name of Lamar who had come from the office of Tennessee Senator Howard Baker. An assistant to Bryce Harlow, Lamar was a quiet, almost self-effacing young man with an attractive wife and a couple of children. He was bright, knew Congress well, and was a pleasure to work with.

After about a year, he told me he was leaving. I asked where he was going, and he said back to Tennessee. To do what? He always wanted to run for public office.

I said, "Lamar, run for office? That's a rough life. You're too nice a guy. Have you really thought this through? And what are you going to run for?"

"Governor," he said.

I stopped giving him advice. Lamar Alexander was elected Governor, then went on to run several times, though not successfully, for the Republican nomination for President. He would have done better to ask me about running for President.

I had gotten to know Warren Adler when he was handling Jewish affairs for the Republican National Committee. He then set up a profitable public relations and advertising agency and founded *Dossier* magazine, which reported on the social scene in Washington. One day at lunch, he said he was giving it all up. He wanted to write novels. "Don't give up your day job, Warren," I warned. "That's a damned chancy way to make a living."

Wisely, he disregarded my advice and went on to a very successful career writing novels, plays and movies, including the hit, *War of the Roses*.

#

I did a lot of work with John Erlichman, a man who had a reputation for being—with Bob Haldeman—"one of the Prussians." Haldeman was indeed a forbidding character. But I got along well with John. He seemed sensitive to the domestic needs of the country (that was his area of responsibility), and, although no liberal, very willing to work with a number of moderate Republicans like me.

I became particularly indebted to him for a personal matter, involving how much of a Jew I was going to be. Shortly after I got to the White House in 1969, the Jewish Welfare Board asked me if I would be Honorary Chairman of United Jewish Appeal for the Government. I was startled. I had never been that observant a Jew, and I contributed to UJA, but just minimally.

The official explained that solicitations within the government were supposed to be confined to the United Fund. But UJA solicited for funds and needed some one "high in the White House to smooth things over in case there were complaints." He assured me that notables like Meyer Feldman had done it for the Kennedy White House and there really wasn't much to do.

I said I wasn't very notable and asked why not Henry Kissinger or Leonard Garment. He said they had both declined. So it seemed that it had come down to me. I told him I had to check with my superiors.

I asked a Deputy Assistant to the President to whom I reported, and he looked worried. Why did I want to do that? That wasn't why Gene Cowen was here. Did I want to be type-cast? Well, if I insisted, he said, I should talk to John Ehrlichman. He seemed certain that Ehrlichman would turn me down.

I asked for a private meeting with John. In his office, he asked, "What do you really want to do?"

"John," I said, "Until he turned me down, I really wasn't so sure. But now, I think I have my back up and I guess I want to do it."

"That's good," he said. "You know, when you're in the White House, whether you want to be or not, you're a role model. I think you should do it." And I did.

Ehrlichman and I got along well after that. One day, during the legislative battle over the Family Assistance Plan, Nixon's welfare reform proposal, he called me into his office, closed the door, and said, "What would you say if I told you the President did not want the FAP to pass?"

I said I'd be surprised because it was a major initiative and something Nixon had gone on television to propose. But I also knew that Republican conservatives were bitterly opposed to that or any other kind of welfare plan. I assumed that Nixon needed them for some other legislation more important to him and this was the tradeoff—not uncommon. So I asked John what he wanted me to do. He said he just wanted to know what we had to do to make sure it went nowhere and that our footprints were covered.

I left, checked around, discovered a surprisingly easy solution and reported back. I told him that the votes were pretty well split down the middle. Most of the Republicans, although a minority in the Senate, were against any welfare plan; most of the majority Democrats wanted one that was more liberal than that proposed by the President; and Bob Finch, the head of the Department of Health Education and Welfare, was urging the Administration to move a little to the left to pick up the Democratic votes we would need to pass a sweetened Nixon plan. I said all we had to do was do nothing. If we did not move, the legislation would die of its own weight (which it eventually did).

He said thanks, and before I left, I said, "John, how many people know about this?"

"Just you and me, Gene, and of course the President," he answered.

"John," I said. "The light is red now. I trust you'll tell me if it turns yellow or green."

He agreed with a laugh.

In 1973, after I had left the White House and after all the ugly Watergate revelations began spilling into the news, I visited John Ehrlichman along with an American Broadcasting Company senior vice president to work out a problem that ABC had with the wage-and-price freeze that the Nixon Administration had recently imposed.

After we settled ABC's business and were heading for the door, Ehrlichman said to my associate, "You know, Gene Cowen is the only one in this White House who could keep a secret." The ABC official had no idea what Erlichman was talking about.

John Ehrlichman was accused of participating in the Watergate cover-up and went to jail. I must assume that whatever he was convicted of, he did. But as far as I was concerned, he was a very decent person and I enjoyed working with him. Some years later, after he got out of prison, he wrote a novel, *The Company*. He sent me a copy with an inscription in the flyleaf, "For Gene Cowen, one of the best [Capitol] Hill men the White House ever held."

A Novel: Chapter Thirteen

The President wanted to see him. The message said that he was to come to "the private office" at eight p.m. You don't ask why the President wants to see you, but you wonder. Navigator asked one of his colleagues if The Man ever fired people in person, and they both laughed.

The Oval office is awesome, with its majestic blue rug with the Great Seal of the United States and the breathtaking view of the Washington monument as a backdrop for the manicured South Lawn. But the Oval Office is ceremonial. Richard Nixon did his real work and serious thinking in a modest office in the Old Executive Office Building.

The OEB was west of the White House. It had once been the old War Department headquarters and looked it—gray, rococo and forbidding. Inside, it wasn't much more inviting. That was where most of the second-level White House staff worked, except for Room 232, which was distinguished from all the other numbered offices in the institutional brown hall only by a desk and a Secret Service man sitting behind it with feigned nonchalance.

The meeting was on the President's schedule; would he go right in.

Richard Nixon was in shirtsleeves with an open collar. On the President's desk were lined legal pads and a telephone. On a credenza behind him, pictures of his family. Nothing else. Undemonstrative, like Richard Nixon.

The Man looked up, smiled, and rumbled, "I like the work you're doing here."

Well, at least he wasn't going to be fired. He mumbled something about being proud to serve in this administration, and then waited to be told what the hell this was all about.

"I'm impressed at how you can take on a confidential job, like that maneuver on the Family Assistance Plan, do your work and, frankly, keep your mouth shut. So I'd like to know if you could take on a different sort of assignment. Not in place of what you are doing, but in addition," Nixon said.

He said, of course he would and was flattered. But what did the President have in mind?

"Well, you know there are lots of people out there—in the media, in Congress, in some of those goddam radical organizations, all kinds of people—trying to bring this government down."

Navigator tried to think of somebody he knew in Congress who was trying to bring the government down, couldn't think of anyone immediately, but said nothing.

"They conspire," Nixon said. They hate me, they hate this government, and they hate you."

Navigator had known one or two people in his lifetime who hated him, but this was the first time he had realized that they were in a conspiracy. *Nod, indicating acceptance, if not agreement.*

"And so we have a few people here who keep their eyes and ears open, do surveillance, and meet once in a while," Nixon said.

The "surveillance" got his attention. He was aware of all the closed-circuit cameras in the White House, and the FBI and the CIA, but he wondered what else The Man was talking about and what they did when they met. *Nod, again.*

"Of course, this has to be kept very confidential. And unofficial. Just you and those people I trust doing surveillance. Not a government function. Well, you haven't said much? Are you in or out?"

He thought for what felt like minutes but was probably more like seconds. He wished he had his pipe, so he could stall while he filled and lighted it. *Surveillance, confidential, not a government function.* A nerve in his lower right jaw began to twitch. *This was the President of the United States, the guy who could command great armies, the man whom other heads of state paid obeisance to. He really had to know right from wrong, didn't he?*

My Life, A Novel

"Yes, sir," he said. "I am honored that you think enough of me to offer me this assignment. I'd be proud to do it."

The President shook his hand, told him that he should forget that this conversation had ever taken place, and the next time he would hear anything about this was when he got a call from John Alden, who would be his contact man. His heart sank.

Gene Cowen

My Life: Chapter Sixteen

I left the White House before the Watergate scandal, and I'd love to say I saw it coming. I didn't. But with the benefit of hindsight, there were signs and portents that should have told me that the place was an accident waiting to happen. There was a cavalier attitude in the building. *We're in the most powerful place of the most powerful country in the world,* Nixon assistants sometimes believed, *so step high and everyone will get out of our way.* Sometimes it was fun, other times not.

One day, we were at a meeting in the White House Cabinet Room, when the President met with an anti-Vietnam War protest delegation. There was a heated exchange with the President, and one of the protesters was getting pretty nasty. I scribbled a note on White House note paper and handed it to a Presidential assistant sitting next to me. It said, "Ed, what can you do with a guy like that?"

"How about assassination?" he wrote under my question.

I was flabbergasted and stuffed the paper quickly into my pocket, then later destroyed it. What kind of a nut writes a thing like that on White House stationery?

Sadly, and for other reasons, Ed later ended up in jail on Watergate charges. When I was at ABC in 1974, I got a postcard from him saying that jail wasn't all that bad, except for the food.

I used to tell people who worked with me that, wherever the White House walked, it left big muddy footprints, so you didn't have the luxury of behaving like every other citizen. But that took discretion and some of the White House staff played a hand that was short in that suit. I once was discussing with Jeb Magruder, assistant to Chief of Staff Bob Haldeman, a problem we were having with a Member of Congress who wouldn't support the President's program.

"What can we do to help?" he said.

"If we could put some pressure on the Congressman through his local newspapers, that would help," I said.

"How about we take out some advertising on the issue in his papers?"

"That's fine, but where are you going to get the money?"

"Money?" He laughed. "We've got plenty of money. Just tell us what you need and for what paper. We'll see what we can do."

"Where the hell do you get the money from?" I said.

Jeb pointed in the direction of the handsome townhouses across from the White House at Farragut Circle and said, "Over there; they're raising money."

"Is all that really legal?" I asked.

"Legal?" Again, he laughed. "Why worry about legal? Hey, we're the government. Whatever we say is legal *is* legal."

Jeb Magruder and others in the White House often wrote memos that they labeled as "eyes only." That was shorthand, for "This is secret, for your eyes only, and burn this after you've read it." Obviously, some people didn't. I assumed that people often forget to destroy hush memos and I had a congenital fear of things in print coming back to haunt.

For instance, Tom Korologos, my associate in Congressional relations, once wrote a memo to Bryce Harlow and sent me an information copy. It said something to the effect that "I met with Chuck Percy, that turd..."

When I got my copy, I took him aside and said, "Tom, I appreciate getting copies of things, but you have to remember that people often file their copies and you're in the White House now. Do you know what happens to White House files after a President leaves office? They go to the National Archives or the General Services Administration. Ten, twenty years from now you might end up being, what, president of Boise Cascade? And Senator Percy might then be, what, President of the United States? Some guy working on a Ph.D. thesis about the Nixon Administration might be leafing through copies of memos in old dusty files and here you are calling President Percy a turd."

Tom laughed and accepted the advice, then remembered it when he stayed on in the Ford Administration after President Nixon was forced to resign. He told me he attended a staff meeting in the Roosevelt Room, looked around the room, waggled his finger and told that story about indiscreet memos.

I also worked with some of the White House principals in what later was to become the great Watergate scandal. When I first knew him, John Dean was the head of Congressional Relations at the Justice Department. He was not terribly good at that job and always seemed to have a conspiratorial air about him, but so did a lot of other people in the Nixon administration, so Dean did not especially stand out.

One day, Bill Timmons, to whom I reported at that time, came walking out of his office quietly cursing John Erlichman. "Damn that bastard," Timmons said. "Would you believe that he called me and said, 'Bill, you know of John Dean's work at Justice. What do you really think of him?' and I, like a fool said, 'I don't think he's worth a shit.' And Erlichman said, 'Then you'll be pleased to know that he's just been announced as Counsel to the President, and we'll be reporting to him!' Can you believe that?"

My own contact with Dean was, interestingly enough, about photography. He found out that both of us were photo buffs, and he liked to talk about our mutual hobby. I remember him most for his enthusiasm for "rolling your own" film. He waxed eloquent about how much money could be saved by buying twenty-five-foot or fifty-foot rolls of Kodak Tri-X black-and-white 35mm film. That was generally film that Hollywood studios sold off because it had been left over in their motion picture cameras at the end of a shoot. As a consequence, it was not nearly as reliable as the more expensive and more carefully packaged film that came directly from Kodak.

I also told Dean that feeding that stock into a still camera was a pain. He explained happily that he enjoyed taking the a big roll of unexposed film into his darkroom and feeding it into cassettes made for that purpose. I thought he was nuts, spending all that time in a pitch-dark room just to save a few dollars on film. But, then again, Dean was a strange guy, as you might remember from his extensive testimony before the Senate Watergate investigating committee.

Egil (Bud) Krogh was cut from a different cloth. He was a young, gentle person whose voice I never heard raised. His specialty was domestic affairs and we would discuss legislation and, occasionally, politics. Bud was deeply religious and the last person I would have guessed would later be involved in the Watergate scandal. In 1973, I

My Life, A Novel

was startled to read that he had pled guilty to crimes involved in the "plumbers" operation and the Daniel Ellsberg break-in.

#

In the two and a half years I worked in the White House, I was with Richard Nixon personally only when other people were present—Senators summoned by the boss, Senators who wanted something from him, or people whom Senators wanted him to see. I didn't have much "face" time with him. (That's an expression made famous during the Monica Lewinsky imbroglio in the later Clinton Presidential years, when other staffers were jealous of the close attention he paid to Ms. Lewinsky's face and other parts.) So what I observed about Nixon was in the context of being with him with others in the room. It never really bothered me that "RN" didn't call me in for private consultations. I was there to represent the White House to the Congress, and I knew pretty much what had to be done (and when I didn't, John Ehrlichman would tell me).

I did get annoyed when I was not invited to some closed briefings by the pathologically secretive Henry Kissinger, and I complained about having "the same damned Secret Service clearance that Henry has." Once, I got very angry when I learned from a Senator that Kissinger had told him about a major military initiative before I knew about it. At the next seven-thirty a.m. Ehrlichman staff meeting, I said, "In the old London *Times*, the editor would instruct his new reporters that 'members of the *Times* must conform to the public misconception that we are the spokesmen for Her Majesty's Government.' So if you want me to represent this government effectively in Congress, please tell me what the hell this government is up to before you tell Capitol Hill."

Nixon was very intense, very intelligent, and I, at least, found him not very pleasant to be with. He seemed to have a conspiracy theory of life, almost a paranoia, so that everyone was a potential enemy. His dealings with Congress were confrontational, especially since Democrats controlled both houses. At one meeting with a large number of Senators, Nixon said with a smile, "Remember, I'm a *Congress* man," with a pause between the two words. No one in the room believed that.

Moreover, I knew of no Senator who could be considered a trusted adviser. Senator Norris Cotton, a New Hampshire Republican and a faithful Nixon supporter on most issues, said to me one day, "Did you know that I'm the President's sex advisor?"

"Oh," I said, waiting for the punch line, "How so?"

"That's because he says to me, 'Cotton, when I want your fuckin' advice, I'll ask for it.'" Cotton roared with laughter when he told the story, but there was a wry truth underlying it.

I often felt uncomfortable about my feelings toward Nixon and attributed it to the fact that, coming from moderate Republican Senator Scott's office, I was suspect by the very conservative in-group around the President. But then I read the following in *Crazy Rhythm* by Leonard Garment, a trusted advisor to Nixon for many years:

"The relationships among Haldeman, Ehrlichman, Kissinger and Nixon were singularly devoted to the breeding and tending of power. They were not friends, not even a little. Indeed, if the members of Nixon's German general staff shared an emotion, it was an intense dislike of Nixon, which he returned."

A Novel: Chapter Fourteen

The original John Alden wooed Priscilla on behalf of Miles Standish. But John was so fair of face and spoke so eloquently that Priscilla fell in love with him, and he spoke for himself. This John Alden was none of that. He was a man of average height and average build in his forties, prematurely gray, somewhat balding and had a rather pinched nose and gray eyes. The only thing not average about him was his tight, narrow lips which it made it difficult to know, when he was smiling, whether he really thought anything was that funny.

He answered the door of their two-story colonial house wearing a barbecue apron that said, "A Rising Tide Lifts All Chefs," which didn't make much sense, but maybe that got him to smile. In one hand he held what looked at first like a spear gun, but turned out to be a barbecue fork. His other hand was extended, and he said, "I'm so glad you could come. Come in."

The call had come to Navigator's home, not to the White House, since this was "not a government function." John Alden had asked if he'd come to the Alden home in Reston for a barbecue supper on Sunday afternoon. "Just you, since I'd like for us to have a chance to talk alone."

It was late September, with Washington's trademark heat and humidity. Navigator had driven his seven-year-old Chevy from suburban Maryland around the Washington Beltway, admiring the trees, which were just coming into good color. The Alden home was a white rambler on a neat lawn, but one that needed watering, and azalea bushes that were well-developed but poorly trimmed—telltale signs of a husband who had too many things on his mind to bother unduly with his yard.

When asked, he told Alden he'd like a white wine spritzer, since the weather was so warm. Alden brought it and poured himself scotch on the rocks. They were standing in a family room that was inexpensively decorated, but in good taste. He admired the curtains which he would bet Maria had made. The barbecuing was going to be done on the patio which led off from the family room.

"And this," Alden said with his tight smile, "is Maria, whom I understand you know."

She stood against the patio door, smiling and offering her hand. She looked properly summery in a flowered blouse and slacks that picked up the reds in the blouse, on which she wore his cameo as a pin. She was trim and fit and proper. Only her eyes betrayed any amusement at the situation.

"Yes, we met a couple of times during the war," he said. "When she served doughnuts, even the USO coffee tasted good."

"Then, why doesn't Maria show you around while I prepare the barbecue?"

Alden left with his apron and spear gun. Maria took Navigator's arm and they walked up a long flight of stairs. Along the stairway walls were attractive photographs of sunsets someone had taken in various parts of the world.

Only when they got to the bedroom did she swing around, press against him and kiss him warmly. It sent a little shiver down his spine and other places.

"Hey," he said. "I'm not really supposed to know you that well. Isn't your husband going to get a little suspicious?"

"Not to worry," she said. "He just assumes we were lovers at some point and that wouldn't bother him. But I'll behave."

"Tell me how you are. How is Anna? What are you doing with your life?" he asked.

"Anna is practicing law…"

"Hey!"

"I'm working as a dressmaker, nine to five, not too bad," she said. "Between us, we earn enough money to pay our mortgage and go to a restaurant once a week. Otherwise, I prepare dinner for John and keep it warm for whenever he gets home. We watch television, go to sleep, get up the next morning, have breakfast. Just the ordinary, as far as those things go."

"And what about the other things that aren't quite so ordinary?" he said.

My Life, A Novel

She smiled, and then the smile darkened. "Well, John is officially in the Army Signal Corps, works very long hours on assignment to the White House, and brings home rather strange friends."

"Still pretty ordinary."

"And John is gay."

He reached into his pocket, filled and lighted his pipe, and waved the smoke away from Maria. Things began falling into place. A single mother in Italy in 1945, yearning to get herself and her daughter into the United States. A gay GI cryptographer, needing cover at a time when homosexuality got you drummed out of the military with a dishonorable discharge. A husband who today didn't mind introducing his wife to a supposed former lover. And John Alden, Army Signal Corps cryptographer, still hanging around with strange friends, the kind of pals who collected explosives, took credit for a plane that crashed in Pennsylvania, and who wouldn't want a fag in their inner circle.

He wondered whether Maria had "focused John's attention" right after that plane crash by threatening to out him from the closet. That also would explain why she had been "seeing other men."

#

They ate on the patio, seated on aluminum chairs, at a picnic table with an umbrella tilted to shade them from the sun. Maria had sliced some good French bread, buttered the slices and warmed them in the oven. She served a simple green salad and sliced tomatoes and onions and offered them with various dressings.

John Alden, wrapped in his rising-tide apron, speared steaks off the barbecue grill and asked whether he wanted his rare, medium, or medium-rare. He asked for one medium-rare and helped himself to roast potatoes.

The food was good but the conversation strained. They talked about the weather and his drive in from Maryland, but carefully avoided anything that might smack of office talk.

Gene Cowen

After they had coffee, John stood up abruptly and nodded to Maria, who looked back at her friend the Navigator and left with the dirty dishes for the kitchen.

"Would you like to come into my headquarters room with me?" Alden asked.

Headquarters room? he thought. Everybody else he knew had a den or a family room, but this guy has a headquarters room.

When they got there, he understood why. When Alden opened the door with a key, it looked like a control tower at a small airport. The lights were harsh fluorescent. Several television screens, dark but menacing, were mounted on one wall. Beneath them were dials, switches and a speaker. On the back wall, there was an impressive reel-to-reel audio taping machine and on the desk in front of it, expensive headphones. Elsewhere in the room were electronic machines that he couldn't identify. But against the left wall, his amateur photographer's eye recognized familiar gear: an Omega enlarger, color filters, boxes of Agfa enlarging paper, Kodak infra-red film, developing trays, spotting brushes and the whole nine yards of goodies for a serious photographer or determined surveillance man.

"Quite an impressive display," he said.

Alden just grunted, walked over to a wall safe, obscured the dial with his body, and carefully spun it back and forth until the safe opened and he drew out a large black leather binder and a legal pad.

"My friend," Alden said, "you're now in a room that does not exist. Nothing we say here can ever leave this room." Navigator nodded his assent and Alden went on. "I work informally with a group of people who are trying to protect this country and the Presidency from the kind of people who are trying to tear it down. It is quite a compliment to you that the President invited you to join us. We do surveillance, which means we listen. We listen to what people are saying. I tape things for the President inside the White House and elsewhere. Some of our members—I call them Plumbers—enter offices and plant small listening devices so we can hear if people are plotting. We also listen to satellite transmissions, and we tune into microwave towers. And I'd like to know from you what you have heard on Capitol Hill. I'd like to refer to what you report on as "Legislative Noise." What have you heard?"

Navigator was better prepared for that question than he had been with Nixon. He said, "Senator Eagleton told me that he hated what he called 'the German general staff' in this White House..."

Alden quickly opened his black binder, turned to a tab labeled "E" and said, "That Commie pinko!"

"...but he said he liked me," he ended, with a smile.

Alden glared and said, "Why?"

"I don't know why," he said, "and what difference does it make why? Isn't it good to have an 'in' with a Commie pinko?"

Alden nodded and wrote on his legal pad. "What else?"

"Senator Mathias of Maryland told me he wasn't going to support the President on the current nomination for the Supreme Court."

"Why would he tell you that?" Alden said.

"Because it's my job to find these things out. Besides, I worked on his last campaign, and he also likes me."

Alden glowered again and took more notes.

"And Congressman Goldstein, a New York Democrat, has a woman working for him who is an avowed Communist," he said, as Alden continued to write.

"How do you know that?" Alden asked.

"Because I had to discuss Congressman Goldstein's legislation with her, and we decided to do it in the cafeteria. She said both her parents were Communists, and she was one almost from birth. She asked me if I knew of the 'theory of the red diapers,' and then she said that when you grow up in that kind of family, Communism flows in your veins..."

"She said all that in a public place?" said Alden, as he shook his hand to get rid of a cramp.

"Oh, yes. She said she was getting dismayed at working in Congress because she wasn't able to make much progress on world revolution in legislation..."

"World revolution?" Alden said.

"That's what she said. So she planned to go next into teaching, where the potential was better among students."

Alden stopped writing and stared into space. Almost to himself, he said, "I think we'd better do something about a person like that."

"Like what?"

"We've got enforcers," Alden said.

Navigator stood up and walked over to Alden, who was obviously startled to see him so close. "Alden, I think we'd better cut the shit at this point!"

Alden pushed his chair back to give himself some breathing room. The relationship had changed and Alden was clearly no longer in charge. His face flushed and a line of perspiration showed on his upper lip. "What are you talking about?"

"I'm talking about you, Alden, and some of your strange friends. I'm talking about 'enforcers' and people who take credit for private airplane crashes."

"I really don't know what you're talking about," said Alden. "I think you're just agitated. Please sit down."

"Damn right, I'm agitated," he said. "Six years ago, your stepdaughter and I got off that plane in Pennsylvania just before it went down. I read the message that your daughter got, taking credit for the crash. I also know you were involved with some of your whacko pals who wanted you to do something that you apparently had sense enough not to do. And I know that you and your family were threatened."

"There's not a word of truth in what you're saying," said Alden. "I don't know anything about the Shafer campaign."

"I never mentioned Shafer," he said.

"I think we should end this meeting right now," Alden said, moving away until he had his back against the wall.

"This is going to end pretty fast, but not until I finish," he said, putting his face into Alden's. "Maria told me that you promised her you were going to keep away from the loonies."

"Maria? How did you...?"

"Oh, shut up," he said. "I talked to Maria after your stepdaughter and I nearly went down with that plane in Pennsylvania. She told me you were going to stay clear of the

My Life, A Novel

loonies with the explosives and crazy ideas. Listen, I've been asked by the President to cooperate with you, and I'll do it—up to a point. But I don't want to be involved with enforcers or dynamiters or anything else that is going to put us behind bars. I'm asking you, in as nice a way as I can..." He backed off a little, to give Alden breathing room. "...to use your head and do the same. Play your political games, if you want to, but for the sake of yourself and your family, unscrew from those fringe elements. People like that eventually get into a lot of trouble, and let me tell you something, Alden—you don't look like the kind of guy who can lie well under oath."

Something he said must have clicked with Alden, who looked sheepish, reached for a handkerchief and mopped his face. "All right. I guess I do go overboard sometimes. I love politics and it's only when I get involved in some of this surveillance that I can do what I do best, which is to use electronic equipment—taping, listening, picking up information. But you're probably making a good point and I'll try to back away from some of those folks. Frankly some of them frighten me, too."

"Just what do you do in the White House—officially, I mean?"

"I operate the internal taping system," Alden said.

"And what do you tape?"

"I probably shouldn't be telling you this."

"In that case, I don't think you should, and I don't want to hear it."

"Anyhow, I tend to the machinery and the tapes. Pretty routine stuff, and I look around for other ways to utilize my skills," said Alden.

"I'm going now. I'm sorry I pushed you so hard just now. But that Pennsylvania plane crash frightened the hell out of me, and I really would prefer to keep away from those people, who want me to die and bring the whole world to an end."

"What whole world to an end?" asked Alden.

"Never mind, it's too complicated," he said. "Thanks for dinner. I'll see you around the White House when both of us are back to our official duties. Happy taping."

Gene Cowen

My Life: Chapter Seventeen

Leaving Nixon

I have framed on a wall at home a very nice farewell letter, dated December 15, 1971, and signed by President Nixon, alongside a picture of the two of us shaking hands and smiling. Most people comment about how, in profile, I resembled him a little. But more interesting is what he was saying to me during that handshake: "Gene, aren't you glad to be rid of those bastards in the Senate?"

Whenever I was in a meeting with Nixon and others, he was doing the talking, unless he was listening to an answer to a question he had just asked. Most people who dealt with him always assumed he had a second agenda, even when he was being pleasant and seemingly relaxed.

Don Hughes had been closely associated with Nixon for years. I first knew Don when he was a crew-cut colonel, taking notes on a clipboard, when Nixon was Vice President in the 1950s. By 1970, it was General Don Hughes and he was military attaché to the President. I saw him then when I was invited to a reception that the President was giving in his honor. I congratulated Don on the President's giving a party for him.

"Yes, Gene," said the general, with a puzzled look on his face. "I wonder why he's doing this."

Maybe I'm taking Nixon out of political context and doing him an injustice. Some people revered him and worked to honor his memory. A former Nixon assistant and later a functionary of the Nixon library interviewed me at length about my reminiscences of my two and a half years in the White House. He was worshipful of the former President but, to me, brought to mind a tired old bearded man with a lantern, searching for someone to say good things about "RN."

Somebody once said, "People have friends, but nations have only allies." He could have added, "And so do politicians." Some people in politics do have friends. But, too often, they are fair-weather buddies who'll hang in there only until their ambitions bring them into conflict. In politics, when the going gets tough, politicians too often get going the other way. But more on that later.

So, in view of my mixed feelings about Nixon, why did I agree to work in his White House? The answer is that for sixteen years I had worked for Republicans in Congress, and I generally agreed with them on fiscal conservatism, a strong military, anti-Communism, and a market economy that encouraged free trade. I also knew that if you choose to labor in the political vineyards, once in a while you have to tend rotten grapes. If something is ideologically repugnant, you really should get out. But since you are dealing with dozens or hundreds of issues, if some are not quite what you'd do in the circumstances, you just hold your nose and console yourself that there are other issues where you might be helping to advance the public good.

Finally, I went to work in that white-painted mansion at 1600 Pennsylvania Avenue because I wanted the exhilarating experience of working in what most people consider to be the most powerful place on earth. And, in the back of my mind was the adage, "The White House is a good place to be *from*."

Going to ABC

Life takes strange twists and every once in a while, I'm reminded how much I was at the mercy of the gods of chance. Wherever I worked before the White House—on a newspaper, in the House, in the Senate—I assumed without thinking that I might stay forever. Then something would change and I'd change jobs. But at the White House, I realized that no one makes a long-term career of being assistant to a President.

So, for a couple of years, I made quiet inquiries here and there and ended up with an interview with Everett H. Erlick, ABC's Executive Vice President. Toward the end of the interview, which seemed to be going well, he asked me to give him the name of one Senator—other than my old boss Hugh Scott—who'd give me a good recommendation.

Figuring I'd show off, I said, "Pick any one."

"Any one of the one hundred Senators?" he asked.

Gene Cowen

I said yes.

The Majority Leader, Mike Mansfield, bless him, gave me an excellent reference and I got the job.

I spent twenty-one good years at ABC. When I got there in December of 1971, I was given the title of Washington Vice President for ABC, Inc., the parent company. That often confused people, since there was also a Washington Vice President for ABC News. So I short-circuited the questions by saying up front that I was really the chief lobbyist.

I started with one secretary, a chauffeur-driven car, and a thirty-seven-hour week. I liked the secretary, felt self-conscious about the limo, and was disconcerted by the short week. At the White House, I had been working about sixty hours a week and had trouble imagining coming to work during daylight and returning while the sun was still above the horizon.

I then went to a couple of people for advice. I asked Nixon Counsel Leonard Garment what to do with all the extra time on my hands. He said with a grin, "Don't worry; you'll adjust."

I asked Bryce Harlow, who by then had returned to Proctor and Gamble, what to do about registering as a lobbyist. On the advice of one of his company's lawyers, my counterpart at CBS had not registered.

Bryce said to me, "I can't tell you what to do, but I'll tell you what I do. Whenever I talk to a Senator or Congressman, whether it's about legislation or about the weather, I'm lobbying. So I register and sleep better for it every night." I did.

#

One of the perks of my job at ABC was luxury travel—occasional trips to company meetings at lovely resort hotels. I wanted Phyllis with me, and she wanted to come, so she decided to retire. Since before our marriage, she had been teaching college English at places like Syracuse and Maryland universities. She was an associate professor of English at Montgomery College, Maryland, when she hung up her chalk.

#

A few months after I joined ABC, the Nixon Justice Department brought an anti-trust lawsuit against the three major networks, largely at the instigation of the Hollywood motion picture studios, who wanted to protect their ownership of prime-time programming. So I met again with Len Garment and asked him why he thought that had happened and whether there was anything I could do about it.

"Gene, you know all the news media, especially the three networks' news departments, give the President a hard time. Richard Nixon, in my experience, takes a primate's attitude about differences of opinion. You knock me down, I knock you down. And, no, I don't think there is anything you can do about it."

I didn't even try.

At about the same time, I was invited to lunch by the Washington correspondent for *Variety* newspaper. Wasn't it too bad, he asked, that right after I came out of the Nixon White House, he takes a shot at the networks?

"Not really," I replied after some thought. "Listen, if there was no news in Washington, you probably wouldn't have a job here, and if there was no trouble in Washington, I wouldn't have a job."

Democratic Convention

The Democratic National Convention in Miami reflected the turmoil of 1972. The streets outside the convention hall were churning with protesters. The police cracked some heads and took their share of thrown flowers and bricks. Inside, the Democratic functionaries were trying to put together a platform and a ticket that reached out to the dissidents and the civil-rights reformers. One of the staff members, who was trying to complete the membership of the platform committee, said to me with a smile, "Well, I think we've covered all bases, but I still need one black Hispanic woman, preferably a lesbian."

The convention floor reflected that turmoil. Many of the young delegates scoffed at the old party regulars, refused to show them the respect the old-liners expected from their juniors, and stepped hard on their feet when they moved down the aisles to their seats. As a result, we got a disproportionately large number of Members of Congress in our little oasis just off the delegate floor.

Senator Vance Hartke of Indiana was one of the old-timers who camped out with us. He was quite a character. Behind his back, people would say, "Indiana has two senators, [Birch] Bayh and Bought."

"Let those crazies take over this party," he said bitterly. "Let them have it and let them lose this election. Then the real Democrats will take it back and have a real political party again."

He also was attracted to pretty, blonde Donna De Verona of ABC Sports. Someone told him that Donna had won an Olympic gold medal in swimming. "I have several golds on waterbeds," he told her with a leer.

Also a regular at our hospitality suite was Senator Thomas Eagleton of Missouri. He would sit quietly in the corner, munching an occasional sandwich, watching our television set or reading. The Democrats nominated Senator George S. McGovern of South Dakota for President, and the next day, they chose Senator Eagleton for Vice President.

"Who?" said my boss Ev Erlick. "That little guy sitting in the corner reading a newspaper all week? They chose him? I hardly bothered to talk to him."

Sadly for the very amiable, well-qualified Eagleton, he was removed from the ticket when it was discovered that he had been treated for manic depression. He was replaced by former Peace Corps director R. Sargent Shriver

When things were quiet in our suite, I got a floor pass from ABC News and wandered around the convention floor, inhaling the charged atmosphere of a convention and chatting with a few Congressmen I knew.

I was accosted by CBS correspondent Roger Mudd, who knew me from the White House, and he struck up a too-casual conversation with me. "Gene, what brings you here?" he asked with a conspiratorial smile.

"Just wandering around," I said.

"Isn't this a strange place for you to be?" he asked, mumbling an aside into his microphone and raising his hand to someone in the CBS news booth above the delegate floor.

My Life, A Novel

"No," I said, wondering if I had violated a newsman's restriction by being an ABC lobbyist wearing an ABC News pass. "I'm renewing acquaintances with a few people."

"For the Nixon White House?" he asked, waving frantically to someone in the CBS booth, trying to get on the air.

I then realized why I was of such interest to Roger Mudd. "Roger, call off the dogs." I laughed. "I left the Nixon White House months ago. I'm no undercover Nixon operative. I really do work for ABC."

His face fell. No story after all.

Jimmy the Greek

At that 1972 Democratic convention, one of the celebrities who found his way into our hospitality suite was John Y. Brown of Kentucky Fried Chicken fame, and with him was Jimmy (the Greek) Snyder, the odds-maker. At that time, Jimmy was apparently hoping to get on the air at one of the networks (he did eventually at CBS, and then got fired for allegedly racist remarks), so he chatted me up and said, "Any time you're around Vegas, look me up."

A short time later, the National Association of Broadcasters held its national convention at Las Vegas. I wrote to Jimmy and we arranged to have dinner.

The night I arrived in Las Vegas, I bought from my hotel's newsstand *The Facts of Craps*, a paperback, for a dollar-fifty. It explained that dice were rolled in ancient Egypt; present-day craps is a game that depends on the frequency with which certain numbers come up on the dice; that mathematicians have known for a very long time the odds of each number coming up (seven, the most often); and that, although over a long period of time, there was hardly any way to beat the odds that a casino would give you, you could have a lot of fun trying. But you must place certain bets and not others if you wanted to reduce the casino's advantage. I allocated fifty dollars to the effort, played for about and hour, won fifty dollars and quit, feeling very smug.

The next night I met Jimmy for dinner. He was an overweight, outgoing, blustery kind of guy with a huge roll of one-dollar bills in his pocket. Seemingly, everyone in Vegas knew him and wanted to bet against him on something. He said he carried the dollars so that he would never have to refuse a bet, signed each bill as he laid it down, and let the person betting against him hold the dollar. Jimmy depended on the bettor's integrity to pay off if he lost.

The dinner was colorful. For dessert, he ate grapes by holding the stalk over his head and nibbling from below. I interrupted his nibble by asking him, "Jimmy, I read this book on craps. What advice could you give me on how to shoot craps?"

"Don't, is my advice." He laughed. "You can't make any money shooting craps." Jimmy said that he would far rather bet on horses or sporting events where, presumably, he could ferret out some inside information and get an edge on the odds. But then he added, "Will you do what I tell you, if I tell you?"

I said yes, and he gave me some pointers. After dinner, armed with that expert advice, I went back to the tables. I lost my fifty dollars. So his first advice was the best. But please note that, for Jimmy the Greek, even his advice was hedged.

A Novel: Chapter Fifteen

Navigator was idly opening his mail as he smoked his first pipe of the morning when a letter dropped out that said, "There's a contract out on John Alden. It's a Mob thing. Lou Jones is the shooter." No signature. No return address on the envelope.

His stomach knotted up with memories of the message that had come after the plane went down during the Shafer campaign. "Damn," he said out loud. "I thought we buried that years ago. Is that stupid sonovabitch involved in something again?."

His secretary said, "Did you say something?"

"No," he said. "Yes, but I was only thinking out loud. Sorry."

After dinner he called Alden at home. "John, I have to talk to you about something."

"What about?"

"I can't say on the phone. Is Maria home?"

"No, she's out shopping. Can't this wait? You can come down to my office in the morning and we can talk."

"No, it can't wait. And I'm not going to talk about this in the White House. I'll be at your house in about half an hour."

When Navigator arrived at the white rambler in Reston, Alden led him into the family room.

Without bothering with any preliminaries, Navigator said, "John, what the hell are you up to now? Why do I hear you're in trouble?"

Alden's brow furrowed. As he poured himself some Scotch his hands shook. "I 'm amazed know how you always find these things out. But, yes, I've apparently gotten into trouble with that group I have been working with on-and-off for years."

"You mean even now, when you're in the White House?"

"Well, yes. Um, they have some unofficial affiliation with the White House. You remember I told you that I do taping. I'm good at it and I like doing it. Well, they're planning a stunt that involves some surveillance for President Nixon's re-election campaign and they want me in on it. It worries the hell out of me. I tried to back out and they said I'm in too deep and if I back out now I'm going to get hurt. Navigator, I'm worried sick."

"Would this crowd be using organized crime figures to work you over?"

Alden's mouth twisted. "Is that what they're planning? That's not so unusual. I know that the government has turned to organized crime for covert help, at least as far back as World War II. The military developed a cozy relationship with Lucky Luciano when he was in prison during the war. He gave them names of Italian partisans who helped the U.S. forces during the invasion of Sicily. After the war, the government agreed to let him be released and deported to Italy. Nothing new about that kind of dealing."

"Is the government involved in all this?"

"Not really. It's hard to explain but these fellows have a relationship to the White House—. I can't say any more."

"John," said Navigator. "I'm going to try to get your ass out of the frying pan one more time. I don't know why I do this, but I'm going to try."

Alden smirked and said,. "I know why you do all these things for me even though you dislike me. You're in love with my wife, that's why."

Navigator smiled and said nothing. His relationship with Maria was so complex he had trouble understanding it himself. He wasn't about to try explaining it to this pea brain.

"John," he said, "while I work on this, keep your doors locked and your shades drawn. Look carefully both ways when you cross the street. And for chrissakes, stop playing with these nasty big boys. They're a disaster looking for a place to happen."

The next morning, he read the note again,: "It's a Mob thing." That's what puzzled him. *How do you deal with the Mob? And do you want to deal with the Mob? You don't carry the right insurance for something like that.*

My Life, A Novel

He called the ABC News Bureau Chief. "Jack, what do you know about the Mob?" he said.

"You mean organized crime? We've got all kinds of files. Tell me more."

"I can't really go into detail, but someone I deal with on Capitol Hill is worried about a Mob contract to kill someone, and I said I'd ask around." He felt his Pinocchio nose grow longer.

"Wow, that's pretty heavy stuff. Not in my job description, if you know what I mean. But didn't you tell me that you were meeting with Jimmy the Greek Snyder in Las Vegas next week? Ask him. He's got all kinds of connections."

#

At dinner in the Sands Hotel in Las Vegas the following week, he listened to Jimmy the Greek give him advice on how to shoot craps and struggled with how to broach this other subject.

"Jimmy, I wonder if you could help point me in the right direction about another problem I have," he said. "I need a connection with someone who's high up in organized crime."

"Navigator, you've got the wrong guy for that question," said the Greek. "I'm an odds-maker. I don't commit crimes."

"Jimmy, I'm not asking you do anything illegal. I just need an introduction to someone who could do me a favor."

Jimmy thought for a moment and then said, "If I got you a name, could you introduce me to someone at ABC who might want a fat old odds-maker for his sports shows?"

Navigator agreed to get him an introduction.

Then Jimmy said, "I can put you in touch with Meyer Lansky. He owes me."

Jimmy made some calls, and a meeting with Meyer Lansky was set for ten p.m. in the Desert Inn on the next night.

#

`Navigator put on a pale blue, summer wool suit with a blue-and-white-striped, buttoned-down shirt and a blue-and-white striped necktie. You have to look right for a meeting with a crime boss.

It was nighttime, but the sidewalks still radiated heat from the oven-baked day. Everywhere he walked, garish signs proclaimed: "Girls, Girls, Girls," "Women Mud Wrestlers," "Slots with the Biggest Payoffs."

This was Neon Town. But it was also Mob Town. The Mob bosses were discreet, however. Big stars like Frank Sinatra, who had a piece of the Sands, were the front men for "the guys back east" who were the major owners of virtually all the principal hotels and casinos. Navigator felt safe walking these streets at night because the Mob held down the crime. They tolerated no "trash" crowding their turf. The big money was to be made in the casinos, and the guys back east didn't allow any free-lance criminals to spoil a good thing.

One brightly lighted billboard proclaimed that Donald O'Connor was performing at the Sahara. Another blared that Buddy Hackett was on stage at the Riviera. Navigator recalled that a different Riviera had been a significant name in Meyer Lansky's career.

Lansky was a Russian-Jewish immigrant who had worked his way up from robbing grocery stores in the Lower East Side of New York to become one of the leading organized crime figures of the early Twentieth Century. Lansky, despite his reputation for being the "brains" of the Mob, was just a mobster with a good brain, who knew how to make money both legally and illegally. His specialty was running gambling casinos, and he did that so well that in the 1950s, the Cuban dictator Batista arranged for him to take charge of the corrupt Cuban gambling houses and clean them up. Lansky was tough, but his compatriots and employees considered him fair and trustworthy.

He was so successful in overseeing the Cuban casinos that he put all his money into the construction of a luxury hotel casino, which he called the Havana Riviera. It did well until Fidel Castro took over Cuba and then ran him and the other foreign businessmen out. Now, Lansky was in Las Vegas, trying to make a comeback.

My Life, A Novel

Navigator stood in the Desert Inn casino and looked for the reception desk. There was no entering or leaving any Las Vegas Hotel without going through the casino. The local joke was that, in case of fire, you still had to go through the casino to get out. The place was brightly lit and noisy. No daylight ever invaded a casino. No clocks were on the walls. The slot machines clanged away. Whenever a player hit a jackpot, bells rang and lights flashed. Noise, lights and fun—that was the mantra.

The reception clerk asked if he was expected. He said yes. The clerk called ahead, and then sent him up to Room 919.

On the ninth floor, a heavyset man in a dark suit patted him down and pointed to the door. Navigator walked into a large room furnished with plain brown armchairs and a matching couch against one wall. At the far end, sitting behind an unadorned desk, was the former crime chieftain. He had no nicknames like his flamboyant associates, just Meyer Lansky.

His early pals were long gone. Bugsy Siegel had been shot down in Beverly Hills in 1947. Lucky Luciano was in Italy. Mickey Cohen was in prison. But the aura of those and other gunmen clung closely to this aging man sitting behind the desk.

He wore a well-cut but simple black suit, a white shirt and a dark-patterned tie. His face was pinched, and dark lines under his cheeks outlined his mouth. There were no papers on this desk and probably none inside it either. Meyer Lansky kept all his books and did all his computations in his head. That was a secret of his success and one of the reasons why, despite years of trying, the FBI had never been able to convict him of any crime.

"Mr. Lansky," said Navigator, "thanks for seeing me. Let me tell you why I'm here."

"I know why you're here, *boychick*," said the somber figure behind the desk. "You have an Italian girlfriend who's married to a schmuck. John Alden works at wiretapping. He's involved with a bunch of amateur fascists who play dirty tricks for Tricky Dicky Nixon, John Alden is in over his head and got crossways with some of the fascists, so they put a contract out on him. Did I leave anything out?"

Navigator caught his breath. This guy's sources were unbelievable. "No, sir, but that woman is not my girlfriend."

"All right. So she's your sister. I don't care about the detail. Why do you bring this to me?"

"Because I don't want Alden killed and I wondered..."

"You think I go around killing people?" said Lansky. "I'm a businessman. I run gambling casinos. That's a tough business, but I've never killed a person in my life. But I've spent half of my life dodging the lies they tell about me in the newspapers and now on television. Wherever I go, reporters and photographers hound me. I go out to walk my dog, and the bastards start taking pictures and pushing microphones in my face. That's where you work, isn't it? For a television network? Why would I help you? Give me a reason."

Navigator flushed as he realized that he had never thought through that question. *Why on earth should this gangster want to help me?* he thought. *I just represent the people who are harassing him. If I were he, I'd throw me the hell out of the office. So maybe I better go before he gets his muscle from outside the door to do it.*

Navigator rose quietly and said, "Thanks for seeing me."

As he put his hand on the doorknob, he heard, "Maybe there is a reason."

Navigator turned to look at a man who suddenly didn't seem so forbidding.

"Can you call off your dogs?" said Lansky quietly. "Can you get them to leave me alone? I'm a sick old man."

Navigator said, "I'll tell you the truth. I don't know. The news department doesn't like us corporate types telling them what to cover and what not to cover. But I can try. If you'll give me a hand with Lou Jones, I'll sure as hell try."

"I've heard that you tell the truth, so that's something. I know Jones. You try and then let me know. Then I'll try," said Lansky.

"Should I call you here at the hotel?"

"Call me?" said Lansky, smiling bitterly. "With my phones tapped where I work and where I live? No, don't call. Do your thing and then come back and tell me, just like we're talking now."

My Life, A Novel

Navigator walked out to the street, then rapidly, past the neon signs and the people strolling along carrying drinks in their hands. He bounded into the Sands Hotel and headed straight for his room, picked up the phone and got through to his Bureau Chief's home in Washington.

"Jack," he said, "I certainly appreciated your suggestion that I talk to Jimmy the Greek."

"You didn't wake me up at two a.m. to thank me."

"No, Jack, I didn't. But I've been put in touch with Meyer Lansky and need to know what you know about him."

"Aw, shit. Get to the point, my friend. What did you really need to know?"

"I need to know how important he is in the news and who you've got assigned to cover him."

"He's an extinct volcano," said the Bureau Chief. "Once upon a time, the guy was big. He was supposed to be the mobsters' mastermind. Like Cyrano de Bergerac's nose, his reputation preceded him into a room by fifteen minutes. But now, all his Mob buddies are either dead or deported. And Meyer lost his ass when Fidel threw him out of Havana and kept the hotel that Lansky put all his money into. So he's trying to make a comeback in Las Vegas as a casino operator. And the Feds have given up trying to convict him of something, ever since their case against him for income tax evasion was thrown out of court. We don't have anyone assigned to him anymore. I have more important things to cover. As for you, Navigator, I smell something funny. But I'm not going to say any more, because I need you every once in a while to help straighten things out for the news bureau on the Hill."

"Jack, you've answered all my questions. Go back to sleep."

"If I can't, I'm going to call you tomorrow at two a.m. and curse at you."

The following morning, Navigator was back in the lobby of the Desert Inn. It was eleven a.m., and the casino was going at about half-blast. The sun was shining outside, but none of it penetrated the casino. Just like something in outer space, a casino has no time.

Gene Cowen

Bleary-eyed middle-aged ladies were feeding coins into the slot machines, and several gray-haired men sat in front of the blackjack tables, saying, "Hit me," from time to time.

Bells started ringing at the slot machine to his left, and a florid-faced woman shouted. "Wowee! Look at all them quarters. There must be a hundred bucks there." She turned toward Navigator. "Can you help me? This cup won't hold all those quarters.!"

He went off for a small bucket to contain her stash. "Congratulations," he said, as she poured nickels. "How much money did you put into that machine?"

"Oh, you. You sound just like my husband," she said and she turned her back without thanking him for helping with the return on her investment.

Navigator, still smiling, went up to Lansky's room, was frisked again, and was admitted. "I'm pleased to tell you that ABC News is off your case. Can you help me with Lou Jones?"

"Consider it done," said Lansky.

"Will you tell me when it's really done?"

"You're a guy who plays straight, but you're not a very good listener. It's a done deal. Now we're even."

Navigator looked puzzled. Lansky got up from his desk and put his hand on Navigator's arm. "*Boychick*, I know the guy who owns Jones," he said with a slight smile. "If he says, 'Jump,' Jones says, 'How high?' If you don't hear from me, Jones is off the Alden contract. The schmuck doesn't deserve it."

My Life, A Novel

My Life: Chapter Eighteen

Leonard & Isabel

Leonard Goldenson was the founder and chief executive of the American Broadcasting Companies. The bright young Harvard graduate had been operating Paramount Pictures' motion picture theaters when, in 1949, the Supreme Court held that a company that both produced and exhibited movies was in violation of the antitrust laws. Paramount spun off its theaters and Goldenson bought them.

At about the same time, the FCC ruled that NBC had to divest itself of one of its networks. Lifesaver king Ed Noble bought the Blue Network and renamed it the American Broadcasting Company. In 1953, Leonard bought the struggling ABC network and operated both the theaters and network as a unit. His American Broadcasting Company was the third network in a two-and-a-half network economy and, as Warren Buffett said many years later, "It was a joke until Leonard took it over and made a real network out of ABC." Through hard work, determination, wit and guile, Leonard built a formidable communications empire.

With it all, Goldenson had the personality of a pussycat. He was always "Leonard" to his employees. He was unfailingly cordial with everyone and seemingly never lost his temper. When unpleasant things had to be done, somehow he found someone else in the company to wield the hatchet.

Each problem seemed to him just another interesting challenge. Once I picked him up at Washington National Airport and gave him a rundown of the various legislative heartaches we were having in the Capital. At the end, he nodded, beamed at me, and said, "Yes, Gene. But we're making money!"

Even in 1982, after we lost a bruising legislative battle in which the networks and the Hollywood studios fought over who should control the rights to prime-time programming, Leonard reacted with characteristic understanding. At a company meeting at a resort hotel shortly afterwards, he assured me that I had done the best I could under very difficult circumstances. Then he swatted me affectionately on the rump—like a football coach. If it hadn't happened with both our wives present I would have wondered about that sweet guy.

His wife Isabel, however, was tough and outspoken, often probing into company affairs and literally terrifying some ABC employees. When I attended company meetings where she appeared, she nearly drove ABC staff mad with demands that her and Leonard's rooms needed amenities and facilities that were nowhere to be found.

One ABC employee told me that during an Olympics that was being covered by ABC, she so infuriated the driver of her chauffeured car that he jammed on the parking brake and walked away from the car in the middle of a driveway.

But I got along well with Isabel. Ardently pro-Israel, she was pleased to learn that, at the White House, I had been honorary chairman of the government division of the United Jewish Appeal. She and her husband were founders of United Cerebral Palsy and, in that capacity, she would appear often in Washington to urge more government assistance for vocational rehabilitation. I often accompanied her and listened as patiently as I could to her discussions about health issues and her opinions about the world in general.

One day, she called me from New York and asked if I would set up a lunch for her and the wife of commentator Howard K. Smith at the Madison Hotel. "Gene, would you like to join us?"

I said I would. I went quickly to the hotel's Montpelier restaurant and spoke to the maitre d', whom I knew. "I have this problem. I want to reserve for lunch for my boss's wife," I said, and he smiled knowingly. "I'd like that corner table next to the window, and I want you to assign one very good extra captain to our table. I'll pay for it, but I want him to stand behind Mrs. Goldenson's chair like a footman. Whatever she asks for, he must say yes. No hesitation, no rolling of the eyes, just yes."

At the lunch with Mrs. Goldenson and Mrs. Smith, the footman stood silently behind Mrs. Goldenson's chair. This dish was too cold; back it went and was quickly replaced. Too much draft? Suddenly, no more wind down her back. A spoon was spotted; back came one unsullied. The meal ended without incident.

When we took our leave of Mrs. Smith, Mrs. Goldenson and I got into the chauffeured car that would take us back to the office and she said, "Gene, I've eaten at the Montpelier often before, but this was the first time I ever got decent service."

Howard Cosell

I always liked Howard Cosell. He was the abrasive, controversial ABC sports announcer, best known for broadcasting ABC's "Monday Night Football" with two other announcers. He was so thoroughly hated by some fans that they occasionally threw bricks at their television screens when he was on camera. One even fired a shotgun at the screen in frustrated protest against what Howard himself characterized as "that prototypical New York Jew."

It was hardly anti-Semitism that inspired the rage. It was the confrontational nasal broadcaster who insulted people, sometimes denigrated the sport, and made himself a champion of unpopular causes, such as the right of Cassius Clay to change his name to Mohammed Ali and refuse military service.

But still, I liked him. We first met when ABC was about to broadcast "Monday Night Football" from Washington, and I arranged for our office to hold a pre-game VIP reception at RFK Stadium. I asked all three of the MNF on-air stars to attend, but only Howard arrived, and he quickly made himself the host, chief greeter and principal attraction. Howard was the big draw at those parties, second in popularity only to the food and booze which were so much better than the hot dogs and beer that fans could get in the stands.

As long as Howard had a crowd around him, he was happy. He posed willingly for pictures with fans and was especially gracious with children who wanted to be photographed with the famous man. Howard, who had left the practice of law for broadcasting, was very bright. When on the air, all sports announcers have the benefit of data fed to them from computers. But Cosell also would call up from memory information, such as what number a player had on his shirt when he had played for another team, what he had said to Cosell in the locker room before another game, and what then had happened on the field.

Gene Cowen

"How do you keep all those data in your head?" I asked him one day at lunch. "Do you use a mnemonic system?"

"No, Gene," he deadpanned. "Just a superior mind."

But Howard had his dark side, which kept him anxious and irritable much of the time. He liked to generate controversy, but resented when people struck back. Once, before a game, he took me aside and said, reaching into his jacket pocket, "Gene, look at what this lousy Midwestern bastard said about me." He handed me a clipping from a small newspaper by a sports columnist whom I had never heard of, who had raked Howard over the coals for something he had done or something he was supposed to have done.

"Howard," I said, "you live by the sword, you die by the sword."

"I'm thinking of suing," he muttered. He didn't.

From time to time, he confided that he might run for the U.S. Senate. He didn't do that either. Toward the later 1970s, when he was getting more controversial and more paranoiac, he had bodyguards with him. No one ever attempted to attack him at our parties.

The parties themselves were fun, and I used them for what I considered low-key lobbying—no legislative discussions, just gaining good will by providing an event that the legislators enjoyed. We had as guests Members of Congress, their senior staffs, occasional Cabinet officers, and White House officials. I would tell some of my lobbying colleagues that they were welcome to come to our "in place to be" before Redskins football games, as long as they were accompanied by someone from Congress.

Outside the broadcast booth, Howard often used his wicked sense of humor. In a restaurant, when he spotted someone he knew, he would raise his voice and say something embarrassing about him. Marty Rubenstein, an ABC news vice president, tells the story of the time he entered the ABC cafeteria in New York and heard Cosell, from the other end of the room, say in a booming voice, "You know, there are too many Jews at ABC and the board intends to do something about it. They can't do anything about Goldenson, he's the president. They can't do anything about Erlick, he's general counsel. But Rubenstein, he has to go!"

Marty said he wanted to shrivel up.

Howard would occasionally make unheralded appearances in Washington to testify at sports-related hearings, and that would give me heartburn because I was never sure what he'd say. But once I was involved and it got quite serious. In the early 1970s, ABC began broadcasting boxing matches of the top professional boxers, based on the boxers' ratings as published in *Ring Magazine*. There were allegations that the ratings were fixed and, although ABC had nothing to do with that, we were a prime target for a Congressional committee that wanted to look into the problem.

The House Communications Subcommittee invited ABC to testify (not a subpoena, but a command, nonetheless). The witnesses were to be Jim Spence, senior vice president of ABC Sports, Howard Cosell and Everett Erlick, my boss, who was executive vice president of the parent company, ABC, Inc. Erlick and I briefed the witnesses—what to say, what not to say, when to answer a question, why never to volunteer, and so forth. Briefing is very important for an adversarial proceeding, and a well-prepared witness will usually do well, while one poorly briefed could stumble into a minefield.

Howard was his usual feisty self, promising to "tell it how it is," and generally sounding resentful that anyone should question his integrity. It had me worried.

On the way up to the hearing, I rode in the same car with Howard and his wife Emmie. "Howard," I said, "be aware of one thing. This committee counsel, who will lead most of the questioning, is a very ambitious guy and not very nice—so much so that the members of his own committee dislike him. They resent his trying to take control of their committee. I don't think there's going to be any problem, because neither you nor ABC has done anything wrong, but the counsel is certainly going to make it sound as if someone did something wrong. Don't say anything that will make the committee feel it has to defend its own counsel. Don't volunteer anything that hasn't been asked specifically of you. And roll with any smart-guy remarks he might make in order to set you off."

"Damn it!" he shouted. "I'm not going to let some pissy-assed kid make his reputation by climbing up my back. If I feel like saying something I'm going to tell it just the way it is."

"Howard!" said his wife sharply. "Listen to the man."

Dead silence. He was subdued; I hoped for the best.

At the hearing, our three witnesses were seated as a panel, with Howard flanked by Spence and Erlick. The hearing began with no surprises. Spence testified that ABC used *Ring Magazine* ratings; if they were wrong, we had no way of knowing; we were just as upset as this committee when we discovered the problem.

Then, however, when Jim Spence was winding down and answering a question, Howard thought of something, interrupted, and began expounding loudly about corruption in sports, especially boxing, and on and on at length.

My heart sank. We had warned him of the perils of volunteering. Running off at the mouth is an invitation to further questions, and Lord knew where that might lead.

Suddenly, Howard stopped in mid-sentence. The puzzled committee chairman asked him if that was all. Howard said, yes, that was all, and stayed silent.

The hearing ended. We were all elated and decided we'd gotten away without losing any skin. But I was just as puzzled as the committee chairman. Later, when Erlick and I were alone, I said, "Ev, what happened to Howard? He started running off at the mouth, and then stopped in the middle of a sentence."

"I kicked him," said Erlick.

"You kicked him?"

"Yes. I hit him a good lick in the shin."

#

Howard Cosell left ABC television in 1985 and died ten years later at the age of seventy-seven. Broadcasting is worse off for his departure. ABC Sports, in particular, is much in need of this kind of mouthy irritant. I watch ABC's coverage of auto racing and wonder at its small-bore focus on the sports coverage and disregard for news coverage at the same events.

For instance, during a recent race, an Indy-car crashed into a fence and parts of the wreck hurtled into the stands. The announcer referred in passing to the fact that there may have been some injuries among the spectators, but nothing more, and race coverage continued.

The following day, newspapers reported that several people in the stands had been killed. But ABC cameras, which home in quickly to cover every wreck and every oil spill on the track, didn't focus on the mayhem on the other side of the fence, presumably because of some understanding the network has with the race sponsors.

It's hard to imagine that if Cosell had been in the announcing booth, he would have let the cameramen get away with that monkey-no-see-no-hear-no-speak attitude.

ABC

When I first took over the job as Washington Vice President of ABC, I told my boss, Ev Erlick, "I think I know everything I need to know about this job, but not a thing about television or radio."

"Don't worry," he said. "You'll learn. Read a lot."

So I went to a library and took out about year's worth of copies of *Broadcasting* the bible of the industry. My eyes glazed over after reading about six-months' worth, so I called on Sol Taishoff, the founder, owner and publisher of the magazine, and a dominant and delightful character. Sol, fiercely proprietary about his publication, immediately became one of my good friends because I'd had the foresight to study up on his magazines.

I had an office on Seventeenth Street, with depressing prints of Hogarth's drunks in London's back alleys on the walls, a secretary, and a chauffeured car. But, despite my boasting to Erlick, I really was not sure exactly what I was supposed to do.

This was 1972, a Presidential election year and a year of political conventions. I was ABC's man in charge of "government relations," which meant lobbying. ABC News, of course, was going to cover the two major conventions, so it seemed logical that we should tie on to them in some way. I persuaded our management to let me set up a hospitality suite for Members of Congress and their senior staffs at both conventions. The logical place for such a suite was just off the delegate floor, so legislators who were delegates could stop by for some food and drink.

Easier said than done. I was asking for prime real estate from the scarce amount allocated to ABC News, and the negotiations got tense at times. Invariably, in the years I was with ABC, I had to win two falls out of three with ABC News every time. But we did get our space, a room only about the size of a large family room, with a bar, bartender, a table full of small sandwiches (I told the caterer to give me only "one-handed food," things that Congressmen could grab up, gulp down and leave), and a TV set that was tuned only to ABC.

Shortly after I came to ABC, the White House invited me to serve on the committee that chose its interns. After a committee one day, Steve Hess and I walked back downtown and discussed the Watergate scandal that had just engulfed the Nixon administration. Steve and I had worked together in the White House and left at about the same time. He became a distinguished "President watcher" and, at the Brookings Institution, wrote several books about the historic role of the Presidency.

I asked Steve how the Watergate disaster could have happened.

"Gene, you know I've was with Richard Nixon for a long time," he said. "I was with him when he was Vice President and stayed with him when he ran and lost for governor of California. During that gubernatorial campaign, we'd sit in our hotel room each night, talk over what had happened that day, and he'd often dictate statements that he wanted me to get out later that night. Most of the time I'd do that, but sometimes I'd reread one he had dictated and think, *Phew, he doesn't want to say anything as awful as that!* So I wouldn't put the statement out. If he'd ask me about it later, I'd apologize and get it out quickly. Often, he'd just forgot about it, and the statement never got out, thank God. Richard Nixon needed someone to protect him from himself. But in this White House, he didn't have anybody who was willing to do that, more's the pity."

A Novel: Chapter Sixteen

On April 15, 1972, two cars drove up to a white rambler home in Reston. Six men got out of each car and fell in behind a bald-headed man with a mustache, who apparently was their leader, and who had a document tube under his right arm. He strode up the walk, brushed past the azaleas and rapped on the front door. When John Alden opened it, he nodded once and led his troop into the family room.

When the Leader's laser glare focused on Alden, Alden quickly looked away and motioned everyone into seats.

The Leader said, "Alden, you okay? You're on board? No more reservations?"

Alden nodded.

"Good. You know these five people who you worked with before," he said, motioning to three men in suits, plus one with a seriously scarred face and another in a T-shirt and jeans. Pointing to the sixth man, he said, "And this is Lou Jones. He's new to our effort."

He pointed to a beefy, red-faced man who stared knowingly at Alden, his aborted target of only a few weeks earlier.

As Alden took drink orders, Maria arrived in the room with her daughter behind her.

The Leader looked at Alden and said, "I'd prefer it if your family would give us some privacy."

Alden asked his wife and stepdaughter to leave.

The Leader pulled his chair up to a coffee table and unrolled a large blueprint from the document tube. He put a cigarette into his mouth, patted his pockets, but couldn't find a match.

Jones reached over, lit the cigarette with his last match and dropped the empty matchbook cover into an ashtray.

"We all know why we're here," the Leader said, "so let's get down to business. We have another plumbers' job. This is no different from the entry we made on Ellsberg or any of the others, but bigger. The target is the Democratic National Committee headquarters at the Watergate, tomorrow night."

"What's a water gate?" Jones asked.

"The Watergate is a mix of an office building, an apartment house, and a hotel on Rock Creek Parkway and Virginia Avenue, next to the Kennedy Center," said the Leader. "It's a monstrosity of poured concrete with half-buttresses sticking straight up, as if some one started to build a church and then changed his mind. The Potomac River runs along the west side of Rock Creek Parkway, so you get a nice sunset with the light bouncing off the river. Since that lights up the whole place, nothing should happen until it's full dark. This operation goes down on May 27. Sunset will be 8:26."

The Leader pointed to the blueprint. "Here's the hotel on the north of this complex. I want you to get a room at the hotel on Friday, and then, overnight, the six of you work your way through the garage to the office building."

"You follow the Yellow Brick Road," said one of the suits.

"What yellow brick road?" said the Leader.

"It's really red," said the suit, "but it's a walkway marked in the garage that leads you to the Kennedy Center as you move south. Everyone calls it the Yellow Brick Road—from *The Wizard of Oz*, remember?"

"Oh, for chrissakes!. Would you like us to paint a sign saying, 'Plumbers this way'?"

"I just thought…"

"Stop thinking and listen. Climb up six flights of stairs to O'Brien's office."

"Who's O'Brien?" said Jones.

The Leader looked at him for a moment and then said, "He's the chairman of the Democratic National Committee. That's the object of this exercise. We need to find out what they're planning for the Presidential campaign, who they talk to, where their money is coming from, and so forth. Put devices in O'Brien's office and any nearby offices where they won't be found. But stay alert to Watergate security. There's one guard who makes his rounds from a guard station in the hotel basement about once an hour. He works his way south toward the office building. It takes him about fifteen minutes. So watch him from a secure position and if you start right after he completes his rounds, that ought to give you forty-five minutes to do your thing."

"Is he armed?" Jones asked.

"I don't think so," said the Leader.

"Well, just in case, I'm going to be carrying," said Jones.

"The hell you are!" the Leader shouted. This was the first time he had raised his voice. It ricocheted around the room. Alden shifted in his chair.

"No weapons! Are we clear on that? This is not going to turn into a fire-fight. You're to go in, plant devices, and get out. That's all," said The Leader.

And, thought Alden, *if—God forbid—you're picked up carrying a gun, you're in really deep shit.*

"Any questions?" said The Leader, rolling up the blueprint.

Alden said, "You haven't mentioned me in this."

"Right," said The Leader. "These devices, if they're placed properly and working all right, will transmit to a receiver at the Howard Johnson's Motor Lodge across Virginia Avenue from the Watergate. They'll be monitored by one of our men. He will tape the audio and get the tape back to you, Alden, and you make copies for me."

The Leader stood. "Okay, that's the plan. Thank you everybody. Good night."

#

Maria's voice woke Navigator out of a sound sleep. "Don't say anything. Please, just listen."

He shifted the phone to his other ear and looked at the clock, which said three-thirteen a.m.

"I'm desperately afraid. I'm sure I'm under surveillance. I assume my phone is bugged. Yours may be also. Please meet me at twelve-thirty tomorrow on the north side of 19th and K Streets. We can go somewhere for lunch and talk. Tap on your phone once if you can meet me, twice if you can't. I hate to do this to you, but I need help."

He suspected he knew what this might be about, and he wanted to tell her that he no longer worked for the White House and that he didn't want to get involved. But this was his Maria, and he couldn't turn down her plea for a meeting. So he tapped the phone once and hung up, tried to fall asleep and couldn't.

He rolled out of bed at six a.m., bleary-eyed and irritable, made his own breakfast and read the *Washington Post*. He worked for a television network organization, one with a low tolerance for its officers getting involved in national political campaigns and no tolerance at all for them getting swept up into screwball surveillance operations. Well, maybe he could hear Maria out and tell her that and figure out some way to turn her down.

He was at his office by eight, read his mail, glanced at the clock, dictated some letters, glanced at the clock again, returned a few phone calls and, at noon, he left the office and walked four blocks to 19th and K Streets. He was early, so he circled around, looking to see if he recognized anybody or could find Maria. He wondered again at all the secrecy, saw nothing unusual except a man in a sandwich board labeled, "Defend Men's Rights," refused the pamphlet the man offered him, and then saw Maria on the northeast corner.

She smiled slightly when he saw him, kissed him on the cheek, held tightly onto his hand and led him across K Street and down a flight of stairs into an underground shopping mall. She maneuvered him inside the door and stood there for several minutes, looking closely at everyone who came in. Then she went down a corridor to a ladies room, motioned to him to stand outside the door and went inside.

He saw a bag lady in a tattered dress go into the ladies room. Then two teenagers, giggling about some guy who had been trying to "hit on" one of them, but no one else before Maria walked briskly out, took him by the hand again and led him up a different flight of stairs that brought them out onto L Street.

They walked past three doors and entered a restaurant with a sign pasted in its window that said, "Today – Opera – Five

My Life, A Novel

Voices – Four Musicians," and waited for a young woman in a peasant dress to seat them.

She pointed them toward a small table a couple of rows back from the tiny stage. But before they were seated, Maria shook her head and asked to sit at another table further back, between tables already occupied. As they sat down, Maria's wallet and makeup spilled out of her purse onto the floor. As she gathered them up, she looked up under each chair and the table and ran her hands surreptitiously under most of the surfaces.

After a waitress left them with a menu, he smiled and said, "Can I talk now?"

"Wait until the music starts," she said.

Four musicians in well-worn suits and a young blonde woman in a glittery blue gown trooped out onto the stage. The singer, a pleasant soprano, began with an aria from *La Traviata*.

Maria, holding the menu in front of her mouth, said, "I'm not crazy."

"I didn't think you were."

"This situation has gotten out of hand."

"You mean with your husband and his loony friends?"

"Yes," she said. "But it's much more than that." Then she told him of the meeting at her house. "Navigator, these people are involved in Nixon's Committee to Re-Elect the President. I'm sure they are doing bad things. They don't trust me, so they have bugged our phone and our house, and they follow me often. But that's not the worst of it. They've got John deeply involved, and now Anna is helping him. She's the one who told me some of these details. That's really what's killing me. If anything happened to that girl, I'd die."

"Where are they doing these bad things?" he said.

"Anna tells me that this crew of theirs—they call themselves 'plumbers'—are planning to plant bugging devices in the Democratic National Committee headquarters at the Watergate. Then someone at Howard Johnson's across the street will listen to what they get, tape it, and give it to John to make copies for the people at the Nixon re-election committee.

Gene Cowen

John is going to be talking to one of the plumbers who will be carrying a walkie-talkie, and he enlisted Anna to help him monitor police radio calls from his operations room in our house."

A tenor joined the soprano and they began the duet from *The Merry Widow*. It was obvious why Maria had picked a noisy place like this and why she was covering her mouth with a menu. But he suspected that a professional bugging specialist would laugh at those precautions, and could screen out extraneous noise and pick up conversation. He was too concerned about Maria's daughter being caught up in this scheme however, to bother about who else, if anyone, might be listening to their conversation.

"When is this all going down?"

"I don't know. I only know what I get from Anna."

"Why on earth would Anna let herself get involved in this?" he said.

"As I told you before, she thinks she has some obligation to her stepfather, and so she's trying to stay involved to keep him out of trouble."

"That's absurd," he said, as the singers launched into something from *The Barber of Seville*. "All she's doing is getting involved in something that might get her into a terrible jam. Should I talk to her?"

"It won't do any good. If she won't listen to me, she won't listen to you." Her eyes glistened. She fingered the cameo around her neck and looked around the room.

"Maria, look," he said. "Maybe I can talk to John. Maybe...oh, I don't know what, but maybe I can do something. Let me think overnight, and then I'll make a call or two."

Maria pressed his hand against her face. He paid the bill without either of them having eaten anything and they left separately.

On the way out of the restaurant, he put some coins into a newspaper vending machine on the corner and tucked a copy of the *Washington Post* under his arm.

At the office, he picked a Peterson pipe off his pipe rack. It was a shiny burl with good grain, a straight stem and the

My Life, A Novel

traditional Peterson bit—hard rubber and heavily reinforced to keep teeth-grinders like himself from biting through. With a pocket knife, he scraped out of the bowl the charred carbon that had accumulated after many smokings and knocked it out onto a cork knob in the center of his pipe ashtray.

He opened the can of Walnut tobacco on his desk—not very exotic tobacco, but his favorite after trying probably half the other mixes on the market—and slowly filled the pipe. Then he turned a lighted Zippo lighter sideways over the pipe's bowl and drew in deeply. Good taste, good smell, and soothing smoke curling up from the bowl. That should help him think. Lord knew, there was plenty to think about.

Alden, the idiot, had gone right back to cavorting with his loony buddies. Only, this time, the stakes were higher and he had Anna involved. Penetrating the DNC was serious stuff. In campaigns, people in all political parties often got involved in the "intelligence work" of spying on the other side. That occasionally developed into the more serious high jinks that some people called "dirty tricks"—planting hecklers in an opponent's audience, doctoring photographs, distributing fake literature to make the other side look bad—none of which was very nice and some of which was illegal. But none were hanging crimes, and they were seldom prosecuted. About the worst that usually happened was that the offended party would file a complaint with the weak-kneed Fair Campaign Practices Committee, would generate one day's publicity, and then nothing at all would happen.

But here, Maria was telling him about these characters' planning serious violations of law: breaking-and-entering, bugging, wire-tapping and Lord knows what else. He didn't give a damn about Alden. That lame-brain could rot in jail as far as he was concerned. But Anna was in real peril. And it was Maria who was asking for help.

On the other hand, with the job he had now with a broadcasting network, he had to walk on little cat feet and not leave any footprints. But that didn't mean he couldn't talk to Alden and maybe scare the shit out of him. Alden scared easily

Gene Cowen

and, who knows, maybe that would help. He'd call first thing in the morning and see if he couldn't head off some of this.

He knocked out his pipe, opened the *Washington Post* and began to read just below a dateline which said it was Friday, June 16, 1972.

My Life, A Novel

A Novel: Chapter Seventeen

    The art deco clock in the Watergate Hotel restaurant told Lou Jones that it was ten p.m. He and his five compatriots had just finished a leisurely lobster dinner and were lighting up cigars and cigarettes. No one was drinking. They were dressed in the business suits you'd expect them to be wearing at the posh restaurant, and they seemed to be in no hurry. But they kept glancing at the clock on the wall.
    At eleven, they paid their bill and left. Scarface took an elevator to the basement. The other five took another elevator to the second floor and entered a room.
    There they opened valises and from them carefully put into one attaché case several voiced-activated devices that were capable of picking up and transmitting all talk, including telephone conversations. Into another case went lock-picks, door jimmies and $2,300 in hundred-dollar bills.
    Into another, went forty rolls of unexposed film, two 35 mm cameras and three pen-sized tear gas guns.
    Jones clipped a walkie-talkie onto his belt, turned his back on the others and slipped a Smith & Wesson .38 caliber pistol into the belt, then buttoned the jacket over it before he turned around. The bulges looked as if they were all part of the walkie-talkie.
    Then they sat around smoking until the phone rang at twelve-fifty a.m. and Scarface reported from the basement, "Smokey the Bear just completed his rounds."
    They rose, picked up the attaché cases, rode down the elevator to the garage, and walked purposefully but slowly along the "Yellow Brick Road," as if they were businessmen on their way to their cars.
    The garage was empty of people and their footsteps echoed as they moved south. Ventilation was poor and Jones said he thought he could smell cigarette smoke. When they got to the

stairwell at the foot of the office building, all six pulled on rubber surgical gloves and Jones taped open the door. It was 1:01 a.m.

They climbed the stairs, and each time they got to a closed door, Jones taped it open. At the sixth floor, the stairwell led directly to a door that said, "Democratic National Committee" and something cheery and forward-looking about the George McGovern campaign for President.

One man pushed a jimmy into the door latch, which popped open as if it were the top of a beer bottle. "These clowns are living in a dream world," he said. "They know nothin' about security."

Inside the office, they opened some file drawers, looked over papers and began photographing.

Jones said it was about time for the security guard to make another of his rounds and that he was going to watch from a secure position to see what he did when he got to the entryway of the office building. He walked down the stairs.

#

Joe Hall hated his job. Ever since he was a kid, he had wanted to be a policeman, but after high school, he'd tried twice and failed twice to pass the District of Columbia police exams. Well, he had never really been a good student and, what with one distraction and another, he had not applied himself to the tests. So he'd had to settle for security guard duty. But it paid reasonably well for a twenty-four-year-old and he got a uniform with a patch that said "Watergate Security." *Better*, he thought, *than guard duty in a prison.*

But the hours! Eleven p.m. to six a.m. The nights seemed never to end, and all he had to do was walk from the Watergate Hotel, punch his security key into a clock in the basement garage, then follow the "Yellow Brick Road" that was really red to the apartment building where he punched in again, go to the stairwell at the bottom of the office building, punch in again, all through the night. It could drive a man to drink, which he did a

My Life, A Novel

little of, or to smoke, which he did too much of. He pulled a cigarette out of his pack of Chesterfields and lit it with a match.

As he looked for someplace to throw the spent match, he saw that the door to the stairwell had been taped open. *Damn those cleaning people!* he thought. *They're too lazy to hold a frigging door open when they come through with their trash.* Last week they had put a wedge under the door and this week it was tape.

He peeled the tape off, closed the door, and moved back toward the hotel. His watch said it was 1:35 a.m. on a boring Saturday morning, and he still had more than four hours to go.

#

Jones stood in the deep shadow of a support post and watched Hall remove the tape. Once Hall was well on his way back west toward the hotel, Jones taped the door open again and started on his way back to the sixth floor. He pulled out the walkie-talkie and checked in with John Alden.

#

Security guard Hall made it halfway back across the garage to the hotel, reached into his shirt pocket, and couldn't find his cigarettes. "Damn," he said out loud and tried to remember where he might have left them.

He got all the way back to the stairwell entry to the office building when he saw two things: his cigarettes and the door that he had untaped, newly retaped. He broke into a run for his guard office in the hotel and called the Washington, DC Police Department at 1:47 a.m.

#

Jones was speaking on his walkie-talkie to Alden, filling him in about the operation, telling him how stupid the Democratic National Committee was about security, when Alden suddenly interrupted: "Jesus Christ! The police just got a call!"

"What kind of a call?" said Jones.

"My daughter is listening to a police scanner radio, and there's a report of a break-in at Watergate," said a quavery Alden. "Mayday! Mayday! Jones, tell everyone to get the hell out of there."

"Okay, will do," said Jones, but he walked down the stairs, not up to the sixth floor. He was carrying a gun and had to get the hell out of there. If he went to the sixth floor, he'd be trapped along with the others. He moved quickly into the basement and exited south, where it faced the Kennedy Center. As he passed a waste can, he pulled the gun from his waistband and dropped it into the can.

He was walking along Virginia Avenue by the time an unmarked police car, with its light flashing but no siren blowing, pulled up to the Watergate Hotel. A block further on, in front of the George Washington University Hospital, he hailed a cab.

#

Three District policemen met Security Guard Hall at his guard station and accompanied him through the garage, south along the Yellow Brick Road to the office building. Hall silently pointed to the tape on the stairwell door. The policemen nodded and motioned to him to stay right there.

Then they drew their guns, climbed the stairs and followed the trail of taped doors to the Democratic National Committee. They pushed open the jimmied door, saw some movement and shouted that they were police and no one was to move.

One man jumped up from behind a desk, saw the guns, put his hands in the air and cried, "Don't shoot!"

My Life, A Novel

A Novel: Chapter Eighteen

On Saturday, June17, Navigator called Alden several times but got no answer and wondered why he couldn't get through. On Sunday, he found out why. The *Washington Post* carried a story with a headline, "5 Held in Plot to Bug Democrats' Office Here." It described the break-in and reported that five men were charged with attempted burglary, possession of implements of crime, and attempted interception of telephone and other conversations.

He tried again for the next several days, but there was still no answer at the Alden residence. On Friday, he read that the police were looking for another Watergate burglar, who was thought to have gotten away, and they were believed to be questioning a White House cryptographer and his stepdaughter, who might have been involved in the conspiracy.

He immediately got into his car and drove to the little white rambler in Reston. The woman who opened the door looked haggard and her eyes were red-rimmed. Maria was forty-six years old and looked like sixty. She brushed her fingers through her disheveled hair.

"You didn't answer your phone," he said.

"I've been afraid to," she said. "It's either been the news people or the White House or the Nixon committee, and I don't want to talk to any of them. Navigator, do you realize what happened? Anna may go to jail. John may go to jail."

He asked where Alden was, and she led him into her husband's operations room. Alden was sitting in the chair from which, only a few days before, he had been conducting his surveillance operations. He was staring into space. His belt was unbuckled; his shirt, unbuttoned, hung loosely over his shoulders. He had a blanket over his lap. A TV was tuned into a daytime soap opera, but the sound was turned down. Alden had a bottle of liquor at his elbow and a half-empty glass of what had earlier been Scotch on the rocks before the rocks melted so that it looked like he was drinking a urine specimen.

Alden registered their appearance, then turned to face a wall. Discarded newspapers were stacked at his feet. The telephone had been pulled out of its jack on the wall. Here and there was the detritus of meals eaten over several days and only fitfully cleaned up.

"We don't know what to do, Navigator," Maria said.

"Have you talked to a lawyer?"

"No."

"What do the police say?" he asked.

"They have questioned John several times. They know that he had had some contact with the burglars. They got a warrant and confiscated his scanner radio. They suspect that he was in touch with the break-in crowd. They've talked to Anna, and she admitted listening to the radio at the time of the police call," she said.

"Why on earth did she do that?"

"Because she insists that there was nothing wrong in doing that. But they're threatening to charge her as an accomplice in the break-in."

Navigator looked at Alden. "What are you going to do?" he asked. He watched as Alden picked up the bottle and added some Scotch to his watered-down drink, and then he walked over to Alden and knocked the glass out of his hand and took the bottle away.

"Well," said Alden, "have you got an idea what I should do?"

"It would help if you would tell me what happened on Saturday morning at the Watergate."

"No," said Alden. He got up, holding his trousers around his waist with one hand, and reached into a file drawer for another bottle of Scotch.

Navigator walked over to Alden and kicked the drawer shut on his hand. Alden grabbed his hand and began to cry.

Navigator pulled Alden up out of his chair and pushed him against the wall. "You're in deep shit, Alden, and you're much in need of a friend. I don't see many other people standing in line waiting to be your friend. You might not like me, and I don't

My Life, A Novel

think all that much of you. But tell me what happened and I might be able help."

Alden thought about that for a long while, shook his head to clear it a little and finally, resigned, said, "All right." He described what he knew of the break-in, who was there, how he'd tried to alert them to the police and how everything seemed to fall apart for reasons he could not fathom.

"Who were you talking to on the walkie-talkie?" he asked Alden.

"Lou Jones."

Jesus!, thought Navigator. *How did that bastard get back into the picture? If they were working with Jones, no wonder this turned into a disaster."* I didn't read about him being picked up," he said.

"He wasn't," said Alden. "He got away. The son-of-a-bitch never got the others out. He was saving his own ass."

"Do you know where he is?" he said.

"Yeah, I might. He left a matchbook cover here at the house the last time he was here. It was from the Charleton, a motel on Rhode Island Avenue."

"Okay," he said. "Now I maybe have an idea."

Alden looked blank. He was beyond caring.

"First, get yourselves a good lawyer."

"What could a lawyer do for me now?" Alden said.

"Let him negotiate a deal for you—a trade-off."

"What kind of trade-off?" Alden asked.

"You trade them Lou Jones for you," he said.

"Jones?" said Alden, suddenly coming to life. "That guy's a killer. I'm afraid of a guy like that."

"Are you prepared to go to jail?" he said. "You have nothing else. Trade in Jones and see what a good lawyer can extract."

Alden looked around the room, nodded, got up slowly, and began cleaning up the mess.

#

D.C. Police Sergeant Bruce McIntyre walked into the prison and asked to see one of the men who was serving a three-year

Gene Cowen

sentence for his participation in the Watergate break-in. McIntyre hoped that one of the perpetrators might have seen Jones pick up a gun that night, but so far, the other four conspirators he'd talked to either hadn't seen or didn't want to admit it.

A man in loose-fitting prison garb was brought into an interview room and McIntyre sat down opposite him.

"We've got your missing friend," he said. "Lou Jones. We picked him up, and we've got a witness who'll testify that he was with you in the Watergate. So we've got him there, but we want something more. We found a gun with his fingerprints in a trash can about a block away from Watergate, but we're trying to place that gun with him at the break-in. Carrying an unregistered gun when committing a felony should add five to ten years to his sentence. Can you help us with that?"

The man said nothing, waiting to hear what the deal was.

"Some friend you got there in Jones," said McIntyre. "He got the alert from Alden that the police were coming, but he just left to save his own ass, and then let the rest of you to take the fall. Can you help or can't you? I don't have all day."

"Why should I?"

"Because you want justice done," said McIntyre.

"Cut the shit."

"I can recommend that your sentence be commuted."

"Listen," said the man. "I watched Jones turn his back while he was putting a walkie-talkie into his belt, and I saw him put that Smith & Wesson into his belt. But I'm not going to testify to that unless I get something more than your damn recommendation. I want a firm deal with the district attorney to take time off my sentence. I have a lawyer. I'll put you in touch with him. Let's see what we can work out. If the deal is solid enough, I'll testify."

McIntyre left the prison and drove back to the white rambler in Reston. Maria, grim-faced, let him in and sat in a corner while Alden and he talked.

"Alden, here's the deal," he said. "I got what I wanted on that gun, and I'm depending on you to testify. But all I can offer you is that we won't prosecute your stepdaughter."

Maria heaved an audible sigh of relief.

"What kind of a deal is that?" Alden shouted. "I thought I was going to get something out of this."

"You will," said McIntyre. "We'll hold off with your prosecution until you come up with something more."

"More what?" said Alden, perspiring and still shouting. "What the hell do you want me to say?"

"Alden, you know more about this deal than you've revealed so far. So, think and come up with the rest of it, and then we'll see about whether we prosecute you for the conspiracy we all know you were part of."

"Thank you, sergeant," said Maria, trying not let the deal on Anna fall apart. "We'll be further in touch."

McIntyre left, smiling to himself. He had no idea whether Alden was holding back information or not, but he liked sweating a bastard like that.

#

Jones was convicted and sentenced to eight years in prison.

In the 1972 election, notwithstanding all the scandal, Richard Nixon was re-elected with a handsome majority. But on March 23, 1973, when Judge John Sirica was sentencing several of the convicted conspirators, he read a letter from one of them, which charged that the White House had been conducting a cover-up to conceal its connection with the break-in and that the defendants had been urged by the White House to plead guilty and remain silent.

By May, the focus of the widening investigation shifted to the U. S. Senate, where the Select Committee on Presidential Campaign Activities began public hearings.

Navigator climbed into his Chevy and drove to the white rambler in Reston. Maria greeted him at the door with a hug, and they sat and talked in the family room.

"Is Anna okay?" he said.

"Yes, dear, thanks to your suggestion. Jones is serving an eight-year sentence, and the District Attorney agreed not to press charges against Anna. But John is still sweating. The police keep asking him to come up with more information, preferably something that might tie this crime directly to President Nixon, and he doesn't know anything more. What else can he tell them?"

"Can I talk to him?" he said.

They walked together into Alden's now-denuded operations room. The walls had the shadowy outlines of all the electronic and photographic equipment that was now gone. Alden hadn't bothered to cover the pock marks of the screw holes in the walls, but he had moved another few chairs and a desk into the space, giving it the look of a shabby den.

Alden, who had never been very heavy, looked as if he had lost fifteen pounds. His hair was gray and disheveled and his face drawn." I'll give you this, Navigator," he said. "We were able to get a deal to keep Anna out of jail. But you seem to have forgotten about me. What do we do now?"

"Just what the hell do you do in the White House, really? You remember, I didn't want to hear about it when you first mentioned it. I think it's time you gave me a few details."

"I service the machinery that tapes conversations in the President's offices," Alden said.

"Which conversations?"

"All of them," said Alden. "In 1971, we installed the machinery in the Oval Office and the Cabinet Room of the White House, in the President's office in the Executive Office Building, and on four of the President's personal phones."

"Holy God!" he said. "Who turns them on?"

"They're voice-activated," said Alden. "Any time anyone speaks, the tape starts running. About all I do is install fresh tapes every morning, check the ones that I had just taken off, and then file them by date. As I told you, it's pretty humdrum, boring work and I was looking for something more exciting to do."

"And Nixon knows about this?"

"The taping? Of course, he does," said Alden.

"You mean, when I was in his office in the EOB and he asked me to get involved in your surveillance activities, all that was on the tape?"

"I guess so," said Alden. "I don't listen to the tapes. I just service them."

Navigator began going over in his mind what he had said at that meeting. Nixon had been talking about those who were "trying to bring down this government" and having a "few people who keep their eyes and ears open and do surveillance." All he could remember doing was nodding his head and agreeing to work with Alden. Didn't sound to him like a crime, but it bothered him nonetheless.

"And is this taping still going on?" he asked.

"Oh, yes," said Alden. "But what does this have to do with my problem?"

"And who do you report to?" he said, disregarding the question.

"To the Secret Service, which is in charge of the machinery, and occasionally to Alex Butterfield, an Assistant to the President."

He looked at Alden and smiled. "You've got a pretty good lawyer?"

"Well, he was able to get Anna out of a jam when I agreed to testify against Lou Jones, but he hasn't been able to come up with much since then."

"You've got something for him," he said.

"About this taping?"

"Yes. You can trade them the World's Fair for your puny little ass."

"Why the hell should the police be interested in the taping?" said Alden.

"Because," he said, "the Senate investigating committee is digging into evidence that might tie Watergate directly to the President. Now you're telling me that you can steer them to the ultimate evidence. For them, it would be as if they were flies on the wall, listening to what Nixon knew and when he knew it. If they had taped the President surreptitiously, it would have been a crime. But if Nixon was taping himself, the investigators might have found the smoking gun. Have your lawyer put together a meeting between the police and the Senate investigators and

Gene Cowen

see if they can get you off the hook in exchange for information on this taping."

A week later they did, and on June 13, 1973, Senate investigators asked Alex Butterfield to tell them about the taping at the White House. He did, and the rest of the scandal began unfolding. On August 8, 1973, Nixon announced his resignation. He left office the following morning.

My Life: Chapter Nineteen

Grassroots Lobbying

Although I said during my interview for the ABC job that, except for broadcasting, I thought I knew everything I needed to know about the lobbying job, I really had to start by reinventing the wheel. My predecessor on the job was a former head of affiliate relations who knew very little about the nation's capital and did little.

ABC, as a network, had a lot of prestige in Washington and virtually nothing else. Members of Congress respond to their own constituents, and reaching them involves grassroots activity. ABC had hardly any constituents of Members of Congress; we had a handful of people running the network in New York and even fewer in Los Angeles, and that was all. Company officials rarely made any contributions to Congressional campaigns, and ABC had a news department that, in the course of doing its proper business, frightened the hell out of many legislators. ("The only time we get on your news is when we're in trouble," said one Congressman.)

So I started building a grassroots lobbying organization. The most obvious candidates were those who received the same kind of paychecks I did: employees of the five television and seven radio stations owned by ABC. I set up a program in which the station managers would come to Washington once each year. We'd invite their Senators and Representatives to dinner. Those who couldn't make dinner, we'd invite to a lunch, and for all the rest, we'd schedule morning and afternoon appointments.

It was low-key lobbying. We'd tell the legislators about the news and public affairs the stations were programming in their constituencies, ask the legislators if there was anything they'd like to tell us, shake hands and leave.

The Members of Congress liked the contacts. It put a human face on the station and gave them a name to call if they had any questions or complaints—and they often had plenty of both. And, of course, it also gave us the warm press-the-flesh contacts that I needed. When real legislative problems arose—vote for this, vote against that—I or people who worked with me in Washington would do the heavy work. (I would occasionally tell Senators and Representatives that ABC was concerned ninety percent with what was happening on the tube and ten percent with what was happening on the Potomac.)

At first, the station managers grumbled about being forced to take time away from their jobs, but eventually most came to enjoy meeting the legislators and getting a point of view somewhat different from their obsessive focus on meeting quarterly budgets.

But after those five television and seven radio stations that ABC owned outright, there was a lot more that needed to be done. ABC had more than two hundred stations affiliated with the network. Those were stations which the network did not own, but which, rather, had a contractual relationship to broadcast network programs.

A television network doesn't broadcast directly to your home. It "feeds" its programs to its affiliates, which in turn broadcast into their own viewing areas. That's how you see programs that you receive over the air. Those affiliates, owned by other entities, have a relationship somewhat similar to that of a Chevrolet dealer and General Motors. GM provides the product and they sell it.

In broadcasting, it's a love-hate relationship, in which the affiliates depend on their supplier and therefore have a concern about its health. But they also wrestle constantly with the "behemoth in New York" about what programs they must carry and how much money changes hands in the process.

I figured that if we could get our affiliates working on our side most of the time, it would more than offset those times when they opposed us. So I encouraged our affiliates to organize, and I advised, pleaded and cajoled them about Congressional issues which should concern both the affiliates and the network. Eventually, we had a good, aggressive, affiliate government-relations organization.

Finally, there was the whole rest of the broadcast industry. By virtue of my position at ABC, I had a seat on the board of the National Association of Broadcasters, which represented virtually all television and radio stations in America. Getting those folks to be on our side was a high-wire act, but even so, we often succeeded.

My Life, A Novel

Eventually, ABC was pleased at how well the Congressional relations programs worked to its advantage.

It worked—that is, until about the time I retired in 1990. Then, the affiliated stations decided that, on many issues, their business interests diverged from the network's, and they opposed us too often and too effectively. My senior management waggled fingers at me for "creating a Frankenstein."

Retirement

I retired twice. In 1990, I retired as Washington vice president of Capital Cities/ABC, and then returned as a consultant and retired again in 1993. The first departure brought lots of encomiums, parties and bittersweet farewells. The second was more subdued, but both times Thomas Murphy, the delightful CEO of Cap Cities, came to the observance.

In my adult life, I've done a lot of different things, but for the past forty-nine years, most of it has involved working with the U.S. Congress—covering Congress as a reporter, working for members of the House and the Senate, being Deputy Assistant for Congressional Relations in the Nixon White House, chief lobbyist for a broadcast network company, and even now, director of legislative affairs for a non-profit organization. By now, I should be disenchanted with that circus on Capitol Hill. But, in reality, I love the place.

There is a certain flawed majesty about Congress, to which Americans send people from their midst to represent their concerns. Congress has its barnacles—personal scandals and sins of commission and omission—but fundamentally, it is largely made up of decent hard-working men and women who fight like hell to get elected and then try to do their best in the unwieldy structure of a national legislature. It often takes a lot of pushing, persuading and conniving to get a consensus, but somehow it works and laws eventually do pass.

Shortly after I got to Washington in 1952, I wrote a thesis for my masters degree in history about a nineteenth-century politician in Syracuse, N.Y. I am struck by the similarity in the basic principles of American public life back then and today. In those early days of the

Republic—with no radio, no television and no Internet—politicians used street rallies, torch-light parades and pamphlets. But they still made special appeals to minorities, such as the Irish who were building the Erie Canal, advertised heavily in newspapers, tried to deliver blocks of their supporters to the polls, and provided precinct workers with "walking-around money," in case some voters needed further persuading.

Today, as in those days, many people wonder: 1) Do politicians listen to the people who elected them? 2) Do they care about their jobs? 3) Or are they just a corrupt bunch of bastards? The answers are: 1) yes, 2) yes, and 3) only a few.

Here are some principles and people that I believe influence a Member of Congress:

First Principle—by a long shot—is that politicians are influenced most by what they hear from their *own* constituents, the people who put them into office and who can vote them right out again. For instance: When I was working for Senator Scott, he was visited one day by a delegation of irate Pennsylvania chicken farmers. Government farm subsidies had driven up the price of grain, which was feed for their chickens, and they wanted something done about it. I stood in the back of the room while they complained bitterly and urged that Scott "put those people in jail."

I didn't laugh there, but I did when I met with the Senator immediately afterward. "Wow!" I said. "Don't they know you're not going to put people in jail?"

"No, they don't, Gene," he said, "and we can't, but we are going to do *something*, aren't we?"

We did: the Senator introduced a bill to eliminate the grain subsidies (which went nowhere).

The point here is that, no matter how irrational a constituent's suggestion may be, if he feels strongly enough about it to come to Washington to meet with his Senator, the legislator better do something, anything.

Another for instance: in 1970, while I was still working for Senator Scott, he lent me to Congressman Charles (Mac) Mathias to be second-in-command of Mathias' successful campaign for the Senate. By 1972, I was in the Nixon White House and drew the assignment of finding out why Mathias ("your friend, Gene") was not supporting the President's nominee for the Supreme Court.

"Mac," I said, "the President has sent up Judge Carswell's name for the high court, and you tell us you can't support him. Dammit, my friend, if you are unimpressed by the choice, doesn't the President rate at least as much consideration as those people in the opposition who are importuning you to vote against Carswell?"

Mathias put his arm around my shoulder, and said, "Gene, you worked on my campaign. You know the people who supported me. Let's go down the list: organized labor, Jews, other minorities, doves on the Vietnam war. Would any of those people want me to vote for that turkey?" He voted against Carswell, and so did enough other Senators to defeat the nomination.

The point is that if a Senator's constituents are strongly in opposition—and they let him know it—even the President of the United States does not have enough clout to turn the Senator around.

Second Principle that motivates politicians: Money. Running for federal office can cost millions of dollars, and the law permits a candidate to raise private funds to finance the campaign. You can contribute a certain limited amount of money directly to a candidate, give money through a political action committee, or give your money through a political party. There's no question that if you are a contributor to a Member of Congress running for re-election, he will pay serious attention to your entreaties, maybe even vote the way you ask.

But let's go back to the First Principle. If I were asked to solve a Lady-and-the-Tiger riddle, in which I had to decide who would have more influence with a politician: 1) outsiders who contributed money or 2) constituents who turned out in force to meet with the legislator, I'd pick the arm-waving constituents every time.

Third Principle: Party Leaders. Yes, the President of the United States and Congressional party leaders often prevail on major votes. That's largely because they appeal to party loyalty or have something important to offer, such as a bridge or a courthouse in the legislator's district. Or they can threaten to withhold some of those things. But, again, those leaders prevail with a legislator only when there is not a tidal wave of constituent opinion going the other way.

Fourth Principle: Strongly held views. Obviously, if a Senator or Representative feels very, very strongly about a subject, he or she will vote that way. But think about yourself. How many issues do you feel very, *very* strongly about? I don't mean your getting annoyed at a story on television about the lack of funding for an eldercare center, or reading in the papers that the price of stamps is going up again. I mean intensely felt issues. There are really not that many. Perhaps abortion, or gun control, or whether we go to war. And most members of Congress will have expressed themselves long before about their own strongly held beliefs and probably got elected to office in the first place because most of their voters agreed with them.

Fifth Principle: lobbyists. These are people who are paid by someone to advocate an issue. They're not all bad (I was one). They represent such benign organizations as the American Red Cross, public broadcasting and churches and universities, all the way to such controversial folks as the tobacco industry and the National Rifle Association. Just as in Congress itself, there are some bad apples, but most of them are decent hard-working people. They argue their case, and the legislator then votes with them or against them, depending largely on the persuasiveness of their argument.

Sixth Principle: the tree that falls in the forest. This is a vital qualifier to the First Principle—that politicians are influenced most by what they hear from their constituents. If a tree fell in the forest and no one saw it fall and no one heard it fall, *it didn't fall*. No matter how strongly you feel on a subject, if your Congressperson doesn't hear from you and lots of other yous, if you and they are not writing, e-mailing, visiting him or her, *then the tree didn't fall*. I'm sorry to have to say this, but you are to blame. You have not made the politician aware of the strength of feeling in the constituency, and you have left the door open for the money, party leaders and lobbyists to come marching in and influence the vote.

The legendary Speaker of the House Sam Rayburn is supposed to have indoctrinated freshmen Congressmen with the following advice about answering mail: "If you get a letter from a contributor, you should answer it within a week. If you get a letter from a businessman in your district, answer it by the next day. But if you get a letter written on a piece of brown paper bag from a old woman in your district who said she hasn't gotten her Social Security checks for two months, you'd better answer it while you're still holding it in your left hand."

Gene Cowen

A Novel: Chapter Nineteen

It was a beautiful November day in 1981, and Washington's summer heat and humidity were well past. The trees were in full color and Navigator was looking forward to one of his catch-up weekend days with Maria. They stayed in touch by spending a Sunday together every few months, sometimes at a movie, sometimes having brunch, sometimes driving around, and often just walking in a pleasant place and talking about what had happened since they last played-catch up.

He was now driving a year-old Oldsmobile, a testimonial to his better-paying job and his new-found sense of affluence. Maria leaned back against the headrest and watched Rock Creek Parkway roll past the windshield as if it were a travel documentary. Her hair had been going gray for years now. She was fifty-five years old, an attractive "American lady," with the same bright eyes and animated face that he always enjoyed looking into. Maria's firm body showed that she worked to keep it that way, but she could do nothing about her Mediterranean hips, even though most men would have told her that it added to her muted sexuality.

They talked idly about Iran's releasing the American hostages and marveled over the fact that President Reagan had survived an attempted assassination outside the Washington Hilton Hotel. He sensed that she had something else on her mind, but he had learned to wait patiently until it surfaced of its own buoyancy.

As they approached a shaded picnic area with an empty parking lot, he slowed the car and looked over at Maria. She nodded and he pulled in and parked.

They got out and walked slowly along the footpath. She put her hand lightly on his arm. The trees in Rock Creek Park were a patchwork of red, orange and brown leaves that spread themselves into an arbor over their heads. Dappled sunlight played on the ground and the tree trunks tiger-striped the brown leaves.

Navigator picked up a small rock and idly tossed it into the bushes ahead of them. A squirrel, who had stopped gathering nuts and was observing them suspiciously, dashed off through some ivy and hid behind a tree trunk.

"Navigator," she said, "Did you see what he did?"

"He or she," he said.

"Don't do that," Maria said. "I'm serious."

He put on his serious face and listened for whatever it was that was going to come bubbling to the surface.

"That squirrel could be you," she said. He just listened. "That was poison ivy he ran through. A squirrel can go through things like that that are dangerous to us, and it doesn't bother him at all. That's like you. You can go through all kinds of things, and they don't bother you. But if it were me, and I went through poisonous leaves like that, I'd certainly come down with a hellova rash."

He still said nothing, but they stopped walking and he looked intently at her.

"That's the story of our lives, you know," she said. "How long have we known each other—thirty-six years? In all that time, you have survived, grown, even prospered. You've gone through a war and didn't die."

"I told you, I can't die or the world would end," he said.

"Stop that," she said, her face flushing. "You promised me once you wouldn't say that again."

"Until I can get a star to move."

"Yes. Now let me get back to what I'm trying to say," she said.

He took her hand and nodded.

"What I'm trying to say is that you have survived all that time, and I have come down with one case of poison ivy after another. No matter what I've tried over the years, I just seem to have walked into trouble. So I've decided that was because I once made a big mistake."

"I thought we were going to forget about what you were doing when I met you in Rome."

"No. That's not the mistake I mean. Do you remember the second time we met at my house?" she said.

"That was in 1945," he said. "I was too young to remember."

She laughed, but it was covering up something else. "I said I wanted to marry someone and get out of Italy with my daughter, but you were not the right guy. Do you remember that?" She looked into his eyes. "That was my mistake. You *were* the right guy, and I was too dumb to know it."

The squirrel decided he was now safe and resumed his hunt for nuts. A sparrow swooped down and landed on a branch in front of them. A few more leaves fluttered down. And they walked silently.

"Maria, my very dear friend," he said. "It was not to be."

"I suppose so," she said, looking off to the right as if there were something to see there while she prepared to say what came next. "But you know I love you, don't you?"

"And I love you, babe, but maybe not the same way," he said. "You're my fantasy girl. Someone I love knowing. Someone I can be with and share experiences with, dream with. We're good friends or, better yet, *compares*, an Italian word you taught me a long time ago. Good buddies, who can turn to each other."

"Well," she said, "that's another thing. I told you about being a *compare* when I said I owed you and would always be there to help you. But, dammit, I've been the one who always needed the help, and you've been there for me. I don't like the way that worked out."

He put his arm around her and they walked. "Let me say about your love what I said about your offer to help me whenever I needed you. I accept it as the tender and delicate thing that it is, and—if you'd permit me—I'd like to put into my pocket for such time as I might want to take you up on it."

She turned, kissed him lightly, and said, "Somehow, I knew you'd say something like that."

My Life, A Novel

They sat beside each other as Navigator drove back to Reston. The sun had set, leaving behind only a rosy glow on the horizon. But the glow did nothing for either of them as they mulled over what had just happened.

I feel like a shit, Navigator thought. *I've known this woman for all these years and now she bares herself to me and I punch her in the stomach. Just as if she were a common whore. Just like my co-pilot did thirty-six years ago, only it took me longer and my punch had to hurt that much more. But what the hell was I supposed to do? I love my wife and I'm not about to cheat on her. Why can't Maria just continue being a best friend? Why can't we just be pals? Why can't a woman be more like a man?*

He laughed bitterly to himself. *You idiot, you sound like Professor Henry Higgins in* My Fair Lady. *She can be a "pal" if she's only a fantasy. You can shape a fantasy as if it were Playdough. But once a fantasy turns real and you start to handle it, it responds like any woman. Then you're in trouble when you try to throw away the real, live, tingly, appetizing Playdough of a woman.*

Maria, staring glumly at the windshield, said to herself, *Your problem, Maria, is that you're just a damn fool. What did you expect him to do? Chuck his wife and children for a reformed whore? Be thankful you're still friends, good friends. So let's pick up life where you left off. You have one good friend who won't let you be any more than that and one not-so-good husband who sleeps only with men. There must be a word to describe someone like me. How about a female eunuch?*

"You know, something interesting will happen in the sky tonight," Navigator said out loud, just to take their minds off what both of them were thinking. "There will be a Leonid meteor shower. It happens when the Earth passes through the tail of the Temple-Tuttle comet, and the tiny dust particles burn up as they pass through the earth's atmosphere. The shooting stars can be spectacular."

"Just promise me one thing," Maria said.
"Promise?"
"Promise me you won't talk to them."
"Talk to who?"

"The stars."

"You really know how to hurt a guy," he said.

"Tell me about it," she said.

He looked over at her as the car moved under a street light. But she wasn't angry. She had a funny twisted grin.

"It's nice to know that a bright, puritanical guy, who seems to do everything right most of the time," she said, "is just a cuckoo at heart."

#

When they got back to Reston, the sun had gone down and the night sky was dotted with stars. Alden was in the house. He seemed relaxed and in as good a humor as he ever permitted himself to be. He said that he'd love some iced tea.

Maria went into the kitchen and Navigator looked around the house that had been the scene of so much turmoil. The family room was still tastefully decorated with inexpensive furniture, the fireplace mantel had pictures of Maria's family in Italy, and alongside the windows hung long beige drapes that Maria had made.

One of the drapes moved, and when Navigator walked past the fireplace and drew the drapes away from the wall, he found himself looking into the face of Lou Jones. Jones was standing there, grim, unsmiling, unmoving, except for feverish eyes that looked from Alden to Navigator. Jones's jacket was open and the butt of a pistol jutted from his waistband.

Alden's face turned gray, and he began to shiver. Navigator looked at the andirons in the fireplace and tried to estimate whether he had the courage to try to grab one and do something with it without getting himself shot.

Jones followed his gaze. "Don't even think about it," he said, drawing the gun and leveling it at Alden. "One of these bullets is for the stoolie over there who's shitting in his pants. I've got more in this clip. If you want me to add you as a corpse, just make a move toward that fireplace."

"Listen, Jones," said Alden, "you really don't know the whole story. I never expected that you would go to jail."

"The hell you didn't, bastard," Jones said. "What you didn't expect was for me to finish my eight years and come looking for you."

"Jones, think a little before you do anything. Think about—"

Alden never finished the sentence because Jones fired. Alden took the bullet in the center of his chest, and he was dead before he hit the ground.

Maria came back through the doorway with a pitcher of iced tea, looked quickly at Alden's body on the floor, then at Navigator, and threw the pitcher at Jones's back.

"Don't!" Navigator shouted.

The pitcher missed, but the tea sloshed down Jones's back as he turned and fired point-blank at her.

Navigator grabbed an andiron in both hands and swung it like a deadly baseball bat. He hit Jones in the back of the neck and he could hear bones crack. Jones fell to the floor, inert, his head twisted back over his shoulders, his neck broken. Navigator kicked the gun out of Jones' limp hand and turned to Maria, who was crumpled on the floor with blood pumping from her chest.

She wasn't breathing.

He jammed a handkerchief into the bleeding hole in her chest and pressed his fingers against the pulse in her neck, but there was no pulse.

"Oh, God, babe. Why did you do that? You didn't have to do that." He was crying now and tears ran down his face and dripped onto hers as he cradled her head in his lap. "You thought I would get the next bullet. You still owed me. You were finally paying me back.

"But now you're gone. My sweet fantasy is no more. You were in my mirror world. We all live in one universe. But there is another one out there. A mirror world. That's where I'd go when there was nowhere else to go. And I'd find you there. My fantasy girl. The only trouble was," he said, pressing his lips to her forehead, "you were too real. I found my fantasy, and then had trouble dealing with a real live one. You talked back and laughed at me and made me deal with your lousy husband. A fantasy is not supposed to do that."

Navigator gently removed her necklace and its cameo and dropped them into his pocket. He leaned over Jones' body, satisfied himself that that the bastard was dead, spat once in his general direction. He stood up, stepped over Alden's body, and telephoned the police. Then he opened the glass doors, and walked onto the patio.

The sky was alight with falling stars. Bright white, yellow and orange were stabbing at the heavens. It was more spectacular than the Fourth of July but more chaotic. It looked as disoriented as he felt. Somebody up there was speaking a language of light that was both beautiful and horrible.

"Stop," he said softly. "This is no time to celebrate. Stop! I'm supposed to be able to make you stop. I brought down the…" The white, yellow and orange were joined by flashing red lights that bounced off the trees and the sides of the house. Navigator turned back through the patio doors to let in the police.

About the Author

Gene Cowen was Washington Vice President of the American Broadcasting Company, deputy assistant to President Nixon, chief of staff to a U.S. Senator and an assistant to a Congresswoman. Before that, he was a reporter for the Syracuse (NY) *Herald Journal* and its Washington bureau. He has bachelor's and master's degrees from Syracuse University. During World War II, he was a combat navigator and was awarded the Air Medal. He and his wife live in Washington, D. C.

Printed in the United States
1174700003B/255